——————— ★ ———————

Eyes flashing, mouth stretched taut in a rictus of hate, Gwen Baker grabbed the Present-from-Paignton paperknife out of Sixsmith's desk tidy and swung it high. His arms shot up to ward off the blow. But he wasn't the target. The knife plunged down with such a force it passed clean through the tabloid spread out on the desk and dug deeper into the woodwork.

"That's *her!*" spat Ms. Baker. "That's the bitch who's trying to kill me."

Joe's gaze slid down the still-quivering knife and saw that its point had neatly sliced through the cleavage of raven-haired beauty Meg Merchison.

——————— ★ ———————

"Joe is a wonderful new character, full of wit and intellect..."

—*Baldwin Ledger, KS*

"Hill has been dubbed one of today's best British mystery writers."

—*Booklist*

"...the most enterprising new hero since Super Mario Brothers."

—*Kirkus Reviews*

REGINALD HILL

BLOOD SYMPATHY

WORLDWIDE®

TORONTO • NEW YORK • LONDON
AMSTERDAM • PARIS • SYDNEY • HAMBURG
STOCKHOLM • ATHENS • TOKYO • MILAN
MADRID • WARSAW • BUDAPEST • AUCKLAND

BLOOD SYMPATHY

A Worldwide Mystery/August 1996

First published by St. Martin's Press, Incorporated.

ISBN 0-373-26210-8

Printed in U.S.A.

ONE

THE MAN CAME IN without knocking.

He was in his mid-thirties with gingerish hair and matching freckles. He wore a chain store suit that didn't quite fit and an agitated expression that did.

He said, 'I want to talk about killing my wife.'

Joe Sixsmith removed his feet from his desk. It wasn't a pose a man of his size found very comfortable and he only put them there when he heard footsteps on the stairs. Clients expected to find private eyes with their feet on their desks, and as a short, black, balding, redundant lathe-operator was likely to disappoint most of their other expectations, it seemed only fair to satisfy them in this.

On the other hand, customer satisfaction could be a liability when the customer was confessing murder.

If that was what he *was* doing. Could be he was merely looking for a hit-man. Time for the subtle questioning.

'Pardon?' said Sixsmith.

'And her sister, Maria. She's there too.'

'There? Where's there?'

'At the tea-table,' said the man impatiently.

'Dead?' said Sixsmith, who liked things spelled out.

'Of course. Aren't you listening? They're all dead.'

Sixsmith thought: *All?* and looked for a weapon. There was a Present-from-Paignton paperknife in the desk tidy. Casually he reached for it, felt the man's eyes burning into his hand, and plucked out a ballpoint instead.

He said, 'All?'

He could be really subtle when he wanted.

'Yes. My parents-in-law too. Mr and Mrs Tomassetti.'

'Could you spell that?' said Joe, feeling a need to justify the pen.

'Two s's, two t's. My sister-in-law is Maria Rocca. Two c's. Is all this necessary?'

'Bear with me,' said Joe, scribbling. The pen wasn't working so all he got were indentations, but at least it was activity which gave him space to think of something intelligent to say.

He said, 'Is that it? I mean, are there any more? Dead, I mean?'

'Are you trying to be funny.'

'No, not at all. Hey, man, I'm just doing my job. I need the details, Mr. . . ?'

The man slid his hand inside his jacket. Joe pushed his chair back till it hit the wall. The hand emerged with a card which he dropped on to the desk. Joe picked it up, then put it down again as it was easier to read out of his trembling fingers. It told him he was talking to Stephen Andover, Southern Area sales manager of Falcon Assurance with offices on Dartle Street.

Suddenly Joe's mental darkness was lit by suspicion.

He said, 'Mr Andover, you're not by any chance trying to sell me insurance?'

The light went out immediately as the man's freckles vanished in a flush of anger and he thundered. 'You're not taking me seriously, are you?'

'Oh yes, I surely am, believe me,' reassured Joe. 'I just had to be sure . . . Listen, Mr Andover, you've been straight with me, so the least I can do. . . The thing is, I'm in the business of solving crimes, not hearing confessions. You see there's no profit in it, not unless you're a priest, or a cop maybe, and I've got to make a living, you can see that . . .'

But Andover wasn't listening.

'This was a stupid idea,' he said bitterly. 'I picked you specially, I thought being a primitive you might understand, but I'll know better next time. God, you people make me sick!'

He left the room as precipitately as he'd entered it.

Emboldened by the sound of his steps clattering down the stairs, Sixsmith called, 'Hey, "us people" ain't no primitive, friend. "Us people" was born in Luton. And you can shut up too!'

This last injunction was to a black cat with a white eye-patch which had raised its head from a desk drawer to howl in sleepy protest at all this din. He clearly didn't care to be spoken to in this way, but as a huffy exit would take him away from his nice warm refuge, he decided not to take offence, washed his paws as if nothing had happened and went back to sleep.

It seemed a good example to follow but Joe Sixsmith suffered from a civil conscience and in the remote contingency that Andover really had chainsawed his family, someone ought to be told.

He picked up the phone and dialled.

He asked for Detective-Sergeant Chivers, but as usual they put him through to Sergeant Brightman. Brightman was the Community Relations Officer and Joe got on well enough with him, except that he didn't take his detective ambitions seriously. Worse, he'd met Joe's Auntie Mirabelle at a Rasselas Estate Residents' meeting and they'd formed an alliance to persuade Joe back into honest employment. Sixsmith suspected Mirabelle had persuaded Brightman to put an intercept on his phone.

'Joe, how're you doing? What can we do for you?'

'You can put me through to Chivers.'

'You sure? You're not the flavour of the month there, I gather.'

More like smell of the decade. Whenever their paths crossed, Chivers usually stubbed his toe on a boulder. But at least this meant he took Sixsmith seriously.

'Please,' said Joe.

'It's your funeral. See you at the meeting tonight?'

Joe's heart sank.

'You going to be there?'

'That's right. The Major asked me along to report on the latest statistics. Good news, Joe. You seem to be getting it right on Rasselas. Wish we could say the same for Hermsprong. But I think we'd need to torch it and start again. See you later. Hang on.'

A few moments later Joe heard the unenthusiastic grunt with which DS Chivers greeted criminals, his wife, and private eyes.

At least the story Sixsmith had to tell provoked a more positive response.

'You what?' said Chivers incredulously.

'That's what the man said,' replied Joe defensively. 'Look, OK, so it's probably fantasy island, but I've got to tell someone, right?'

'Haven't you got a pen pal you could write to?' said Chivers. 'All right, what's the address? You did get an address?'

'Of course,' said Joe with professional indignation and crossed fingers as he searched for Andover's card. He found it and saw with relief that it did give a private address in small print.

'Casa Mia,' he read carefully. '21 Coningsby Rise.'

'Coningsby Rise? Very posh. I got a feeling you're wasting my time, Sixsmith. As usual.'

'Hey, posh people commit crimes too,' protested Sixsmith.

But the phone was dead and with a sign of relief, Sixsmith returned his attention to the pressing problem he'd been dealing with when Andover arrived.

It was *The Times* Crossword.

He'd started doing it recently to impress the better class of customer, but he'd rapidly realized he had no talent for the task. Other people's clues baffled him. Reluctant to abandon what seemed like a clever ploy, he'd started filling in words of his own choice, then working out clues to fit them. This way he always looked close to completion, though actually finishing one had so far proved beyond his scope. The trouble was that in reverse of the normal process, his method meant the more you filled in the harder it got. He invariably ended up with at least one non-word. Today's was *sbhahk*. It could mean something to an Eskimo, he supposed, but to an under-employed PI it was just another small failure.

He glanced at his watch. Four o'clock. Too early to go home. There could be a late rush, though he doubted it. Things were very slow. In the last recession it had been the kind of people who hired lathe-operators who got hit. This time, it was the kind of people who hired private eyes.

Time for a cup of tea, he decided. He went into the small washroom which allowed the estate agent to charge him for 'a suite' and filled his electric kettle.

As he re-entered the office he saw the briefcase.

It was black leather with brass locks and it was leaning against the chair Andover had sat on.

'Oh shoot,' said Joe Sixsmith.

He stooped to pick it up, then hesitated.

Suppose it was a terrorist bomb?

'Why would anyone want to bomb me?' he asked the air. 'I don't tell Irish jokes and I try not to be rude about other folks's religions.'

Whitey raised his head cautiously from his drawer, twitched his ears, then subsided.

Sixsmith got the message. Nuts left bombs without motives, and whichsoever way you looked at it, Andover was undoubtedly a nut.

So what to do? His mind ran through the possibilities.

Ring the police, who would clear the building and the block while they waited for the Bomb Squad. He imagined the scene. Dr Who type robots clanking across the floor. Stern-faced men in flak jackets talking into radios. Long queues of traffic, and anxious, curious, aroused faces peering from behind barriers to glimpse what was going on.

Then the anticlimax when an officer appeared with the briefcase in one hand and a bunch of insurance invoices in the other.

To hell with that!

Gingerly Joe reached out towards the case, paused, telling himself it was better to look stupid alive than stupid dead, reversed the proposition and reached out again, paused again with his hand almost touching the locking catch, drew in a deep breath...

And shrieked as a voice said, 'Ah, you've found my case, then.'

In the doorway stood Andover. He looked neither like a terrorist nor a lunatic. In fact if anything he looked rather sheepish. But Joe was still taking no chances and retreated hurriedly behind his desk.

Andover came into the room and picked up the briefcase. It didn't explode.

'I thought I must have left it here,' he said. 'To tell the truth, Mr Sixsmith, I'm glad I had an excuse to come back...'

The phone rang, postponing the possibly homicidal reasons for Andover's gladness.

'Hello!' said Joe.

'Chivers,' growled the phone.

'*Sergeant* Chivers. Well, hello, Sergeant. You got some news for me, *Sergeant?*'

'Look, I know what my rank is,' said Chivers. 'About that info you so kindly passed on?'

'Yes?'

'There's definitely been a crime committed.'

'You're sure?' said Joe, looking fearfully towards the patiently waiting Andover.

'Certain. And you know what crime it is, Sixsmith? It's called wasting police time! To wit, Detective-Constable Doberley's time. He's just got back from the Andover residence where he found Mrs Gina Andover and her sister,

Mrs Maria Rocca, having tea with their parents, Mr and Mrs Tomassetti.'

'You mean they're alive?' said Joe, dropping his voice.

'Of course they're alive! I know that Doberley sings in the same church choir as you, Sixsmith, but that don't mean he's so far gone he can't distinguish the quick from the sodding dead. And here's something else. On his way out, Doberley met the brother-in-law, Carlo Rocca. They had a little chat. Your Mr Andover was mentioned. Doberley asked if he'd been acting funny lately.'

Sixsmith saw that Andover was opening his briefcase. He had a very strange look on his face. He certainly looked like a man who was acting funny now.

Chivers went on, 'Rocca was very forthcoming. Said that his brother-in-law had been talking a bit strange in the last few days, going on about dreams and slitting throats, all sorts of crazy stuff.'

Andover's hand was sliding into the case.

'That's what I told you, Sergeant,' hissed Joe urgently. 'That's why I rang . . .'

'Yeah. Trouble is, you got the wrong number. So do me a favour. Next time you get a nut in your office, ring the psycho department at the Royal Infirmary!'

The phone went dead.

And Mr Andover slowly withdrew his hand from his case.

It held a tube of indigestion tablets.

He belched. His funny look disappeared. He popped a tablet into his mouth and smiled apologetically.

'Nervous dyspepsia,' he said. 'I've been suffering a lot lately. Look, Mr Sixsmith, I wanted to say I'm sorry for my behaviour earlier. I realized once I had time to think about it that I must have made quite the wrong impression. It's my job training, you see . . .'

'You mean, you really were trying to sell me *insurance?*' Joe cut in.

'No, of course not. What I mean is, on the training courses, they teach you that the most important thing is, hit hard. Get the customer's attention. You follow me?'

'Not really,' said Joe.

'What I mean is, I wanted to talk to someone about...this thing. And I got very anxious about it, so I just let my training take over and when I came in here, I may have been a bit over-dramatic... Look, I know in my mind that Gina's safe at home, and Maria and Momma and Poppa Tomassetti too, but sometimes what you feel is realer than what you know, do you know what I mean?'

'You're losing me again,' said Joe. 'Why don't we go somewhere and have a coffee...'

While reassured that he wasn't facing a multi-murderer, he still liked the idea of having more company than Whitey, who with a look of great resignation had re-entered his drawer.

Andover glanced at his watch.

'I don't think I've got time,' he said. 'My brother-in-law's picking me up at half past. He borrowed the car today to go for an interview in Biggleswade and we arranged to meet at my office, but when I realized I had to come back here for my case, I left a message for him to come on here, I hope you don't mind.'

'Be my guest,' said Joe. 'At least sit down while we're talking.'

A man in a chair is less of a threat than a man on his feet.

Andover sat down and resumed talking.

'The thing is, I've been having these dreams. At first they were vague, undetailed. I just used to wake up with a general sense of something being very wrong, and this stayed with me all day. A sense of something unpleasant somewhere over the horizon. Then they started getting clearer. And clearer. And...well, what it boils down to is this. I arrive home. I go in the house. No one answers my call. And there they all are. Gina and Maria and Momma and Poppa...sitting round the coffee table...and there are cups and saucers and a half-eaten Victoria sponge cake...and they're all dead, Mr Sixsmith...*they're all dead!*'

His voice which had almost faltered to a halt suddenly rose to a shout.

'Ah,' said Joe with a briskness born of a determination not to do anything which might suggest he wasn't taking Andover seriously. 'So what you came to report to me was not a murder but a dream of a murder.'

'Yes, that's right,' said the man, back to normal level. 'But more than a dream, I'm sure. Such vividness, such detail, has got to be more than just a dream. I'm convinced it's a warning, Mr Sixsmith. I believe unless I do something, it will happen. And if it happens, it will be my fault. A sin of omission, or even God help me, of commission.'

'Pardon?' said Joe.

Andover leaned across the desk and fixed him with a gaze which would have sold freezer insurance to Eskimos. Perhaps that's what *sbhahk* meant.

'This is the worst of my dream,' he said. 'I'm not sure when I wake up if I feel like I do simply because I've found the bodies or whether it's because I'm the one who killed them!'

Joe glanced at his watch.

'Will your brother-in-law come up for you or will he be looking for you outside the building?' he asked.

'He'll wait outside. I'll see if he's there, shall I?'

Andover came round the desk to look out of the window.

Joe, who didn't fancy being outflanked, stood up too and sauntered to his filing cabinet.

'Can't see him,' said Andover. 'I hope he hasn't got held up at Biggleswade.'

It was on the tip of Joe's tongue to say, no, Mr Rocca had arrived home about half an hour ago. But on second thoughts it didn't seem a good idea to let on he'd brought the police into it.

He pulled open a drawer of the cabinet in the interests of verisimilitude and said as he examined its contents (two tins of cat food and a tennis ball), 'Why'd you come to me, Mr Andover? Why not go to the cops?'

'You're joking. They'd just laugh at me,' said Andover.

Joe thought of DS Chivers and couldn't disagree.

'But I had to talk to someone professionally,' Andover went on. 'I don't mean a shrink. Someone who'd take what I said seriously, and maybe investigate, not just prescribe a lot of pills... but it had to be someone truly sympathetic...'

'Like a primitive, you mean?' said Joe, recalling their first exchange.

'Look, I didn't mean anything. I'm not racist. I married into an Italian family, for God's sake! It's just you once did some work for our Claims people and I remembered what they said about you...'

It had been a last-minute job. A negligence case against a private clinic by a man who'd ended up in a wheelchair after a simple cosmetic operation had left Falcon facing a million pound payout. Suspecting, or at least hoping for fraud, they had decided to keep a close watch on the patient. Then the claims investigator concerned had fallen off a ladder and, needing a replacement in a hurry, Falcon had hired Joe. He, however, between the briefing and his office, had contrived to lose the file.

Reluctant to admit his incompetence, he had managed to recall not the patient's details, but the name and address of the doctor who'd performed the operation. Thinking to bluff the other essential details out of her, he'd called at her house in the Bedfordshire countryside. When there was no reply to his knock, he'd wandered round the back in case she was in the garden and found that indeed she was, being humped in a hammock by a large red-headed man, whose temper proved as fiery as his hair. Joe had fled to his car, literally falling in, and the first thing he saw from his worm's eye view was the lost file under the seat. There was a photo of the suspect patient pinned to it. He was a large man with red hair.

It had been a nice scam. The lady doctor had made the right incisions, coached the guy in his responses, fixed him up with drugs to help fool the insurance experts, and told her sympathetic colleagues that it had all been too much for her and she was emigrating to Australia to start afresh.

'So I came recommended,' said Joe.

'Sort of,' said Andover. 'Some people said you were just lucky. But one or two reckoned there had to be something else, something intuitive, a kind of natural instinct that made you head straight for the doctor. I mean, no one else would have dreamt of suspecting her, not in a million years. So when I got to wondering who I could talk to about investigating dreams, not any Freudian crap, but the sort of dreaming which was like a real world you could move in, maybe manipulate, all I could come up with was you.'

He spoke with a resigned bitterness which wasn't very complimentary, but Joe was not about to be offended. In fact he was starting to feel rather sorry for the guy, which wasn't all that clever, seeing that there was no honest way to make a client out of him, even if sight of Joe hadn't put him off the idea.

'Mr Andover, I'm sorry, I'm strictly a wideawake PI. Could be what you really need is a travel agent, take a nice holiday. Now if you don't mind I'm closing shop, time to head home for my tea . . .'

'Yes, of course. I'm sorry, I've been foolish. It was just that I nodded off after lunch today and I had a dream with such intensity, I had to do something . . . Where on earth is Carlo?'

'Perhaps he's having trouble parking?' suggested Joe.

'Not Carlo. He still drives and parks like he was in Rome. He'd be right out there in the street if he was coming. Mind if I call my office?'

He picked up the phone and dialled without waiting for an answer.

'Debbie? Hello. It's me. My brother-in-law been in yet? Thank you.

'Damn the man,' he said putting the phone down. 'I can't afford to be late tonight. Gina and I are going to the theatre...' He looked at Joe speculatively. 'You wouldn't happen to be going my way, Sixsmith?'

Joe sighed. He was, vaguely, in so far as the concrete block-houses of the Rasselas Estate were within mortar-bombing distance of the mock-Tudor villas of Coningsby Rise.

'Come on,' he said.

The old Morris Oxford had a few rattles and squeaks, but none of them to do with the engine. An aptitude for cross-words Joe might not have, but when it came to machinery, he could make an engine purr like Whitey in anticipation of a fish supper.

Casa Mia was impressive, even in an area that reeked of Gold Cards and overdrafts. Maybe it was the bold decision to abandon the traditional black and white half-timbering and go for scarlet and gold that made it stand out. Must be money in the insurance game, thought Joe. Though not enough left over to spend on a decent tailor?

'There's room to turn at the top of the drive,' said Andover.

Joe drove in. No sign of any other car, so presumably Carlo Rocca had set out to pick up his brother-in-law. Tough.

Andover got out by the classically porticoed porch which looked like it had been recently stuck on to the studded oak front door.

'Like a drink?' he said.

'No, thanks,' said Joe firmly.

'OK. Thanks for the lift. 'Bye.'

Andover went inside. Joe carefully negotiated the ornamental cherry which marked the hub of the turning circle in the gravelled drive.

Ahead was the gateway. Behind, he hoped forever, was Mr Andover and his crazy dreams. He noticed that someone had recently done a racing start here, scattering gravel all over the elegant lawn.

'Mr Sixsmith!'

He heard his name screamed. In the mirror he saw Andover rush out of the house, waving his arms and staggering like a closing time drunk.

It felt like it might be a good time to follow the example laid out before him and burn rubber.

Instead he stopped, said to Whitey who'd reclaimed the passenger seat reluctantly given up to Andover, 'You stay still,' and got out.

Andover was leaning against the cherry tree, his face so pale his freckles stood out like raisins in bread dough.

'Inside,' he gasped, then, as if in visual aid, he was violently sick.

Joe went towards the house, not hurrying. He had little doubt what he was going to find and it wasn't something you hurried to. Also he felt his limbs were moving with the strange slow floating action of a man in a dream. Someone else's dream.

The front door opened into a panelled vestibule, tailor made for sporting prints and an elephant-foot umbrella stand.

Instead, the walls were lined with photos of bright Mediterranean scenes framed in white plastic, and the only thing on the floor was a woman's body. Her throat had been slit, more than slit, almost severed, and the handle of the fatal knife still protruded from the gaping wound.

There were open doors to the left and the right. The one on the left led into a kitchen. On the floor were strewn the shards of a china teapot in a broad pool of pale amber tea.

Gingerly Joe stepped over the body so he could see through the doorway on the right. It led into a lounge, and he was glad his sense of professional procedure gave him a reason for not crossing the threshold.

There were three more bodies here, an elderly couple and a youngish woman. The couple were slumped against each other on a garishly upholstered sofa. The woman lay on her side by a low table on which stood four cups and saucers, and a half-eaten Victoria sponge.

All three had had their throats cut.

Sixsmith turned back to the hallway. By the main door was a wall phone, with a fixed mouthpiece and separate earphone, like the ones reporters use in the old American movies. Carefully cloaking his fingers with his handkerchief (something else he'd seen in the movies), Joe dialled the police.

'DS Chivers, please.'

'Sorry, the Sergeant's out on a call, sir. Can I help?'

'I'm at a house called Casa Mia, number twenty-one Coningsby Rise—'

'Hold on, sir. We've had that call already, that's where the Sergeant's gone. He should be with you any time now.'

'This is real service,' said Joe.

He stepped out into the fresh air and drew in a deep breath.

Andover was sitting with his back against one of the porch pillars, his head slumped on his chest.

'You OK?'

The head jerked in what could have been an affirmative.

'Good,' said Joe, then walked across to the cherry tree, where he was following Andover's earlier example when the first police car screamed up the drive.

TWO

IT SEEMED THAT four bodies got you more than a sergeant, which was just as well.

Chivers, first on the scene, clearly saw Joe Sixsmith as a prime mover in all this mayhem. In fact it turned out that when he was passed details of the phone call saying, 'My name is Stephen Andover. I have just murdered my wife and her family at 21 Coningsby Rise,' he had wasted several minutes trying to ring Joe's office. Once he grasped there really were four bodies in the house, he was much inclined to arrest Andover on the spot. Joe protested that the man had been in his company for the past half hour or more.

'So we've got ourselves a conspiracy, have we?' snapped Chivers illogically, and was cautioning Joe when Detective Chief Inspector 'Willy' Woodbine arrived.

Built like an old style pillar-box, he had a matching reputation for getting his message across. Now he listened to a résumé of the known facts, told Chivers not to be a twerp all his life, and put out a general call to pick up Carlo Rocca, age thirty-four, stocky build, with long black hair and a heavy black moustache, perhaps wearing a slouch hat and a grey topcoat with an astrakhan collar, and driving an F registered blue Ford Fiesta.

Then he went into the house presumably to look for clues.

Chivers glowered after him.

Joe said, 'Can I go now?'

'No you bloody well can't! We'll need a statement, and I'm sure that Mr Woodbine will want to question you personally. Doberley, get your useless body over here!'

Joe looked round to see Detective-Constable Dylan Doberley trying unsuccessfully to keep out of sight by pretending to search the shrubbery. Known inevitably as Dildo, Doberley was an old acquaintance of Joe's from their co-membership of the Boyling Corner Chapel Concert Choir. Now they also had Chivers's wrath in common.

'Yes, Sarge?' said Doberley.

'You seen what's in there, my son?' demanded Chivers. 'You realize they must've been having their throats slit while you were starting up your car? Call yourself a detective! Defective is more like it. Take a statement from Sherlock here. Then get yourself off round the neighbours and check if they saw anything suspicious, and I don't mean you!'

Taking Joe's statement didn't take long as he'd already been mentally rehearsing it to keep his personal involvement down to a minimum. When they were finished Doberley said, 'I'd better get on to the neighbours before he starts yelling again.'

Keeping out of Chivers's way seemed a good idea, so Joe joined the detective as he walked down the drive.

'On a short fuse today, your boss,' he said conversationally.

'He can blow himself up for me,' said Doberley bitterly. 'What's he think I am anyway? Psychic? OK, I saw them, but they were all happy as Larry, jabbering away like they do, all arms and spaghetti bolognese—'

'You mean they didn't speak English?'

'Of course they spoke English! The two young ones spoke it just like you and me. The old pair sounded a bit more foreign like, and it was when they got a bit excited, they all started spouting Iti.'

'Excited? You didn't tell them—?'

'That I'd come to make sure they wasn't dead? Don't be stupid. I told 'em I was crime prevention come to warn them there'd been a lot of break-ins round here lately. That was enough to set them off, particularly the old boy. Right little Musso he was, wanting to know why we didn't hang people and why he couldn't keep his own personal machine-gun in the house. Lot of good it would have done the poor old sod.

Not when your own son-in-law's just going to walk right in and slit your throat. If it was the son-in-law did it, that is.'

Joe grinned at the sad little straw Dildo was clutching at and said, 'He didn't strike you as suspicious, then?'

'No, he bloody didn't!' exclaimed Doberley. 'I was just walking back to my car when this blue Fiesta turns into the drive. It stopped and he wound down the window and asked if he could help me. I guessed he was one of the family—'

'Why?'

'Because he would hardly have asked otherwise,' said Dildo in exasperation. 'How do you earn a living, Joe? Also he spoke with a bit of an accent and he looked foreign with that shaggy moustache and slouch hat. I asked him who he was, naturally, and he told me, and I told him who I was, but I didn't shoot him the crime prevention line.'

'Why not?' asked Joe.

'I thought: He doesn't look like he'd scare easy; so I asked about Andover, had he been acting funny recently? And that got him going, all this stuff about crazy dreams and so forth. And that was it.'

He laughed without humour.

'Know what the last thing I said to him was, Joe? I said it would probably be better if he didn't mention this to the ladies or the old folk, as there was no need to frighten them unnecessarily! Oh no, he said. He wouldn't do anything to frighten 'em. Then he went in and did *that!*'

'Like you say, Dildo, we can't be absolutely sure,' said Joe.

'No? What do you want?' said the DC, abandoning hope. 'The angel of the Lord in triplicate? Here, you'd better disappear now, Joe, and let me get on.'

Immersed in their conversation, they had turned into the driveway nearest Casa Mia and were approaching a not dissimilar mock-Tudor villa, only this one was traditionally coloured and called The Pines. Sixsmith could see why Doberley wouldn't want to have to explain his presence either to the householder or, worse, to Chivers. Unfortunately their approach must have been monitored, for now the door opened and a woman came to meet them.

She was in her fifties, tall and angular, with expensively coiffured grey hair and a horsey face that looked like it had been worked on by a good picture restorer.

'Hello,' she cried in the piercing voice of one who expects her own way but isn't so absolutely certain of personal desert that she can be quiet about it. 'Police, is it?'

'Yes, ma'am. Detective-Constable Doberley, ma'am,' said Dildo, making a chess knight's move forward in an effort to conceal Joe. 'Just a couple of questions, if you would, Mrs...er...?'

'Rathbone. Julia Rathbone. Is it about next door?'

'That's right, ma'am.'

'Ah. I thought it would be.'

Sixsmith, not wanting to embarrass his fellow chorister but feeling it would look suspicious if he just took off back down the drive, moved sideways towards a grey Volvo parked in front of the garage and started examining it with that air of suppressed shock policemen usually adopted when checking his Morris.

'Why'd you think that, ma'am?' asked Doberley.

'Because I saw your cars arrive, naturally. But besides that, I've always said it would end in tears ever since they moved in.'

'You mean the Andovers?'

'No, of course not. He's all right, not quite top drawer, of course, but at least he's English and knows his manners. Can't imagine how he got mixed up with his wife, Gina, isn't it? If they'd met on holiday, perhaps...I mean she's just so...*colourful*, like one of those ornaments that look so delightful in Andalucia but when you get them home, it's straight into the attic. Can't do that with a wife, of course, not unless you're called Rochester. But it appears she was born over here, in Tring, I believe, and that's where he met her, so it can't be down to sunstroke and vino, can it?'

Dildo Doberley, with a single-mindedness Joe admired, kept hold of the original thread which had led him into this verbal tangle.

'So why would it end in tears, Mrs Rathbone?'

'When the other came. That Rocca. My dear man, one look at him and you knew here was trouble. Do you know, he once told me if ever I was thinking of changing my hi-fi, to let him know and he'd fix me up with the best bargain I'd get in Bedfordshire. Well, I knew what that meant, back of a lorry stuff. No, thanks, I said. And he's still undischarged, you know, and likely to stay so from what I've seen.'

There was a great deal more of this. Doberley stuck to his guns manfully and what it boiled down to in his notebook, or would have done if Joe Sixsmith had been making the notes, was that the real money in the family derived from old Tomassetti. He'd built up a thriving business in the fur trade with outlets all over Beds, Bucks, and Herts, till seeing that public opinion was moving strongly against wearing dead animals, he'd sold up, retired, and bought Casa Mia, inviting his eldest daughter and her husband, Stephen Andover, to join them there with the understanding that the house would pass to them after his death.

'The house was called Cherry Lodge when he bought it,' said Mrs Rathbone. 'He changed it to Casa Mia. Down at the bridge club we said that Cosa Nostra would have been more appropriate, especially once the Roccas turned up.'

Carlo Rocca had married Maria, the younger and wilder daughter. Even-handedly, the old man had pushed a large chunk of money their way at the same time as he went into the Casa Mia arrangement with the Andovers. Rocca, then a salesman in a hi-fi and television store, had used his expertise and the money to set up his own shop in Luton's new shopping mall. For a while things had prospered. Then recession began to bite, interest rates went up, sales went down, and six months earlier Rocca had been declared bankrupt.

'That was it. Everything had to go, the shop, the stock, his car, and of course they had to get out of their flat, I mean, even our crazy social services won't pay for a luxury apartment, will they? So Maria came to see her father, I think for more money. But he said no, he wasn't going to chuck good money after bad, but she was family—you know what they're like about family—and she could come to live with them in Casa Mia, and her husband too, if they wanted. So they did. Well, I knew it would lead to trouble. And it has, but what kind of trouble, Mr Doberley? Here am I telling you everything I know, and you're not telling me anything!'

Her eyes were bright with expectation.

Doberley, perhaps hoping to shock her into brevity, said flatly, 'I'm afraid there's been a fatality, ma'am.'

Her eyes went into super-nova.

'A *fatality?* You mean he's killed one of them?'

'We don't have any more details, the investigation's at an early stage...'

'But it has to be him. Of course it's him. I saw him!'

'You saw...what did you see?' demanded Doberley.

'I saw Rocca come running out of the house. Earlier this afternoon. I was in my bedroom and you get a good view over the shrubbery to the front of Casa Mia. Rocca came running out of the front door, jumped in the car and took off like one of those joyriders, you know, wheels skidding, gravel flying everywhere. I remember thinking: That will ruin their lawnmower if they're not careful. Who's dead?'

Ignoring the question, Doberley said, 'You're sure it was Rocca?'

'Oh yes. He had his hand up to his face as if he felt he was being watched and was trying to hide, but that ghastly moustache and awful gangster's hat are unmistakable. Which of them has he killed? His wife? They were always rowing. The poor old mother must be so distressed. Perhaps I ought to go across and see if there's anything I can do...'

'I don't think that would be such a good idea, Mrs Rathbone,' said Doberley.

'Why not? Look, I'm not just being nosey, I really like the old lady...'

'I'm sure. Only she doesn't need comforting.'

Something in the policeman's tone got through.

'You don't mean ... not her too ... oh God.'

She had gone quite pale beneath the make-up. Sixsmith waited to see how far Doberley would go with his revelations, but the DC clearly felt he had gone too far already.

He said, 'I think my superiors would like to talk to you, Mrs Rathbone. Perhaps we could go inside and I'll contact them on your phone if I may.'

He ushered the woman into the house in front of him, turned to close the door and mouthed, 'Get lost!' at Joe.

It seemed like good advice.

Back at the Casa Mia everyone was busy, or looking busy. He looked for Chivers in the hope of getting leave to leave but the Sergeant was nowhere to be seen. In any case, the Morris Oxford was completely boxed in by a fleet of official police vehicles. Untroubled by all this activity, Whitey was fast asleep. It seemed a good idea. Joe slid quietly into the back, closed the door and curled up on the old travelling rug he kept there for warmth on all-night stake-outs.

It was impossible not to think about the killings. From what the nosey neighbour said, it sounded pretty open-and-shut. A house full of tensions, Rocca the wide boy chafing at having to toe the line to get the old man's charity, his wife perhaps reckoning her sister was getting the better deal from their dad; the old man, dominant, patriarchal; explosive Latin temperaments; exploding Latin rows ... no wonder poor old Anglo-Saxon-repressive Andover started having weird dreams!

One thing was sure; there was no case fee in it for J. Sixsmith PI, Inc. And he was glad there wasn't. Tracking unfaithful wives and credit defaulters might be dull but at least it let you sleep easy.

A wink was as good as a... His eyelids closed... He drifted into a deep dark untroubled sleep...

But there was something in that darkness. Figures seated around a table, mere silhouettes at first, but gradually sharpening, and then their features emerging like a landscape at dawn...

'Oh shoot!' said Joe Sixsmith in his sleep. Once more he was looking at the slaughtered quartet, and they were looking back at him, their sightless eyes locking on his, as each in turn raised a lifeless hand first to their bleeding throats as if in hope of staunching the wounds, then higher to cover their mouths as if to hold back their screams of terror and agony.

But there was no holding them back. Out they came, high, piercing, unearthly, and Sixsmith felt a weight pressing on his chest and the scream was so close it seemed to be inside his own head...

He awoke. Whitey was sitting on his chest bellowing into his ear that it was long past his tea-time and what was he going to do about it?

'Don't do that!' snapped Joe, sitting up and precipitating the cat to the floor. But when he looked at his watch he had to admit the beast had the right of it. He got out of the car and stretched.

'You still here?' said DCI Woodbine, coming out of the house with Chivers in close attendance.

'That's right,' said Joe mildly. 'But I would like to go soon if I can. I've got a meeting tonight, also my cat's getting a bit hungry.'

'Four people dead and all he can think about is his cat,' sneered Chivers.

'You got something against cats, Sergeant?' said Woodbine sharply. 'I've got four Persians and I tell you this, I wouldn't dare keep *them* waiting for their dinner. So you push off, Mr Sixsmith, whenever you're ready.'

He thinks it's all wrapped up, thought Joe. And so it probably is. Witnesses, motive, and a suspect with an Italian accent and a Mafia moustache driving round in a car whose number will be plastered across the nation's telly screens tonight.

Woodbine ordered the vehicles blocking his exit out of the way and personally waved him out. Joe almost blew a kiss at Chivers but didn't quite have the nerve.

'There you are, Whitey,' he said as he drove home. 'There's no accounting for tastes. Even cops can love cats.'

But Whitey was unimpressed. A deepdown racist, he regarded Persians and all foreign breeds as illegal immigrants, sneaking over here to take English mice out of English mouths. So now he merely sneered and yelled even louder for his tea.

THREE

WHENEVER JOE SIXSMITH felt the sharp elbows of Anglo-Saxon attitudes digging in his ribs, he reminded himself that these people had invented the fried breakfast.

He liked the fried breakfast. He liked it so much he often had it for tea too. And sometimes for his dinner.

He'd been warned that addiction to the fried breakfast could kill him.

'There are worse things to die of,' said Joe.

Whitey enjoyed the fried breakfast too, which was just as well.

'No fads and fancies here, man,' Joe had warned him on first acquaintance. 'You've joined the only true democratic household in Luton. We eat the same, drink the same.' Which principle was sorely tested the first time Whitey caught a mouse and pushed it invitingly towards him.

They shared half a pound of streaky bacon, three eggs, two tomatoes and a handful of button mushrooms when they got back from Casa Mia. Then they split a pint of hot sweet tea sixty-forty and Joe settled before his twenty-six-inch telly to let the early evening news scrape the last traces of the day's horror from his personal plate into the public trough.

In fact there wasn't all that much about it. The politician and pony scandal still got main billing, and a crash landing on the A 505 came second. It was only a light plane and there were no fatalities, but a woman trying out her new camcorder had caught the whole drama in wobbly close-up and the resultant images must have been irresistible to the picture-popping TV mind.

If there'd been a camera to record what Joe Sixsmith had seen, he didn't doubt that the Casa Mia killings would have been top of the pops, but they had to make do with exteriors and a close-up of Willy Woodbine confidently anticipating an early arrest and inviting viewers to look out for, but steer clear of, Carlo Rocca, who could help the police with their inquiries.

There was a photo of Rocca which looked like a fuzzy enlargement from a wedding group. Joe doubted if it would be all that much use except to anyone with a grudge against some fellow with a prominent moustache.

'Now, sport,' said the presenter. 'Luton have made a late change in the team for their key league match tonight...'

Sixsmith sighed and felt his season ticket burning in his wallet. Trust the Major to call a residents' meeting on a night when Luton were playing at home. That's what came of being brought up on rugger and polo. Thoughts of truancy drifted through his mind, then drifted out. The Major he could avoid, but not Auntie Mirabelle.

Still he had time for forty winks before he needed to think about going...

He relaxed in his chair, closed his eyes...and was back in Andover's dream. At least he tried to make himself think of it as Andover's dream (which meant he knew he was dreaming), only it had his own little variation of the corpses raising their hands to their mouths and screaming...no, not screaming...this time they were making an insistent bell-ringing noise...ah, now they were screaming...

He awoke to find Whitey bellowing in his ear that the phone was ringing and wasn't he going to answer it?

He yawned and reached for the receiver.

'Hello,' he said.

'Joe, that you?' demanded the unmistakable voice of his Aunt Mirabelle.

'No, Auntie, it's a burglar,' said Sixsmith.

'It wouldn't surprise me. You play with pitch, you going to get defiled, doesn't the Good Book tell us so?'

'Yes, Auntie. And you've rung to tell me not to forget I'm due at the Residents' Action meeting, right?'

'You so clever, how come you can't get a proper job?' she said briskly. 'The Major says, make sure that nephew of yours shows up on parade. People are starting to think they can't rely on you, Joe, and that's bad.'

'People?'

'Yes, people. The Rev. Pot just the same. He says: Is that Joe singing in my choir or is he not? This is no public house singalong we're trying to do, this is Haydn's *Creation*. That took the Lord seven days, how many days you think it's going to take you?'

'I'll come to choir practice tomorrow, I promise, Auntie. And I'll be at the meeting tonight.'

'See that you are. I got someone I want you to meet.'

Joe groaned inwardly, said, 'Goodbye, Auntie,' put the phone down, and groaned outwardly. He loved his aunt dearly but her efforts to direct his life were a trial, particularly since she'd decided that what he needed to get his head right and drop this detective nonsense was the responsibility of marriage. A stream of candidates had been channelled his way, most of them extremely homely and slightly middle-aged. Mirabelle would sing Joe's praises to anyone, but even a loving aunt reckons a short, balding, unemployed nephew in his late thirties can't be choosey. The odd ones who were comparatively young and attractive always turned out to have some hidden disadvantage, like a string of kids or convictions for violence.

'Whitey, you look after the place. Anyone tries to get in, you bark like a dog.'

The cat looked suitably disgusted by the suggestion and snuggled into the cushion made warm by Joe's behind.

Sixsmith envied him as he stepped out into the shadowy canyons of the estate, specially constructed so that where'er you walked, cool gales fanned your butt. With designs like this, who needed nuclear energy? The meeting was in the community room in one of the newer blocks about half a mile away. Normally he would have walked, but there was rain in the wind so he made for his car.

There were no purpose-built garages at this end of the estate. Back in the 'sixties you weren't expected to own a car if you lived here. There were a dozen lock-ups available in Lykers Yard, a relict of the old nineteenth-century settlement, most of which had been demolished to make way for the high rises. But these were privately owned and let out at rates almost equalling what the council asked for its flats. Joe valued his old Morris, but not that much. It was not a model greatly in demand by joyriders, so, theorizing that crooks didn't like a dead end, he usually left it parked on Lykers Lane facing into the exitless yard. So far it had survived unscathed.

On arrival at the community room, he hung around outside till he heard the Major's unmistakable voice calling the meeting to order. Then he slipped in quietly, hoping thus to avoid the threat of Auntie Mirabelle's latest introduction. But there was no escape. Seventy-five she might be, overweight and somewhat rheumatic, but she had an eye like a hawk, and she patted a vacant seat next to her with an authority that would have intimidated a cat.

On her other side was a woman Joe didn't recognize, presumably Mirabelle's latest candidate. He studied her out of the corner of his eye. She looked to be in her late twenties and had a strong, handsome face, which meant she was either a single parent or a psychopath. Suddenly, as if attracted by his appraisal, she glanced towards him and smiled. Flushing, he turned away and concentrated his attention on the Major who was introducing Sergeant Brightman.

Joe had mixed feelings about Major Sholto Tweedie. In many ways, with his cavalry officer's bark, his hacking jacket, cravat and shooting stick, his habit of addressing anyone black in Bantu, and his simplified view of life as a chain of command, he was a comic caricature of a dying species. After a lifetime spent pursuing wild beasts and women between Capricorn and Cancer till Britain ran out of Empire and he ran out of money, he'd headed home to die in poverty. Landing in Luton, he'd presented himself to the Housing Department saying he understood they had a statutory duty to provide accommodation for anyone in need. A council official, irritated at being addressed imperiously by his surname, thought to get simultaneous revenge and riddance by offering the Major a one-bed flat in the darkest Rasselas block which was scheduled for demolition as soon as there was enough money available to hire the bulldozers.

It was a monumental tactical error. Instead of curling up or crawling away somewhere else to die, the Major, after sampling the conditions, exploded into life. He mounted an assault on the council, at first on his own behalf, but rapidly on behalf of the whole estate. This was not, Joe surmised, because the man's politics had been radicalized, but simply because as an old soldier he knew that a general was nothing without troops.

The council had been gingered into doing repairs, improving the lighting and providing this community room, and the residents had been inspired to united resistance against graffiti, vandalism and general criminality.

You couldn't argue with the results. Sergeant Brightman was reciting statistics to show the continuing decline on Rasselas of break-ins, car thefts, drug-dealing, etcetera. Indeed, by comparison with Hermsprong, its twin estate across the canal, he made Rasselas sound like Utopia.

On the other hand, thought Joe cynically, by comparison with Hermsprong, Sodom and Gomorrah probably came across like Frinton-on-Sea. Nor did he much like the sound of the Major's latest scheme to organize security patrols to deal with offences like wall-spraying and peeing on the stairs. Tweedie referred to 'residents' platoons' but they still sounded like vigilantes to Sixsmith, and to Brightman too, who was trying to steer a delicate path between applauding the Major's leadership and warning him that private armies were against the law.

'A watching brief is all they'd have,' Tweedie cut across the policeman's diplomacy. 'No harm in that, eh? Call the boys in blue first sign of trouble. Now here's what I propose. Battalion HQ, for general surveillance and overall control, myself, Sally Firbright, Mr Holmes and Mirabelle Valentine . . .'

He then ran through a list of sub-groups (which he called 'sections'), pausing for comment after each area of responsibility and list of names. No one offered either query or objection. He'd got them scared witless, thought Joe with cynical superiority till he heard the Major say, 'South-Eastern Sector to take in Bog Lane underpass and the Lykers Yard lock-ups, section leader, Joe Sixsmith; assisted by Mr Poulson and Beryl Boddington . . .'

Joe started angrily in his seat but Auntie Mirabelle's fingers were round his wrist and she murmured, 'Congratulations, Joseph,' as she gave him a smile and a squeeze which defied him to make a fuss.

'Everyone happy?' concluded the Major. 'Good. Section leaders, there'll be a bit of bumph coming your way. Watch out for it. Thank you, everyone. Dismiss.'

Sixsmith shot up like a man who is late for an urgent appointment, but Mirabelle's wrist lock was still in place.

'This your idea, Auntie?' he said accusingly.

'I put in a word,' she admitted. 'But no need to thank me. I thought, with you so keen to do the policemen's work for them, this is a good way to get it out of your system. How're you keeping anyway, Joseph? You look pretty peaky to me. Scuffy too. If your poor dead mother could see you now, the shock would probably kill her. You need someone to take care of you.'

Determined to head off this line of attack, Joe said, 'Mr Poulson I know. Isn't he waiting for his Zimmer? Some vigilante. But who's this Beryl Boddleton?'

'Boddington,' said Mirabelle, with a broad smile which warned Joe too late of the trap that she had laid for him. 'You want to meet her? Why, here she is. Beryl, this here's my nephew Joseph I've told you about. Also your section leader. Joseph, meet your new neighbour and team colleague, Beryl Boddington. Just moved into my block. Beryl's a nurse at the Infirmary. Good job, regular money, career prospects, more than can be said for some people who should know better!'

The woman held out her hand. Beneath her coat Joe could see a nurse's uniform clinging to a sturdy but shapely body. She smiled as he shook her hand. Two smiles without saying a word; I bet she's been coached to show off her teeth, thought Joe unkindly.

'Pleased to meet you, Joseph,' she said.

'Joe,' he said, instantly regretting this tiny invitation to intimacy.

'Joe,' she echoed, smiling again. She did have very nice teeth.

'You two will need to talk about your team tactics,' said Mirabelle.

Joe's mind instantly started lumbering towards excuses for doing no such thing, but Beryl Boddington was ahead of him.

'Sorry, not now,' she said as if he were pressing her. 'I've got to be on duty in twenty minutes.'

'Joseph's got a car, he can give you a lift, ain't that right, Joseph?'

To Sixsmith's jaundiced ear this sounded like a well-rehearsed exchange in a second-rate soap.

He said brusquely, 'Sorry, but I got trouble with my carburettor. I'm just heading back to fix it.'

The nurse said indifferently, 'That's OK. I'll get the bus. See you, Mirabelle.'

'Don't forget the choir practice,' said Mirabelle. 'Rev. Pot's desperate for sopranos.'

'I'll see. But with shifts, it's not easy. 'Bye now.'

The nurse turned and left.

Mirabelle said, 'Joseph, why are you so rude?'

Sixsmith might have felt a little guilty if it hadn't been for the revelation that his aunt was mounting a second front at the choir.

He said, 'Don't know what you mean, Auntie. Excuse me. I need to talk to Sergeant Brightman.'

The Sergeant greeted him accusingly.

'Joe, that's a real hornets' nest you stirred up. You've got everyone running around like mad downtown.'

'Hey, Sarge, I didn't kill them,' protested Sixsmith. 'How's it going? They got this Rocca yet?'

'Give us time, Joe. It's only you PIs in books that get instant results. Real police work takes a bit longer. Isn't that right, Mirabelle?'

Joe realized his aunt hadn't let herself be shaken off so easily. Fortunately the Major, whose keen military eye had quickly recognized good warrant officer material, seized her and said, 'Belle, my dear woman, we must talk about disinfectant for the back stairs. I gather the council's still dragging its feet.'

'That's right. And did you see the mess they left last time they emptied the bins?'

Sixsmith headed for the door. A man who didn't grab his chance to escape deserved to stay locked up.

Outside he found the forecast rain coming down in earnest. His headlights picked out a figure leaning into the wind-driven downpour. It wasn't till he was past that he realized it had been Beryl Boddington.

He hesitated, then said, 'Oh shoot!' and pressed on. She probably hadn't spotted him and to stop now would be a tactical error of monumental proportions.

But he still felt guilty.

He parked his car in Lykers Lane and set off at a brisk trot for his block. There was a taxi outside the entrance. An Asian woman in a sari with a small child in her arms got out, followed by a boy of five or six carrying a large plastic bull with purple horns. The taxi-driver grabbed a suitcase from the boot, then shepherded the party to the shelter of the entrance, stooping over them from his great height as if to protect them from the rain.

Joe knew the man. Mervyn Golightly, one-time fitter at Robco Engineering till the same collapse which sent Joe down the road had dumped him too. He'd put his redundancy money into a cab and he and Joe had a vague deal— 'Any of my customers need a PI, I'll pass them on to you, any of yours need a cab, you pass them on to me.' It didn't occur to Joe that Golightly's presence here tonight might have something to do with this so far unproductive arrangement.

'Merv,' he said. 'How are you doing? This is some lousy weather.'

'Joe Sixsmith,' yelled Golightly, slapping his hand with so much force he almost knocked Joe back out into the wet. 'Now this is fortunate. Lady, this is the man I was telling you about. Luton's answer to Sam Spade and Miss Marple all in one. Joe, I'm dropping a punter at the airport when I spot this lady and her family standing all forlorn, so I ask her, what's up, lady? And she tells me they won't let her husband into this great free country of ours, did you ever hear such a thing? Her and the kids they let through, but her husband they hold on to. What's she supposed to do? She says she needs a lawyer, but where do you get a lawyer in Luton this time of night? You can get laid, you can even get a plumber if you're a millionaire, but a lawyer, no way. Then it hits me, if you can't get a lawyer, next best thing is my friend Joe Sixsmith. So here she is. Name's Bannerjee, do what you can, huh?'

'Merv, I don't see what—'

'You'll think of something. I'm out of here. Regular pickup over in Hermsprong. Exotic dancer, if she's not shaking her stuff in Genghis Khan's in forty minutes, she'll uncouple my tackle. Ciao, bambino!'

He gave the Indian family a smile like a neon sign, waved aside the woman's attempts to open her purse, and folded himself dexterously into his cab.

'Merv, wait!' yelled Joe. 'We need to talk!'

'We'll sort out my commission later, Joe,' yelled Merv. 'See you!'

He gunned his engine and shot away in a screech of spray.

It was time to be firm, decided Sixsmith. He felt sorry for this woman, transported from her Third World rural environment to this cold unwelcoming country, but she had to understand from the start that there was nothing he could do for her except point her to the right authorities.

He said, 'Mrs Bannerjee, I'm sorry. My friend has made a mistake. I don't do immigration work. I'm a private detective. What you want is the Immigrant Advice Centre...'

She was looking at him like he was raving mad.

'What is all this about immigrants?' she demanded angrily. 'I have been living in Birmingham for fifteen years. My children are all born here. I have a National Insurance number, and a job as part-time receptionist at the Sheldon Airlodge Hotel.'

'Oh shoot,' said Joe. He'd made the same kind of bonehead assumption that so irritated him when people made it about him. This was clearly his night for guilt.

He said, 'I'm sorry, I thought when Merv mentioned the airport...'

'We are coming back from holiday, ten days in Marbella, three star hotel. We arrive at Luton, very good flight, only ninety minutes late, and as we go through Customs green light, a man says, will you come this way, please? And he takes us to a little room...please, is there somewhere we could sit down? This has been a very tiring day.'

Joe didn't know if it was written somewhere, never let a woman with two kids and a suitcase into your home, but he guessed it was, probably in the Dead Sea Scrolls or on a pyramid. Maybe it went on to give advice on how to keep them out, but not having the benefit of a classical education he lacked the art. And the heart.

He picked up the suitcase. It was very heavy.

'You'd better come on up,' he said.

FOUR

WHITEY WAS STILL stretched out on the armchair. He kept his eyes closed but Joe knew he was watching. Mrs Bannerjee sank with a sigh of relief on to the sofa. The infant still slept in her arms and the little boy clung on to his bull with one hand and his mother's sari with the other while his huge brown eyes took in the mysteries of this new place.

Joe didn't disturb the cat. Standing was fine. He didn't want this to get too cosy.

'So what happened next, Mrs Bannerjee?' he asked.

She said, 'They took my husband away somewhere else, also our luggage. After a while a lady comes with a cup of tea and orange juice for the children. She asks a lot of questions about our holiday, where we have gone, who we have seen. I ask her, where is Soumitra, my husband? And she replies that he will be with me soon, and goes on asking questions. Then she leaves us alone. After a long time she comes back with my suitcase and tells me I can go with the children but Soumitra must stay. I ask why and she says to help with inquiries. I try to argue but she leads me outside. I do not know what to do. I think perhaps I will phone Mr Herringshaw, my husband's employer in Birmingham, but I do not have his number and besides, it is very late to be disturbing such a man. Our car is in the car park but I have no key and I cannot drive. I think maybe I will take a taxi home but I do not have enough money for such a journey and in any case I do not want to go far in case they let Soumitra go. So I stand there undecided and though I try to be strong, I find that I am crying... Then your friend comes up to me...'

Good old Merv. He hated people being miserable. He'd been worth twice what he got paid at Robco just because of the job he did for shop floor morale.

'Amal, be careful,' said Mrs Bannerjee.

Her young son had gained sufficient confidence to detach himself from his mother's side and kneel in front of the armchair to examine Whitey, who returned the compliment assessingly. The boy's hand went out and touched the cat on the stomach. Joe held his breath. Whitey would claw Mother Teresa if he didn't take to her. But now he stretched luxuriously, offering the whole range of his undercarriage to the child's caress and began to purr like a hive of bees.

'It's OK,' said Joe. 'Look, Mrs Bannerjee. My friend Merv was right in one respect. What you need is help from the law, not my kind of law, but a real lawyer. I may be able to get someone. There's this lady solicitor I know who works at the Bullpat Square Law Centre. If we can get her interested she's very good. But it would help if we had some idea why they're holding your husband...'

'Why do you need to ask?' she demanded scornfully. 'Is it not obvious? They think he is smuggling something into the country.'

Sixsmith didn't care for the scorn and in any case it wasn't all that obvious. If they'd picked up Bannerjee on suspicion of smuggling, why on earth had they turned his wife loose without a much more thorough investigation of her possible complicity?

One reason suggested itself uncomfortably. They might have felt it worthwhile letting her loose and following her to see who she made contact with...

He went to the sliding window which opened on to a tiny balcony crowded with pot plants. Stepping carefully between them, he peered over the rail into the street below. Six storeys down he saw three police cars, sirens muted but with their roof lights still gently pulsating. A little further along was Mervyn Golightly's taxi with Merv leaning against it, protesting loudly as a constable ran his hands up his legs.

'Oh shoot!' said Joe Sixsmith.

The doorbell rang.

He moved quick. He knew the Law's way with a door when they wanted quick access. A short ring in lip service to legality, then . . .

Fortunately he hadn't put the chain on. He seized the handle, turned it and pulled. The burly constable swinging the sledgehammer didn't have time to change his mind. The weight of the hammer carried him into the flat and across the room and out of the open window on to the balcony, where the low rail caught him across his ample belly and doubled him up. For a terrible moment Joe thought he was going to go over. But he let go of the hammer and grabbed the rail with both hands as Joe dived after him and seized the seat of his pants.

Over the man's shoulder he saw the hammer sailing through the night air with the breath-catching majesty of an Olympic medal throw.

Then, like a smart bomb, it revolved slowly as though seeking its programmed target, locked up, straightened up, and arrowed down.

Far below a constable looked up. He opened his mouth in horror, then screamed a warning. The doors of the middle of the trio of police cars flapped open left and right, and two uniformed men hurled themselves out in perfect sync a split second before the sledgehammer passed through the car roof like a cannon ball through canvas.

'Oh shoot,' said Joe.

'Will you get your black hands off my white arse!' snarled the burly man.

Joe could understand his ill temper but that gave him no entitlement to racist cracks.

He let go of the trousers and said, 'Hey, friend, look what you've done to my begonias. Someone's going to have to pay for this.'

Then he turned in search of the bossman.

There were two of them, a DI from the Drug Squad and a Senior Investigation Officer from Customs and Excise. At first they vied for control, but as Joe repeated his story, and Mrs Bannerjee repeated *her* story, and confirmation came from below that Merv the taxi man was repeating the same story, gradually the two men each tried to back out of the limelight, leaving centre stage to the other. The flat meanwhile had been well turned over without result and the searchers were reduced to a close examination of the balcony plants in hope of discovering some illegal growth.

'That is a pelargonium,' said Joe, indignantly snatching a pot from a pair of clumsy hands. 'Who's going to clear up this mess? I want compensation. What right you got to come in here, wrecking my flat, scaring my cat, and terrifying this poor woman and her kids?'

The men looked unimpressed and it was true that Mrs Bannerjee seemed more indignant than afraid, while her daughter hadn't even woken up and the little boy was sitting in a corner with Whitey in his arms, both of them watching the activity with wide-eyed interest.

'I'm going to ring my lawyer,' said Joe. 'But first I'm going to ring the *News*, tell them there's a great story here, cops and Customs men busting an innocent man's place up, not to mention throwing sledgehammers through police cars. Now *that* should really make a headline!'

It was the threat of ridicule which did the trick. The searchers began to do some token clearing up, while Mrs Bannerjee, her kids and her suitcase were being ushered from the flat.

'Where are you taking that lady?' demanded Joe.

'Helping with inquiries,' said the DI who had lost the battle to shed responsibility and signalled this by grudgingly admitting his name was Yarrop. 'Don't worry, she'll be well taken care of.'

Joe doubted it. Having let Mrs Bannerjee run free to see where she went, now presumably they would put her in the same room as her husband and bug their conversation. The last thing on their official minds would be genuine concern.

'Suppose she doesn't want to go?' he said.

'It is all right, Mr Sixsmith,' said Mrs Bannerjee. 'I never wanted to go away from my husband in the first place. Now they say I will see him. But, please, you mentioned a solicitor...'

'I'll see what I can do,' said Joe. 'I'll try to get hold of the woman I told you about. Her name's Butcher.'

'Thank you very much, Mr Sixsmith,' said the woman, smiling for the first time. She was rather pretty when she smiled. 'You have been very kind. Amol, say thank you and goodbye to Mr Sixsmith.'

'Thank you very much, Mr Sixsmith,' piped the little boy to Whitey whom he had released with great reluctance.

He thinks the cat's in charge, thought Joe. Maybe he's right.

The Bannerjees went out.

Yarrop said, 'I'm sorry about this. Can't win 'em all.'

'Well,' said Joe grudgingly, 'at least you can admit a mistake.'

'Mistake,' echoed the man thoughtfully. 'Maybe. It would certainly be a mistake to start disturbing solicitors at this time of night, wouldn't you say? Let's both try to avoid any further mistakes, shall we? Good night now!'

He left. Joe went to the phone and dialled. He had a sense that Yarrop had gone no further than the other side of the door but he didn't care.

A woman's voice said, 'Bullpat Square Law Centre.'

'You really work late,' said Joe approvingly. 'Now that I admire.'

'I know that voice. Is that you, Sixsmith? I heard you'd gone bankrupt.'

'You heard wrong.'

'You sure? I could swear I saw you flogging apples off a barrow in the market.'

'Still can't tell us apart after all these years? No wonder you've got to work long hours to make a living.'

'And I want to get back to it, so why don't you come to see me in the morning. I can maybe manage a two-minute slot around ten?'

Joe said, 'I need you now, Ms Butcher.'

'*Ms?* Such politeness means trouble. But it's no good, Sixsmith. I'm not moving out of here, not even if you've been gang-banged by the entire Bedfordshire Constabulary.'

'Not yet,' said Joe. 'But there's a man called Bannerjee in a fair way to being screwed.'

He explained. There was a long silence.

'You fallen asleep?' inquired Joe courteously.

'Chance would be a fine thing. How do you know this Bannerjee guy isn't a pro dope-smuggler?'

'I don't,' said Joe. 'But I don't think his wife is. And I'm certain his kids aren't. And the way the cops came bursting in here, they're pushing this thing very hard, and that's the way innocent people get squashed against the wall.'

'God, you'll be telling me next you've got a dream. These guys who turned you over, they had a search warrant, I take it?'

'I forgot to ask,' admitted Joe.

'Oh Jesus. The great PI! I expect it was all so sudden.'

'Well, it was.'

More silence.

'And you say they dropped a sledgehammer on to a police car?'

'From seven floors up,' said Joe. 'It went clean through the roof.'

'All right. I'll do it. Not for your sake, not even for the Bannerjee kids' sake, but for the sledgehammer's sake. A story like that deserves some reward.'

The phone went dead.

'Whitey,' said Joe, 'this has been a busy day. And nothing to show for it, except more mess than when you chased that blue-tit that came through the window.'

Whitey gave his are-you-never-going-to-forget-that? mew, and disappeared behind the armchair. He emerged a moment later dragging little Amal Bannerjee's toy bull which he deposited in front of Joe before climbing back on to the chair and going to sleep with the complacent look of one whose duty has been done.

'The poor kid,' said Joe, picking up the bull. He went on to the balcony and looked down. All the cars had gone including the one with the new non-sliding sunroof.

With a sigh, Joe placed the bull carefully among his begonias and started clearing up the mess.

FIVE

NEXT MORNING DIDN'T begin too well.

Joe found he'd run out of provisions for the fried breakfast and had to make do with plum jam on high bake water biscuits which Whitey loathed.

Also he felt very tired. After his third mug of tea, he recalled he'd been woken at least twice in the night by the strident strains of the Casa Mia quartet.

Still, the way business was he didn't anticipate much difficulty catching up on sleep at the office.

As usual, he stopped to pick up his papers at Mr Nayyar's shop on Canal Street which linked Rasselas with Hermsprong. Mr Nayyar claimed to run a speciality store, which meant he sold everything.

'And I've run out of food,' said Joe after he collected the *Sun* and *The Times,* the former to keep him abreast of current events, the latter for his crossword ploy.

Mr Nayyar's real speciality was knowing his customers' requirements better than they did. As he busied himself assembling the rich and varied ingredients of the fried breakfast, Joe browsed through his tabloid, careful to avoid the page with the boobs as he knew these caused Mr Nayyar a problem. Banned from his shelves were any magazines which flaunted flesh, but this principle if extended to papers would drastically limit his trade. So regulars like Joe kept the curves at a low profile till well clear.

The front page headline and three lines of text were still concerned with the horse-loving politician, and the back page concentrated on the A505 plane crash. The pilot, Arthur Bragg, had been taken ill not long after leaving Luton Airport to ferry Mr Simon Verity, a business executive, and his secretary, Miss Gwendoline Baker, to a conference in Manchester. He'd managed to keep control just long enough to flop the plane down on the roadway. None of the three was seriously injured, but they'd all been kept in hospital for observation and the Press concentrated on the woman who'd taken the video, 'Raven-haired beauty, Meg Merchison (29)'.

She said: 'I was trying out my new camcorder on a flock of rooks when I suddenly spotted this light plane diving out of the sky. It was terrifying. I thought at first it was going to hit me, but it levelled off, just missing some trees, and I was able to follow it all the way down on to the road. I never dreamt when I bought the camera it would give me a thrill like this.' There was a photo of the raven-haired beauty astride a gate, caressing her camera sensuously and showing enough leg to give Mr Nayyar moral palpitations.

Lucky lass, thought Joe. Wonder how much she got for the video?

He turned to the inside pages and found that here the Casa Mia killings got a double-page splash. There was a lot of sensational speculation, but nothing new and they were still using the same blurred picture of Rocca that had been shown on telly. There was no mention of Joe. He didn't know whether to be disappointed at missing the publicity or glad at missing the Press.

The shop door opened and two teenagers came in. Dressed identically in T-shirts, jeans and trendy trainers, with hair razored to a crowning crest, they were sexually distinguished only by a faint smear of moustache on the larger one's lip and a bubbling of breast on the smaller one's chest.

Sixsmith recognized the design on their T-shirts, a Union Jack with Maggie Thatcher's face at the crux. This meant they belonged to the True Brits, the leading white gang on the Hermsprong Estate. Joe doubted if they'd enter a Pakistani-run shop looking for anything but trouble, so he kept a close eye on them as Mr Nayyar busied himself with the order.

As the shopkeeper turned his back to weigh some tomatoes, the girl thrust a handful of chocolate bars under her T-shirt. She felt Joe's eyes on her, grinned at him and nudged the boy. He looked towards Joe, bared his teeth in an animal snarl, picked up a music cassette from a display rack and slipped it into his pocket. The girl meanwhile was pushing a couple of packs of panti-hose down the back of her jeans.

'I think that is everything, Mr Sixsmith,' said Mr Nayyar. 'Now let me see, how much will that come to?'

'Serve these young folk first,' said Joe. 'I'm in no hurry.'

'Nah,' said the boy. 'Nothing here we want. Load of Pakky junk. Come on, Suzie.'

They made for the door. Joe moved quickly and blocked their way.

'Hey, man,' he said. 'Aren't you forgetting something? Even junk costs money.'

'What you on about, Sambo?' said the boy. 'You best keep your black nose out, you don't want it even flatter.'

The girl laughed shrilly and said, 'You tell 'im, Glen.'

Mr Nayyar said, 'Please, Mr Sixsmith, it is all right. Let me deal with this.'

Joe looked at him in surprise, then doubled up as the boy, seeing his chance, hit him in the belly and dived through the door. The girl went after him, Joe flung out an arm to grab her but all he managed was to push her shoulder. Unbalanced she staggered over the threshold and fell forward on to the pavement. The boy grabbed her hand and dragged her to her feet. Her forearm was badly grazed and there was a new tear in her jeans through which blood was oozing.

'Come on, Suzie,' screamed the boy, dragging her away. 'You black bastards, I'll get you for this!'

A moment later they heard the roar of a motorcycle engine rapidly fading.

'Mr Sixsmith, you OK?' demanded Mr Nayyar.

'I will be,' gasped Joe. 'Hadn't you better ring the police?'

Nayyar shrugged.

'Why bother?' he said. 'They have other things to do than trouble with petty pilfering from a shop like this.'

'It's still crime,' said Joe. Then as his breath came easier, he looked sharply at the shopkeeper and said, 'You knew they were nicking stuff, didn't you?'

Nayyar looked as if he was going to play at indignation for a moment, then he shrugged and said, 'Mr Sixsmith, people like you and me, we know there are pressures that other people, white people, do not know. Sometimes if we give a little with the little pressures which irritate us, we may hope to avoid the big pressures which can burst us.'

'You mean you don't want to antagonize these kids who come here thieving in case they gang up on you?' said Joe. He shook his head and went on, 'Suit yourself, Mr Nayyar. Just give me my shopping. How much do I owe you?'

'Please, Mr Sixsmith, you have tried to be helpful. No charge today.'

Joe took out his wallet and said firmly, 'You've got me wrong, Mr Nayyar. I'm not a pressure, I'm just a customer. How much?'

Back at the car, he gave Whitey a raw sausage and some radical ideas on the reform of the young to chew over. Then he said, 'Shan't be long. Watch out for joyriders, now.'

Five minutes' walk took him into Bullpat Square. It was a market day and the traders' vans and stalls made it quite impossible to park here. The market customers also tended to overspill into the Law Centre and when he opened the door and saw how crowded it was, he began to turn away. But a voice called, 'Sixsmith! I want you.' And he turned back to see a small bird-like woman of about thirty ushering an elderly couple out of the inner office.

He went inside and said, 'Hi, Butcher. You've gone blonde. What are you up to? Trying to get out of paying your husband alimony?'

'I was always blonde. I've just gone back to my roots.'

She was not much over five two, and skinny as a well-picked chicken wing. She had an initial, C, which presumably stood for something but Joe had never called her anything other than Butcher. She pushed work his way when she could, though there was rarely much money in it.

They'd met when Joe went to the Centre looking for help in the aftermath of his redundancy. There'd been none forthcoming. Robco had done everything according to law and what Joe got was what he had coming, no more, no less. It was when Butcher asked, 'So what will you do now?' and Joe replied, 'How do you go about setting up as a private detective?' that she had started looking at him with more than professional interest.

'First thing is, you've got to be able to wisecrack and to whistle. You know how to whistle, do you, Sixsmith?'

'Pardon?' said Joe, bewildered.

'There's a lot of work to do,' said Butcher and had started the crash course in how to wisecrack like a real Private Eye which was still going on.

Now she said, 'Don't sit down, you're not staying.'

'Look, I was going anyway when I saw how busy things were,' said Joe slightly offended.

'Highty-tighty,' said Butcher. 'I meant you've got business.'

'Sorry?'

'That Bannerjee you put me on to last night, I was able to help. At least I sat with him till they got it into their thick heads he wasn't going to say any more. Then I got his wife and kids into an hotel.'

Joe looked at her with admiration. She must have been up half the night and still managed to look bright as a glass of lager, while a couple of bad dreams left his mind cloudy as homemade ale.

'Did he do it, then?'

'Do what? They're not saying he did anything. The game they're playing now is that this is an immigration case, his papers aren't in order. This is clearly bollocks. He's been living here for nearly fifteen years. He's the sales manager for Herringshaw's, a Midlands rag trade firm. All they're trying to do is put the squeeze on him so that if he does know anything, he'll get so scared about possible deportation he'll cough.'

'And what do you think?' asked Joe. 'Is he straight?'

'I'd say so,' she said. 'He's certainly won golden opinions from his employers. At his request I rang Herringshaw's and his boss, Charles Herringshaw no less, got very indignant and said he'd come down himself to see what he could do. He told me to stay on the case, he'd pick up all the tabs, so I'm in gainful employment at last. I owe you, Sixsmith.'

'My pleasure,' said Joe, who knew that Butcher was forever jammed in a cleft stick of needing well-paid private work to subsidize the Centre without having the time to go out and find it.

She glanced at her watch and said, 'Christ, look at the time. You're late.'

'Me? I wish I had something to be late for. Or is this a not so subtle hint you want shot of me?'

'No, it's tit for tat. That's why I wanted a word with you. I've sent you a client. She wants a good PI so I told her to be at your office at ten-thirty. I meant to ring, but things got hectic, and I didn't realize you kept upper-class hours.'

'Can't afford to keep anything else,' said Joe. 'What's her name? What's she want? Can she afford me? Can I afford her?'

But Butcher only cried, 'Go, go, go!' and opened the door to admit what looked like a tribe of gypsies.

Joe fought his way through them, checked his watch and wallet (the first step to integration is a shared prejudice) and headed back to the car where he found Whitey had unwrapped and eaten the rest of the sausages.

It was dead on ten-thirty as he parked the car outside the office. There was a BMW in front of him. A woman got out. She was elegantly dressed in black culottes and a jacket of pearly grey silk, a severe white blouse relieved by a large pink brooch at the neck. Her short bronze hair looked as if it had been sculpted, an effect heightened by the classic regularity of her face, which however bore a badge of mortality in the shape of a black eye beyond the scope of cosmetic disguise.

'Mr Sixsmith, I presume?' she said.

'Well, I'm not Dr Livingstone,' said Joe, still under Butcher's cinematic influence.

'Yes, that's right,' he hastily added, seeing from her face that this lady was not for joking with.

Her eyes were running over his clothes, his car and his cat like a VAT man's over a ledger. They then turned to the building which belonged to the nineteen-sixties Prince-Charles-hates-it school of architecture.

'Cherry said I shouldn't judge by appearances,' she murmured half to herself, but only half.

'Cherry?' said Joe.

'Cheryl Butcher,' she said.

'Oh, *that* Cherry. Would you like to come inside?' said Joe.

In the tiny dark foyer, he automatically checked his mailbox. As he opened it he felt those assessing eyes watching him and prayed it wouldn't be revealingly empty. He was in luck. There was a Security Trade Fair opening at the National Exhibition Centre the following week and various electronic firms were bombarding him with invitations to come along and check out their bugs.

Clutching the sheaf of envelopes ostentatiously, he ushered the woman into the lift. Whitey howled. He didn't trust the lift and usually they walked up the stairs together. When he realized that good client relations were going to be put before good cat relations he jumped down from Joe's shoulder and set off up the stairs with his tail at a disgusted angle.

'Sorry, I didn't get your name,' said Joe as the lift laboured up three storeys.

'Baker,' she said. 'Gwen Baker.'

It sounded as if it meant something, or perhaps it was just the way she said it.

'And have you known, er, Cherry long?'

'We were at school together.'

'Old friends, then.'

'You could say so. We were thrown together by linguistic affinity. Little girls like that sort of thing.'

This was like one of those crossword clues, the ones which obliged him to invent his own answers. He worked at it and was delighted to have a sudden revelation as the lift shuddered to a halt.

'Butcher and Baker!' he said.

She looked at him sharply as if suspecting she was making a very large mistake. The doors opened to reveal Whitey yawning on the landing as if he'd been waiting for ages.

Inside the office she did her audit act again. He felt like asking her what he was worth. But when he offered her a chair he noticed that she sat down rather stiffly and also that the bruising on the left hand side of her face was accentuated by the pallor of the right.

'You OK?' he asked in concern. 'Anything I can get you?'

'Like all the best private eyes, you have a bottle in your desk, I suppose,' she said.

'Well, no. I was thinking, more a cup of sweet tea, like.'

She smiled for the first time.

'It's kind of you, but no, thanks. Let me put you in the picture then we can decide if we're wasting each other's time.'

It was, he had decided, a wife-battering case. His heart sank. A man who could batter a woman would probably have little qualms about battering a middle-aged balding PI.

But no harm in showing her he was no slouch, deduction-wise.

He said, 'Go ahead. You want to tell me about your husband, I presume.'

He took her by surprise.

She said, 'Yes, but...'

Then he saw those sharp eyes backtracking his line of reasoning, and a twitch of the right-hand corner of her mouth told him he'd got it wrong.

'Perhaps I should begin by explaining I suffered my injuries in a plane crash...'

Of course! That was why her name was familiar.

He jumped in eagerly. 'Yes, Gwendoline Baker. The A505 crash yesterday. You're the secretary.'

'The what?'

'The secretary. To Mr what's it. Verity. Mr Verity.' He could see that he was still failing to impress. 'That's what it said in the paper.'

Her eyes touched the tabloid sticking out of his pocket.

'I hope you don't base all your appreciation of objective reality on what you read in that rag. Let me see.'

He handed it over, feeling like a small boy caught reading a comic under his desk.

A snarl of fury animated her features as she glanced at the back page.

'So you're not Mr Verity's secretary?' said Sixsmith tentatively.

'No, I am not. *Au contraire,* as they say. *He* is *my* secretary. He was accompanying me to a business conference in Manchester. I should be giving a paper there at this very moment.'

'You could send it by special messenger, it won't get there too late,' suggested Sixsmith.

She rolled her eyes upward and said, 'I'm beginning to have serious doubts about this, Mr Sixsmith. One thing is certain. We will get on much more speedily if you refrain from further interruption.'

Sixsmith, relieved that the spectre of the battering husband had receded, nodded agreement. Things were beginning to sound much more interesting. His second guess was that she was going to tell him the plane crash wasn't an accident, but had been arranged by some business rival to get rid of her or at the least keep her away from the Manchester conference.

She said, 'The first thing to understand is that the plane crash wasn't an accident. I'm sorry?'

Sixsmith's inner triumph and regret at letting himself be browbeaten out of a chance of showing her he wasn't an erk, had expressed itself in a plosive grunt. He turned it into a cough and smiled apologetically.

She went on.

'The pilot's illness was induced deliberately with the sole purpose of bringing the plane down and causing my death. Does that cat always stare like that?'

Whitey hadn't followed his usual practice of opening the lowest desk drawer and climbing in, but was sitting upright as an Egyptian artefact, apparently rapt by Ms Baker's speech. Sixsmith felt the direct question entitled him to speak.

'I'm sorry. Is he bothering you? Whitey, get in your drawer. You can listen just as well there.'

'What do you mean, he can listen just as well there?' demanded the woman in some agitation, her hand at her throat.

'Just a manner of speaking,' said Sixsmith. 'You know cats. Sometimes I get the feeling Whitey thinks he runs the business!'

'And you find that remarkable?'

'Not so remarkable as you'd find it if I put him on your case,' laughed Sixsmith.

She smiled thinly, but the answer seemed to reassure her and she let go of the pink brooch which she'd been clutching like a talisman and took a thin gold cigarette case out of her purse.

'Do you mind?' she said, lighting up.

No, but the cat does, thought Sixsmith. He nudged the drawer shut with his knee. Whitey would have to suffer a little discomfort in the interests of business. A potential paying customer was entitled to a bit of atmospheric pollution.

Talking of paying, he speculated how high he dared pitch his fee. Depended what her line of business was. She dressed expensive. Maybe she was in ladies' fashions, nice little earner at the class end of the market, he guessed. One way to find out—the subtle questioning.

He said brightly, 'Why don't you tell me about your business, Ms Baker?'

She said, 'What on earth for? I run an automotive electronics firm, if you must know. But that has nothing to do with the case.'

'It's why you were in the plane, isn't it?' said Joe defensively.

'Yes, of course. But she didn't need access to my company records to know my schedule, did she? No, I've no doubt Gerald told her.'

'Gerald?'

'My husband, Gerald Collister-Cook.'

Sixsmith sighed. He knew he was delaying the *dénouement*, but he also knew that if he didn't get things straight as he went along, you could *dénoue* all you liked and it would still be French to him.

'So Baker is your maiden name?'

'And my professional name. I saw no reason to lumber myself with that double barrelled monstrosity in business. I've just about got the bastards conditioned to dealing with Gwen Baker on level terms. They'd need another decade to come to terms with Gwendoline Collister-Cook, and I can't say I blame them. Can we get on, Mr Sixsmith?'

'I'd like that,' said Joe sincerely. 'You were saying that Gerald probably told *her*. Who is *her*, Ms Baker?'

'Who is her? I'll tell you who *her* is, Mr Sixsmith.'

Eyes flashing, mouth stretched taut in a rictus of hate, Gwen Baker grabbed the Present-from-Paignton paper-knife out of Sixsmith's desk tidy and swung it high. His arms shot up to ward off the blow. But he wasn't the target. The knife plunged down with such force it passed clean through the tabloid spread out on the desk and dug deep into the woodwork.

'That's *her!*' spat Ms Baker. 'That's the bitch who's trying to kill me.'

Joe's gaze slid down the still quivering knife and saw that its point had neatly sliced through the cleavage of raven-haired beauty Meg Merchison (29).

SIX

IT GOT WORSE.

Ms Baker quickly regained control, but the return to her cool, rational manner only heightened the craziness of what was to come.

'She's been having an affair with Gerald. *Affair!* For him, it was a one-night stand, nothing more. Meaningless. We accept such things in our marriage. We don't exchange notes, nothing so louche as that. But we're two adult people, leading lives which often set us far apart, and we both have strong needs. But that bitch wanted more. In fact she wanted everything. But it soon dawned on her that she wasn't going to get it without a fight. Well, I was a match for her there, I tell you. I was well ahead on points. But I didn't realize just how far she'd go, if pushed.'

'The plane crash, you mean?' said Joe, who was beginning to wonder what Butcher's resentment would do if this was what her gratitude sent him. 'She arranged for the pilot to be taken ill?'

'Of course. How the hell else did she happen to be sitting out there with a video camera ready to record it all for her scrap book?'

'You've told the police this, have you?' said Joe hopefully.

'Don't be stupid! How much notice do you imagine they'd take?'

'Well, I mean, they could find evidence, things I can't begin to do. Presumably you suspect the pilot was poisoned and they can get a full medical examination, analyse samples . . .'

'Poison? Who said anything about poison? She'd probably used a poppet.'

'A poppet? Like a lathe-head?'

'A lathe-head? What the hell's that?'

'It's something to do with a lathe,' said Joe cautiously. He usually felt it best to keep details of his past employment away from potential clients, though why he should be worried about alienating Ms Baker he didn't know. He felt a strong pang of nostalgia for the tumult of the tool room, the smell of oil and hot metal, the shouted jokes and laughter of his workmates.

'Is it? Very interesting, I'm sure. But this poppet I'm talking about, Mr Sixsmith, would be a small doll, made out of clay or wax or even rags, looking as much like the pilot, Arthur Bragg, as possible, and incorporating some of his hair or nail clippings or excreta, or something very closely connected with him. And when she saw the plane coming over she'd stick a needle into its belly and waggle it around. Normally that would kill, in which case I would certainly have died also. Only with her hate being directed at me, she couldn't get a big enough surge for that, so she only made the poor man feel rather ill.'

She said all this in the kind of tone suited for delivery of a detailed analysis of automotive electronic statistics.

Joe got up and switched on his electric kettle. He needed a mug of hot sweet tea.

He said, 'You're saying this Meg Merchison is a witch, is that it?'

'Not a term I care for, but use it by all means if it will tighten your grasp of the situation,' said Ms Baker wearily.

'And the reason she didn't manage to kill Mr Bragg was that she was really aiming at you?'

'That's right. The poppet works by providing a focus for deep passionate hatred. But like I said, it's me she hates, not Bragg, so she couldn't generate a big enough charge to really knock him out.'

Joe put two tea-bags in his Chas'n'Di wedding mug and held it up invitingly to the woman. She shook her head.

'If that's the case,' said Joe, 'why bother with the pilot at all? Why not simply do a poppet of you and bite its head off?'

He looked at her triumphantly and for the first time she didn't mock his triumph.

'At last, an intelligent question,' she said. 'She knew it was no use trying to get at me direct. Don't imagine she hasn't tried. But I'm her match there. I'm well protected.'

She unclipped the pink brooch from her blouse and twisted the stone out of its setting to reveal that it was hollow. Inside Sixsmith saw a small wodge of grey stuff, like putty, into which had been pressed scraps and shards of God knows what, and Joe Sixsmith had no desire to share the knowledge.

'You mean, you're a . . . one of them too?' he said.

'I have some knowledge,' she said, replacing the brooch. 'Enough to deal with her kind in the normal course of events. But fighting over a man has never been my scene.'

'So what's all the fuss about?' asked Joe, adding an extra spoonful of sugar to the four already in his tea. He needed the energy.

'You mean, why don't I just let her get on with it? I'll tell you why. Because Gerald's my husband and I don't care to give him up, certainly not to a common little bitch like that. Also, in business matters we have a fiduciary relationship which makes it inconvenient to part company at the moment.'

Joe, who loved clarity above all things except Luton Town, studied this carefully before saying, 'You mean, she'd not only get him, she'd get some of your cash?'

'You could put it like that.'

He smiled his relief at getting back to something like firm ground.

'So what do you want me to do, Ms Baker?' he asked. 'Get evidence that Meg Merchison's trying to kill you by witchcraft?'

'Don't be stupid,' she snapped. 'I need no evidence, and what evidence do you imagine you could get which would satisfy the police? I have problems enough holding my own with my chauvinist colleagues without giving them a field day by letting my name be linked publicly with a witchcraft scandal!'

'So what *do* you want?' asked Sixsmith.

'She's got power over Gerald, there's no other way he'd get entangled with a creature like that.'

'Blackmail, you mean?' he said without much hope.

Ms Baker sighed and said, 'Mr Sixsmith, you cannot blackmail a man into screwing you. No. She has a locket. It belonged to Gerald's mother and that's a very strong link to start with. Look, you can see it dangling between those gross paps in the picture.'

She had to withdraw the paperknife to reveal the heart-shaped locket nestling in Merchison's cleavage.

'It has a ruby cameo design, a cinquefoil, a very strong magical number and image. Inside there will be various items, we needn't go into the details, suffice to say that with the right words spoken over them, they have real power.'

'A love charm, you mean?' said Sixsmith.

'*Love!* But yes, a love charm, if that helps you grasp what this is all about,' she snapped. 'What I want you to do, Mr Sixsmith, is get hold of that locket for me, and fast. This creature is quite mad. What happened yesterday was an open declaration of war. Why do you think she told the media about the video?'

'So's she could make a bit of money, I suppose,' said Sixsmith wistfully.

'No! So that I would know she'd caused the crash. All right, so she didn't kill me, but she hopes that she can frighten me into submission by showing me how far she will go. Well, I won't be frightened off, but if she escalates this thing into a full-scale psychic war, it could take all my time and energy to resist and I can't afford to neglect my business like that. So the simplest thing for me to do is get Gerald back to his right senses for long enough to regain full control of all my finances. Once she sees he's only worth the clothes he's wearing—and I bought most of those—she'll soon lose interest.'

Joe was still trying to find a way out of this madness via reason.

He said, 'If this love charm's so powerful, why doesn't she just use it to make your husband take off with her now?'

Ms Baker's lips drew back from her mouth, showing a pair of long sharp incisors in a smile so unmistakably malicious that for the first time Joe began to consider the real possibility that she was a witch.

She opened her purse and took out a thin silken white cord, about nine inches long with a single complex knot tied in it.

'Because of this,' she said. 'While this knot is tied, Gerald can burn with desire, but there's nothing he can do about it. The knot gets loosened only when he's in my bed.'

Joe looked in horror at the limp white cord. He began to feel a certain masculine sympathy for Gerald the Hyphen.

'And does your husband have any idea that you and Merchison are . . . ?'

'Adepts? Of course not!' She laughed. 'He lectures in political economics at the University of Bedfordshire. What could he understand of such things? You on the other hand, Mr Sixsmith, with your ethnic background . . .'

'I was born in Luton,' protested Joe for the second time in twenty-four hours.

'It's the bloodline that counts,' she said dismissively. 'I was born in Bexhill, but my mother's family have lived near Pendleton in Lancashire since Tudor times at least.'

The detail of the boast was lost on Joe but he got the drift. He opened his mouth to assert indignantly that he was tired of people deciding on the colour of his skin that he must be into voodoo and dreamtime and all that rubbish, but the sight of that knotted cord still dangling from Ms Baker's fingers gave him pause.

'Why'd you go to But...to Cherry, Ms Baker?' he asked.

'I tossed and turned all night in that hospital bed and I knew I had to do something. I needed an agent, but he had to be guaranteed discreet and sympathetic. I thought of my own lawyers but decided they'd be useless. Wrong class of business, you see. Then I remembered Cherry. It was worth a try. I discharged myself from hospital and went straight round to that hellhole she calls a law centre. When I explained discreetly what I needed, she came up with you. She told me you weren't exactly Philip Marlowe but that you had what she called blood sympathy.'

Joe stored this away for future airing with Butcher and said, 'But you didn't go into details of the case?'

'Certainly not. I had enough trouble at school putting up with her scepticism. But I always trusted her judgement of people, and I still do, Mr Sixsmith, despite all the evidence to the contrary. So, will you help me?'

As she spoke with great emphasis, the knotted cord twitched in her hand.

Joe infused a strain of fake regret into his voice and said, 'I'm sorry, Ms Baker, I'm not into theft. It could cost me my licence. I know a couple of break-in artists, though...'

'Don't worry about theft,' she said. 'This locket, as I say, belonged to my husband's mother. The fool must have given it to this tart, but when I spotted it was missing, he claimed it must have been stolen. We had a break-in a few weeks back. I made him add it to the list of stolen property we gave the police. So you would merely be recovering it.'

'Couldn't you just do it yourself, I mean, you with your powers and so forth?' said Joe feebly.

'Impossible,' she said grimly. 'We know when we're within striking distance of each other. No, your great strength is that there's no known connection between us. You can get close.'

'But how...?'

'I presume you usually do *something* to earn your money,' she snapped. 'Talking of which, I shall of course be happy to pay your normal rates plus reasonable itemized expenses. And there'll be a two hundred pound bonus when you put the locket into my hands.'

Joe was not a natural bargainer. In markets he kept his mouth shut as he had been known to haggle a trader's price *up*. But now he said sharply, 'Three hundred,' not because he wanted a better deal but in hope that she'd call the whole thing off.

'All right,' she said. 'And here's something to be going on with.'

To his great relief, the knotted cord slid like a thin white snake into her bag and a bundle of crisp new twenties came out.

'Remember, speed is of the essence,' she said. 'I've no idea how long she'll wait before her next attempt. Here's my card. Get in touch as soon as you've got anywhere. But be careful. She may have me under surveillance.'

Joe knew better than to ask how.

He saw her to the door, then collapsed in his chair.

A plaintive howl reminded him that he'd shut Whitey's drawer.

He pulled it open and said, 'So what did you make of that?'

The cat looked up at him, then a paw snaked out, caught at the banknotes held loosely in his hand and sent them fluttering to the floor.

'I couldn't agree more, Whitey,' said Joe sadly. 'I couldn't agree more.'

SEVEN

JOE SIXSMITH HAD BEEN as indignant as most Lutonians when his native town was included in *The Lost Traveller's Guide,* a series devoted to places unlikely to be visited on purpose. But it was hard to argue with its conclusion that the poles of the city's social life were the Georgian Tea-Room and the Glit.

The latter was a pub, properly named *The Gary Glitter,* and brilliant with memorabilia of that superstar. Here Joe usually enjoyed a lunch-time lager and hamburger to the strains of the maestro's Greatest Hits.

Today, however, he walked on by its strobing doors to the discreeter portals of the Georgian Tea-Room, a distance of about forty yards and fifty years. Here he hoped to find Butcher sinking her vegetarian lunch and her principles, protected by the Tea-Room's prices, ambience and pit-bull-terrier-like proprietrix, from the risk of interruption by past or prospective clients of the Bullpat Square Law Centre.

The proprietrix was called Miss Irma. Joe didn't know if this was a joke, but decided it wasn't when she barred his way and said firmly, 'We're full.'

Joe said, 'Miss Butcher's expecting me.'

With the snarl of a bad loser, she let him pass into the half-empty dining-room. Butcher was easy to spot amid the scatter of pot plants, many of which were being worn as hats.

She looked up from her three-bean salad and said piteously, 'No, please, Sixsmith. Not here.'

'So what's all this about blood sympathy?' said Joe, sitting down.

'What? Oh that. I had to say something to recommend you.'

Joe considered this as he ordered a pot of tea and a wedge of bacon flan from a capped and aproned waitress.

'And that was the best you could come up with?' he said finally.

'What's up? Didn't you get the job?'

'*Job* you call it! You know she's a nut?'

'She's made a million, probably more,' said Butcher.

'I thought you were above money.'

'For itself, yes. As a measure of progress in a man's world, it's sometimes all we've got.'

'How come you two have stayed friends?' he asked.

'I was the only person at school she considered bright as her,' she said.

'Don't be modest.'

'All right, brighter. Academically, at least. I think basically she reckons if she could make a million, I should have been able to make two and she can't understand why I didn't. That's what's kept her interested. Really we've nothing in common, except school.'

'No. She said you weren't in the coven.'

'Ah. So she's still on with that? It's amazing, a woman like that. We all dabbled at school. Adolescent girls go through the phase. But she was the only one who took it seriously. I mean seriously seriously.'

'You guessed it might be something on those lines when you sent her along to me, didn't you?' said Joe. 'Thanks a lot, *Cherry.*'

'She really has got a big mouth, hasn't she? So what's she want you to do? Tail a broomstick?'

'You know I can't talk about it,' he said primly.

'Ah, then you did get the job. And I bet she gave you an advance? First rule of business—get them in hock to you. Great, you can pay for this. I've got to dash. Your Mr Bannerjee wants to see me.'

'They're still holding him?'

'Yes. His boss, Charley Herringshaw, came down from Birmingham to collect Mrs Bannerjee and the kids.'

'That was nice of him. Have they left by now?' said Joe, remembering the little boy's bull.

'I expect so. Herringshaw was going to see Bannerjee first. I fixed it up. And you know what? He actually gave me a retainer cheque upfront.'

'He sounds a real generous kind of fellow,' said Joe.

He meant nothing by it, but Butcher shot him one of those sharp glances she saved for when he said something she thought was clever. As usual, he couldn't see why.

He went on, 'Anyway, that means you're still on the payroll. Good. You can pay for your own lunch.'

'Don't be silly, Sixsmith. I've got better things to do with my money than give it to Miss Irma.'

She gathered her things together and stood up.

'Hey, don't go,' protested Joe. 'I got the kid's bull in the car...'

But she was on her way with a flamboyant wave, partly of farewell, partly to indicate to Miss Irma that her bill was taken care of.

Joe ate his flan slowly, chewing each mouthful thirty-two times, one for each tooth, like he'd been taught. It was good nosh, better than the burgers at the Glit anyway, but the tea was lousy. He stirred the pot in an effort to get a bit more strength into it, then tried an extra spoonful of sugar in his cup to give it some body. His experimentation drew Miss Irma's wrathful gaze, but before she could take any retaliatory action, a new arrival, wearing enough bullion to ballast a galleon, paused at Joe's table and said piercingly, 'I say, you're that detective chappie, aren't you? What on earth are you doing here?'

It was Mrs Rathbone, Andover's nosey neighbour, still clearly taking him for a CID officer.

Joe put his finger to his lips and shushed her imperiously. For a second she looked ready to be offended, then enlightenment crazed her pancake make-up and she cried, 'Oh, I *see*. You're here on a case!'

She pulled out a chair, sat down, looked all round the dining-room, then leaning close to him, hissed in a voice only marginally moderated, 'Which one is it you're watching?'

No one actually made a run for it, though there were undoubtedly a few twitches, possibly more of indignation than alarm. But a pretty young woman with fluffy yellow hair and a striped blouse who'd been having her ear beaten by her older companion turned so sharply she knocked her water glass over. Miss Irma rushed forward to repair the damage, casting an accusatory glance at Joe's table to make it quite clear whose fault it was.

'Can't tell you that, Mrs Rathbone,' said Sixsmith.

'No? Oh, all right. But you can tell me if there are any developments in that business next door. I've a right to know about that, surely. Have you caught him yet?'

'Rocca? No, not yet,' said Sixsmith.

'You're taking your time, aren't you?' she said. 'Not that I'm surprised, using a dreadful photograph like that. Surely there must have been a better one?'

'Why do you say that, ma'am?' asked Joe.

'Come on. A vain creature like that. Why, the house must have been full of photos of him!'

Sixsmith considered this. It wasn't a bad point.

'Maybe he removed them all to make it more difficult to identify him?' he suggested.

'That would mean it was planned,' she said. 'Did it look like it was planned to you? No, typical Mediterranean crime of passion. They're all mentally unstable, you know. It's the sun. What other explanation could there be?'

'He could have done it for the money,' suggested Joe.

'What money?'

'I thought you said yesterday the old man was rich...'

'Oh, yes, no doubt of it. But there's no way any of that money's going to come anywhere near Rocca. You don't

imagine he wasn't forever pestering Mr Tomassetti for cash
to put him back in business, do you? The old man was too
sharp for that. And he took the precaution of making it
clear that when he died, Maria would only get her share of
his money in trust, providing an income for life but with no
access to capital which would be preserved for her children
if she ever had any.'

Sixsmith digested this and his flan together, then said,
'For someone who didn't approve of your neighbours, you
know a lot about their affairs, Mrs Rathbone.'

'I hope you're not being impertinent,' she said sharply.

'Wouldn't dream of it,' said Joe. 'Just curious.'

'Well,' she said, 'let me put it like this. I have learnt in life
that you can never know too much about people, especially
people you do not wish to know. I spoke to the old lady
quite a lot. She was of her kind a not unpleasant old soul.
She reminded me of an Italian cook my family had during
the war, a refugee of some kind, always ready to talk inces-
santly of her family at the slightest provocation. So believe
me, Constable or whatever you are, there was no way for
Rocca to profit from the death of anyone in that house. No,
he simply went mad. Ah, here comes my friend. I'll leave
you to your stake-out.'

'It's a flan,' said Joe as Mrs Rathbone rose to join a stout
party as heavily bejewelled as she was gilded.

Joe called for his bill. Miss Irma clearly didn't trust her
staff with money and you paid her personally as you left.
The yellow-haired woman was in front of Joe at the seat of
custom. As her companion paid the bill he heard the
younger woman say, 'Thank you, Auntie.'

'That's all right. Now you take care of yourself, Debbie.
And keep your distance, that's my advice till you see how
things work out. There'll be talk talk talk, more noise than
the airport, but if you do your work and say nothing, then
at least no one will be able to talk about you.'

'Yes, Auntie.'

Joe paid and followed them out.

On the pavement, the women parted, the older one heading left towards the station, the younger one right towards the shopping centre. Joe was going this way also and he fell into step behind her. After fifty yards or so, she glanced over her shoulder, then turned sharply into Boots. Joe was reminded that he wanted some soap and toothpaste, so he turned in too. He glimpsed the woman in the striped blouse in the cosmetics section, but by the time he made his purchases, she had disappeared.

He went out of a side exit into Dartle Street which ran down to the glass and concrete cube which housed the Central Library. The yellow hair was bobbing along about thirty yards ahead of him. Once more she glanced back. Then she accelerated and quickly put another ten yards between them. Ahead of her a police car drew in to the kerb. A fat young constable got out, stretched in the sunlight and yawned, then made his way purposefully across the pavement towards the Togo To-go Sandwich Bar. Before he reached it the girl with yellow hair seized his arm and spoke urgently. The policeman said something to her, she shook her head, then hurried on. When Joe reached the car, he found his way barred by the constable.

'Just hang about, sunshine,' said the young man as Joe tried to sidestep. 'I want a word with you.'

'What word's that, Officer?' said Joe politely.

'Do you know that young lady?'

'The one with yellow hair? No.'

'Ah, but you know she's got yellow hair,' said the constable.

It wasn't often Joe met someone whose powers of deduction he felt immediately were inferior to his own.

'That's because I can see that it's yellow,' he said.

'Don't try to be smart with me, sunshine,' said the man aggressively. 'Let's be having some details, shall we? You got any ID?'

'What's this all about, Officer?' said Joe.

'It's about you following that young lady,' came the reply. 'She's made a complaint that you're molesting her.'

Joe could see the girl with yellow hair further down the street. She'd stopped and was looking back. And now she vanished into a pale pink office building.

'I think you must be mistaken,' he said, 'or else she's mistaken. Where is she, anyway?'

The constable looked round, then turned back to Joe, his face aglow with indignation, as though suspecting he'd vaporized her.

'You'll have got her name and address?' said Joe, confident that the young man hadn't written anything down.

The constable pushed his face very close and said, 'I asked for ID, sunshine.'

'What's holding the grub up?' said an irritated voice. 'Oh, it's you, Joe. Not reporting another mass murder, I hope?'

The stout constable looked perplexedly at Sergeant Brightman who was emerging from the car and said, 'You know Nelson Mandela here, do you, Sarge?'

'Old friends. This is Joe Sixsmith, Luton's answer to Philip Marlowe. Joe, meet Dean Forton, the Force's answer to Nero Wolfe. What's the hold-up here, son?'

'There's been a complaint. Harassing a girl,' said Forton.

'Joe? You're joking. He'd not know how. And what girl?'

Sixsmith, almost as offended by Brightman's defence as by Forton's accusation said, 'Look, I'm on my way to the library. I can't help it if some hysterical woman is walking that way too.'

'Library? You'll be telling us you can read next,' sneered Forton.

'OK, Dean, that's enough,' said Brightman. 'You going to get those sandwiches or not?'

Muttering, the stout young man headed into the sandwich bar.

'You be careful now, Joe,' said Brightman. 'I know it shouldn't be this way, but it's easy for a chap like you to give the wrong impression.'

Sixsmith glanced at his reflection in the bar window and wondered how anyone with normal eyesight could turn that slight, balding, round-shouldered figure into a mad sex predator.

'Chance would be a fine thing,' he said. 'See you, Sarge.'

When he reached the pink building, he glanced at the plaque listing the firms which had offices here. One caught his eye and he paused to study it.

Falcon Insurance. Andover's firm. And hadn't he rung a secretary called Debbie to check if Rocca had arrived yet...?

He glanced back up the street. Forton had emerged from the sandwich bar. Brightman was sinking his teeth into a crowded baguette, but the stout lad was staring after Joe with surly suspicion.

Resisting the temptation to wave, Joe hurried on.

The library was as efficient as it looked and the Reference Assistant showed no surprise at being asked where Joe could brush up on automotive electronic firms and necromancy. He read for an hour, took a few notes, and fell asleep.

The Casa Mia dream woke him. It was better than an alarm. He looked around, shamefaced, to see if his nap had been noticed, and realized he was not a lonely sleeper. This was where the wrinklies at the other end of the social scale from the Georgian Tea-Room set came to relax.

It was little comfort to feel he hadn't looked out of place.

He rose and headed back for the office.

It didn't smell good. Whitey had used the grit tray, but his glut of stolen sausage had been beyond the deodorizing powers of mere grit. Joe went to the window and threw it open to let in a blast of fresh pollutant. In the street below, a small white car crawled slowly along, its driver either looking for kerb trade or checking building numbers. As the only woman in sight was a brick-built traffic warden reputed locally to be able to remove defaulting vehicles by hand, Joe guessed the latter.

The car double-parked beneath Joe's window and two very large men got out.

He knew at once they purposed no good. If asked, he might have rationalized that men of such bulk did not travel in such discomfort to spread sweetness and light. Also they didn't bother to close the car doors. Only cops and gangsters didn't bother to close car doors.

The warden had spotted them. Mouth open in a predatory snarl which showed a metal tooth which it was rumoured actually grew there, she advanced towards them, her notebook held before her like a buckler, her pencil at the high port.

The men turned and looked at her. That was all. Just looked.

She hesitated. Halted. Turned with the expression of one who has recollected an urgent appointment a long way away, and set off down the street like a steroid-assisted sprinter out of the blocks.

One of the men looked up. Sixsmith jerked his head back so fast he cricked his neck.

'Whitey,' he hissed. 'Not a sound! Not even a suspicion of a sound or it's fish fingers all week.'

He went to the door and locked it. Then he retired behind his desk, sat down and held his breath.

The men must have come up the stairs very quietly because he was totally unprepared when the door handle turned. His heart jumped at the gentle movement and he let out a little gasp.

'Mr Sixsmith. You in there, Mr Sixsmith? We got some business for you.'

He felt them listening. Through the open window he could hear traffic. Then the familiar scream of a jet passing. Like most Lutonians he could easily differentiate the noise of take-off from descent. This one was on its way somewhere exotic. He wished he was on it, even seated in the smoking section next to an airsick Nazi with a recalcitrant child.

Beyond the door he could hear nothing. Nothing but that listening silence.

Or perhaps he was just inventing the listening. Perhaps they had gone. Did he dare to rise and peep through the window in hope of seeing the little white car move away?

He had almost persuaded himself he did, almost signalled his muscles to make the effort, when the phone rang.

He shrieked, just a little, not enough to be heard above the shrilling bell, even if they were still listening. He stared helplessly at the phone, longing to answer it and yell for help; but knowing that to do so would let the listeners know he was still inside.

In any case, with his luck, it would be a double-glazing phone shot.

He had a sense of something moving at the door, but his eye couldn't pin it down. Then he spotted the point of a thin-bladed knife probing through the crack beneath the lock. It was raised, withdrawn, pushed forward again. And the door swung smoothly open.

Joe grabbed at the phone.

'Hello!' he yelled as the two men came in. The first wore a grey suit and had the blank look of a punch-drunk prize fighter. The second wore a blue suit and had the look of the prize fighter who'd punched the other drunk.

'DS Chivers here,' said the phone.

Never had a name sounded sweeter in Joe's ears.

'Hello, *Sergeant*,' he said. 'Nice to hear from you, *Sergeant*.'

'What is it with you, Sixsmith?' said Chivers. 'Every time I talk to you on the phone, you start bellowing my rank. Not trying to be funny, I hope?'

'No, of course not, *Sergeant*,' said Joe.

The man in blue had come round the desk and was pressing his ear so close to the phone Joe could smell Scotch and aftershave, though which he drank and which splashed on was impossible to say. His arm was draped in an apparently friendly fashion round Joe's shoulders. It felt like it had dropped off a marble statue.

The moment to cry for help was past.

Joe said faintly, 'What can I do for you, *Sergeant?*'

'Just stay put,' said the blessed Chivers. 'I'm on my way to see you and I don't want a wasted journey.'

The phone went dead.

The man in grey after pulling open the filing cabinet drawers in a desultory fashion had stepped into the washroom and was combing his well-oiled hair in the mottled mirror.

'Filth?' he said.

'Yeah,' said the man in blue. 'And on its way. I was thinking, with Joe being so busy, maybe we should see him later.'

'See him later,' said Grey, who didn't seem to be a very original conversationalist.

'That's right,' said Blue. 'When it's more convenient. That's a nice cat, Joe. Like cats, do you?'

He was looking down at Whitey who had raised his head from the drawer to complain about the noise, then, like the traffic warden, changed his mind.

'Must like cats,' said Grey. 'Else he'd not put up with the pong.'

'The pong?' Blue sniffed. 'Oh, that's the *cat,* is it?'

Both men laughed.

Joe, with the boldness of one who knows that each passing second brings a detective-sergeant closer, demanded, 'What do you want?'

'What do we *want?*' said Blue.

'What do *we* want?' said Grey.

They looked at each other and laughed again.

'Help, Joe. That's what people pay you for, isn't it?' said Blue. 'That's what we've come for. For help. But we'll catch you later. Goodbye now, Joe.'

'Goodbye,' said Grey.

They went out of the door, closing it gently bchind them. Joe shuddered and went slack in his chair.

The door opened again. Blue's voice said, 'You want to take care of that cat, Joe. Keep it off the road. Dangerous place, roads, for cats.'

And Grey's voice said, 'That's right. Dangerous place. For cats.'

The door closed again.

EIGHT

A GOOD PRIVATE EYE would have made sure he got the terrible twins' car number.

A good citizen would have reported their activities to the police at the earliest opportunity.

Joe did neither, the first because by the time his limp limbs resumed normal service, the little white car was long gone, the second because by the time Chivers arrived, Joe's fractured nerves were beginning to knit together again, aided by a couple of pints of sugar-saturated tea and *The Times* crossword puzzle.

Also he felt rather let down. Had the Sergeant arrived in five minutes, he would have been welcomed as a questing knight, riding to the rescue. Had he arrived in fifteen minutes, Joe would still have felt grateful. But as the clock ticked round for almost an hour, all Joe could think was what a blasted cheek the man had, telling him to stay put as he was on his way!

Thus he didn't even bother to look up from his almost completed crossword when Chivers burst in with more apparent violence than his immediate predecessors.

Joe said, 'Five letter word, blank *b* blank blank j.'

'Eh? What's the clue?'

'Won't know that till I've got the word,' said Joe.

'Sixsmith, are you sure you're in the right business?' said Chivers. 'In fact, are you sure you're in the right town?'

'Sorry, Sergeant?'

'What I mean is, have you never thought of making a new start, all fresh and clean? Somewhere like the Falklands maybe?'

'Has something happened?' said Joe.

'You've happened,' said Chivers grimly. 'I'm a busy man. With a quadruple murder to investigate, we're all busy men. But we keep on getting interrupted. First of all, we're a car short because (and this I find really hard to believe) a sledgehammer dropped on it from your balcony. Then some poncy Drug Squad DI comes in and starts throwing his weight about, wanting everything we've got on you. Then we get a call from Andover demanding to know if we've put you up to harassing his secretary...'

'It was his secretary, then,' said Joe, pleased with himself. 'Hey, man, I worked that out.'

'What? You mean it's true? You *have* been harassing her?'

'Of course it's not true. When did Andover see her? I thought he was struck down with grief.'

'He rang his office this afternoon to make sure his work was being covered,' said Chivers. 'He says Miss Stipplewhite, his secretary, sounded most agitated and when he asked why, she told him that you were spying on her at lunch, then followed her back to the office. Andover wanted to know what the hell was going on, and so do I.'

'Nothing's going on,' said Joe. 'I didn't even know the woman was his secretary. We just happened to leave the Tea-Room at the same time...'

'The *Georgian* Tea-Room?' exclaimed Chivers, his eyes alight with suspicion. '*You* had lunch in the Georgian Tea-Room? Doesn't sound like your kind of place, Sixsmith. And before you get all discriminated against, it's not my kind of place either. In fact, the only reason I'd be seen there would be by way of duty. So was that how it was with you? On a case? If so, which case, 'cos, if you're sticking your nose into the Casa Mia case, it'll give me great pleasure to chop it off.'

'Wrong again. I went there to see Ms Butcher.'

'That bolshy brief from Bullpat Square? Doesn't sound like her kind of place either.'

'That's why she's a regular. She says it's the best spot in town for avoiding real people. Miss Stipplewhite was there with her aunt...'

'You know a hell of a lot for a man who knows bugger all!' said Chivers.

Ignoring this, Joe went on: 'We left at the same time, I headed for the library and her office is on Dartle Street too. She obviously got agitated, she must be all shook up, being close to something like that Casa Mia business... But how did she know who I was? I'm not exactly a household name.'

Chivers said sourly, 'You are in our house. Most likely it was Andover who made the identification when she described you.'

'Which means she was agitated because she reckoned she was being followed by some big black buck whose sole aim was to mug or rape her?'

'Why not? Hysterical women can turn the most unpromising material into Superstud,' mocked Chivers.

'Maybe. But in that case, isn't that how she'd describe me to Andover? So how come he manages to get *me* out of a description like that?'

He looked challengingly at the detective, but Chivers didn't look impressed.

'You try to make everything so bloody complicated,' he said. 'Or perhaps you're just throwing up a smokescreen. Except I don't reckon you're clever enough for that. So I'm going to give you the benefit of the doubt this time. Only remember, if I catch you within spitting distance of the Casa Mia case from now on, I'll go after you so hard, you'll be glad to swim to the Falklands.'

'Pardon me, Sergeant,' said Joe courteously, 'but have you come all the way round here just so you can threaten me personally? You so busy and all?'

'No,' admitted Chivers. 'There are a couple of points we need to check in your statement. Also I'd like your fingerprints for elimination. If that's OK with you.'

Joe rubbed his face to hide his grin. He'd got the picture. Woodbine didn't care for Chivers, he'd spotted that yesterday. And when he'd found out that there were fingerprints in Casa Mia which didn't belong to any of the family and that Joe's prints hadn't been taken, he had dumped the responsibility bang in the Sergeant's lap.

'And *you* go to *him,*' Joe could hear the DCI's voice saying. 'Be courteous. It's your cock-up, remember?'

'No sweat,' he said magnanimously. 'Though I'll need to see them destroyed when you're finished with them.'

'Sure,' said Chivers unconvincingly.

Taking the prints seemed to dilute the Sergeant's illtemper. Perhaps the physical contact with his hands firmly in control of Joe's had confirmed his superior role. When he was finished and Joe was cleaning his fingers in the tiny washroom, Chivers said, 'Now about your statement. Nothing to worry about. It's just this dream thing. For some reason it seems to be bugging Mr Woodbine. He wants to be sure you got the details right as Andover told them to you.'

Carefully Joe went through his story again.

'Yes, and that's what Andover told his doctor too,' said Chivers.

'So what's the problem?'

'God knows. If I did, I might have a better chance of making DCI some day,' grunted Chivers. 'First Mr Woodbine says he doesn't believe in dreams, I mean, in them being forecasts, so to speak. Then he starts wondering why the dream and the reality weren't the same.'

'Yes, I noticed that too,' said Joe. He almost went on to say that in his version, all the bodies were once more round the table, but decided that the fragile truce between himself and the cop would hardly bear the weight of another dream.

'And when I say that if you think dreams are a load of cobblers anyway, there's no point wondering why they don't tie in exactly with reality, he gets all sarcastic.'

'Maybe,' suggested Joe, 'he's got someone over him who's being sarcastic about dreams too.'

The idea seemed to comfort Chivers.

'You could be right,' he said. 'The Chief Super doesn't rate airy-fairy notions. Bodies in cells is what he's all about. Once we finger Rocca's collar, everyone'll be happy. Now what really happened with this sledgehammer?'

Joe told him. The discomfiture of the Drug Squad DI clearly more than compensated for the loss of a vehicle and Chivers was almost amicable as he left. It was perhaps a chance to mention the visit of Blue and Grey, but Joe didn't take it, figuring that all he'd get was if-you-can't-stand-the-heat-get-out-of-the-kitchen routine.

Also time was marching. He wasn't yet certain just how far he was prepared to go with Gwen Baker's job, but there was no harm in going far enough to cover the crisp new banknotes in his wallet.

He'd worked out the best time to take a look at Meg Merchison would be at the end of her working day, between the distractions of work and the security of home. This seemed like a pretty good plan to Joe and he never liked giving up pretty good plans. So he said goodbye to Chivers, picked up Whitey, went out to the Morris Oxford, and headed out of town to the University, which plugged the gap, both physical and cultural, between the former hamlet of Lower Stemditch which was now an executive suburb and the former hamlet of Upper Stemditch which was now an industrial estate.

Joe had more acquaintance with the latter sad change than the former. He'd travelled there every morning for nearly twenty years until that morning when he learned that he wouldn't have to travel there any more. Now he realized without surprise that he'd missed the turn-off to the University and was moving slowly along the familiar road which would take him to Robco Engineering.

There it was. The sign was still up, but the gate was pad-locked and there were nettles and foxgloves crowding against the steel mesh fencing. It looked shabby and derelict, more like a disused prison camp than the thriving, bustling business he recalled.

There but for the grace of God and Maggie Thatcher, not necessarily in that order, he might have spent half the waking hours of the rest of his working life. It had been a fate he was resigned to. No, not resigned. You resigned yourself to something you didn't really care for. He'd been happy here. More importantly he'd been secure too. That's what the bastards had pulled the rug from under. His sense of security.

He'd been happy again on occasion since he'd left. You couldn't deny happiness. Do what you would, it just came sneaking up on you. But he'd never let himself feel secure again.

He was passing through the newer, more prosperous hi-tec section of the estate, though even here he knew recession was starting to bite. Another company sign caught his eye. Sun gold on a Caribbean blue background, BAKER-TRONICS INC. No dereliction here, everything sharp-edged and new-painted, and the car park full of gleaming late registered cars.

Could the woman who ran a state-of-the-art hi-tec business like this really believe that witchcraft stuff?

Why not? he answered himself. It was no crazier than a PI talking to his cat.

Or a man who couldn't solve crossword puzzles setting up as a PI.

There were people coming out of the plate glass doors and getting into the cars. It was going home time. If he didn't get a move on he'd miss Meg Merchison.

He headed for the University.

He'd never actually been here before though he'd passed the turn-off sign twice a day for all those years. Somehow he'd imagined it would be one big building with a main exit outside which a man could sit till he spotted who he was looking for. Instead it turned out more like the industrial estate, a higgle-piggle of unconnected buildings, each with its own label. He kerb crawled past *Oriental Languages, Political Science* (where presumably Gerald the Hyphen worked) and *Mediaeval History,* keeping pace with a young female jogger in a fluorescent green skintight one-piece that started at her thighs and stopped at her thorax and left nothing between to the imagination.

This was getting him nowhere, thought Sixsmith as *Palaeontology* hove into view.

He wound down the window and said, 'Excuse me, maybe you can help me . . .'

The girl looked at him and said, 'I don't believe this.'

'Thing is, I'm looking for a woman . . .'

'You fucking freak. Right on campus. Jesus!'

She was holding a small cylindrical device in her right hand. Her thumb pressed a button on top of it and next moment a hideously high-pitched wailing note ripped through the air.

Whitey, asleep in the front passenger seat, erupted into wakefulness and on to the dashboard where he added his own decibels to the discord. Suddenly the road was filled with young people who seemed to have materialized out of the air. Sixsmith could see mouths opening and shutting but nothing was audible above the pulsating cylinder. One young man took it from the girl and tried to turn it off. Good old masculine know-how proving inadequate for the task, he fell back on good old masculine strength and hurled it at *Palaeontology,* where it continued to scream but at a distance which no longer interfered with communication.

'OK, Josie, what's up?'

'Kerb crawler,' said the jogger, pointing accusingly at Sixsmith. 'Can you believe the nerve of it? This guy propositioning me in broad daylight?'

'Come on,' said the young man. 'You're not that ugly.'

This drew a few masculine laughs but only indignant exclamations from most of the females, who had a lynch mob glint in their eyes.

'OK, fella,' said the young man, trying to re-establish his political correctness. 'Out you get. Someone call the police.'

'No, hang about,' said Sixsmith who had taken the precaution of locking the car doors as soon as he grasped the potential danger. 'I only want to ask the way.'

'That's what they all say,' cried a broad-shouldered woman who looked like the one who'd be pulling on his legs. 'Get him out of there. Let's show him and his kind what they can expect if they hassle us!'

This seemed to win general approval. The youngsters pressed close around the car and there were the beginnings of a chant of 'Out, out, OUT!' when a youth with the bespectacled earnestness of the true seeker after scientific knowledge said, 'What do you imagine he does with the cat?'

This caused a more general laugh and Sixsmith seized on the slight reduction in tension to say to the first young man, 'Listen, when I said I was trying to find a woman, what I meant is, I'm looking for Meg Merchison, she's a lab assistant here, she was in the papers . . .'

'Yeah, I know. You mean you're another sodding reporter?'

'That's right,' said Sixsmith who would have admitted to being worse things if it meant getting out of this stupid situation.

'It's all right, everyone,' called the youngster. 'Josie's got it wrong as usual. It's just another sodding reporter about that plane crash video.'

There was a groan of disappointment and someone shouted, 'I've called the cops.'

'You'd better uncall them, then,' said the youngster.

The crowd began to disperse. The girl, Josie, looked angrily at Sixsmith and said, 'Well, I still think he was propositioning me.'

'Yeah, sure, Josie. You stick at it, girl, it'll happen one day,' said the boy cheerfully.

The girl stalked off to retrieve her alarm which was hiccoughing to silence under a dying azalea.

'Hey, thanks, man,' said Sixsmith. 'Now where will I find this Merchison woman?'

'She works in the Animal Path lab, take the next left, then right, and it's the single-storey white building straight ahead. But you're a bit late, aren't you? Anything she could sell, Meg must've sold already.'

'Human interest,' said Sixsmith. 'You know her, then?'

'I use the lab, yeah. And when you see something as lush as that around the place, you make yourself known.'

'Any luck?'

'No way. She knows her own value and is definitely SCR meat, not even a scrap of bone for a poor starving student.'

'Oh yes?' said Sixsmith. 'Anyone in particular?'

The youngster looked indignant and said, 'Come on! You think I'm going to peddle muck to the tabloids?'

Sixsmith opened his wallet, took out one of Gwen Baker's nice new notes.

It vanished into the protector of public morality's pocket.

He said, 'There's a guy called Collister-Cook, he's an economist, I think. One of my mates reckons he caught him with his head up Meg's lab coat in the Preparation Room.'

'The Preparation Room?'

'That's where she prepares the specimens for us poor students to work on. Kinky, huh? All that blood and guts!'

Not necessarily, thought Sixsmith as he drove on. It depended whether Gerald the Hyphen did it because of the blood and guts or in spite of them.

One thing occurred to him. If Merchison wanted to lay her hands on a rabbit's foot, toad's eye, or snake's tongue, she was ideally placed.

The boy's directions were good but he didn't need them. The first thing he saw when he turned the final corner was Meg Merchison and if he'd just been cruising around on spec, he'd still have spotted her. In the flesh she was even more striking than on the back page. Close to six feet tall, she was standing on the pavement outside the white-painted lab, her raven-black tresses winnowed by the same wind which pressed her thin blouse against her thick breasts and drew her loose skirt between her long legs.

Lady, thought Sixsmith, if you wanted me, you wouldn't need no witchcraft.

He drew up alongside her and rummaged in the glove compartment for the small instamatic camera he carried there. It was less for detective work than in case of accident. It was a tip he'd got from Butcher. 'You have a bump, first thing you do is start taking pictures. Doesn't matter if there's no film in, it scares the shit out of the other guy, even if it's your fault.' He hadn't set out with any firm idea how he'd approach Meg Merchison, but as so often happened, God in the shape of the young student had shown him the way.

Clutching the camera in his hand, he got out and approached the woman.

'Miss Merchison?' he said. 'Could I have a few words? I'm a journalist...'

She gave him a look of such undisguised incredulity that he felt constrained to expand on what he'd rather have slid round.

'...freelance; well, actually I'm just getting started, and when I read about you in the papers...'

'I'll give you a tip,' she said. 'When you read about something in the papers, that usually means there's been someone there before you. Try to remember that. It could help you a lot.'

Sixsmith smiled. He liked to smile at people who made superior jokes. It put them under an obligation.

He said, 'I know that the plane crash story's gone, but what I was after was more human interest...'

'Human interest?' she said as though the phrase puzzled her.

'That's right. I saw your photo and I thought...'

He tailed off, not quite sure what a freelance journalist might have thought. But she was smiling, showing white teeth that looked specially designed by experts for noctitudinal nibbling.

'Oh, *that* kind of human interest, you mean?' She put her face so close to his he could feel her warm breath.

'You're no more a journalist than I am, are you?'

Oh hell, he thought. She's probably seen me and Baker talking in her crystal ball or something. Her hand was on his lapel. She's after a hair! One hair and a lump of clay, and she'll have me in intensive care!

'No,' she went on. 'All you thought was maybe you could con me into letting you take a couple of saucy snaps. Well, no way, buster. You'd better stick to poking your lens through changing-room windows!'

The hand on his lapel suddenly thrust him backwards so hard that he crashed against the car.

The impact woke Whitey who'd just managed to get back to sleep after the jogger's alarm. He appeared at the open window to snarl his opinion that enough was enough and what did a cat need to do to get some sleep round here anyway?

At least, that was how Sixsmith interpreted the intercession.

But Meg Merchison took a step back, her eyes fixed on the snarling black head which with its white patch around the left eye looked not unlike some South Sea devil mask.

She's scared, thought Sixsmith, recalling Baker's reaction to Whitey's stare. These people reckon cats have got the power or something and Merchison thinks Whitey's springing to my defence.

He said firmly, 'It's OK, Whitey. Nothing to trouble yourself with here, my man.'

The cat's snarl turned into a yawn to show that he certainly wasn't troubled and what on earth did Joe think he was on about? Then he subsided on to the seat and closed his eyes once more.

Sixsmith decided this psychic line was one he might usefully pursue. He said, 'No, honestly, Miss Merchison, I don't want to take your photo. It was just that when I looked at your picture in the paper, I got this feeling that there was something more going on than the story told me. I often get these feelings, sort of psychic you could call them . . .'

She now returned her gaze from the car window to his face.

'*Are* you a freelance journalist?' she asked.

He might have been wrong about the crystal ball, but he didn't doubt the ability of those piercing violet eyes to distinguish fact from fiction.

'No,' he said pulling out one of his cards. 'My name's Sixsmith. I'm a private inquiry agent.'

'And you think I'm worth inquiring into, is that it?'

'Like I said, I just sometimes get a feeling. Blood sympathy, some folk call it. It's like sort of ambulance chasing, I suppose. I'm sorry.'

He made as if to get into the car.

She looked to left and right, and said, 'Doesn't look as if my ride's coming. How about you giving me a lift home?'

Joe Sixsmith opened the passenger door, scooped up Whitey and dropped him on to the rear seat.

'My pleasure, ma'am,' he said.

NINE

As THEY DROVE ALONG, Meg Merchison lit up a cigarette and Sixsmith opened his window, not too ostentatiously, but she noticed.

'Scared of the secondaries, huh?' she said, puffing a jet of smoke in his direction.

'Not me,' he said. 'Used to be a forty-a-day man and there's no going back. But Whitey doesn't care for it.'

'No?' She looked at the cat who'd retired to the back seat. Then she shrugged, leaned across Sixsmith so that he felt her breasts resting heavy on his left arm, and threw the cigarette out of the open window.

She then settled back in her seat and Sixsmith said, 'We are going in the right direction, are we?'

'Depends on what you're aiming at,' she mocked. 'You don't know where I live, then?'

'Why should I?'

'You're a detective. You could've been trailing me for weeks for all I know.'

'You reckon?'

She looked at him, then laughed her full-throated laugh. 'Maybe not,' she said.

She was very restless, but it was not an irritating restlessness. Even in repose she was like a luxury sports car, parked for the moment but with its engine running. She reached forward and opened the glove compartment and began to rummage among the debris.

'Anything I can help you with?' inquired Sixsmith.

'Just nosey,' she said. 'Where's your gatsby?'

'Eh?'

'Your gun. I thought PI's always carried a gun in their glove compartments.'

'It's at the cleaners,' said Sixsmith.

'A wisecrack! I was beginning to have serious doubts. You spend a lot of time at the doctor's. Nothing communicable, I hope?'

She'd found some old appointment cards.

'I had trouble with my back,' he said.

'He fix it?'

'He gave me some tablets to fix the pain till it fixed itself.'

'That's about their limit. Mechanics, most of them. You still get trouble?'

He shrugged, winced.

'A twinge now and then.'

'Yeah?' She reached out her right arm and he felt her fingers probing around the top of his spine.

'Talk about tense!' she said. 'You could bounce rocks off that. Relax!'

He felt her fingers caressing his flesh in tiny circles.

'That better?' she said after a while.

'My back feels better,' he admitted. 'But it's not doing anything for my driving.'

'Another joke! Maybe you're for real. Next left.'

She withdrew her hand. It felt like a serious loss.

'The house with the red door,' she said.

It was no gingerbread cottage in the woods with a cauldron bubbling over an open fire, but a tall narrow house in a long Victorian terrace.

She got out of the car in a single sinuous movement.

'Well, come on,' she said. 'Don't just sit there. We've got unfinished business.'

'Sorry?'

'This blood sympathy of yours. I'd like to hear more about it.'

She ran lightly up the steps to the door. Sixsmith got out, said, 'On guard,' to Whitey and followed her.

The house had a rich spicy smell mingled with something more animal. It reminded Sixsmith of the alley that ran in back of The Golden Peony's kitchens in the Heifitz Centre.

'Is that all yours?' asked Sixsmith, who could see no sign of the expected division into flats.

'That's right. I sometimes take lodgers, but at the moment there's just little me. Not looking for lodgings, are you, Joe? Don't mind if I call you Joe, do you?'

'No. And no,' said Sixsmith. 'You rent, or does it belong?'

'It's all mine, by right of inheritance. What we need is a drink.'

She led him into a high-ceilinged sitting-room furnished with heavy Victorian armchairs in chapped leather. Sixsmith sat down carefully but found the upholstering sound and comfortable. The woman went to a huge sideboard and produced a matching bottle of whisky and a pair of tumblers.

As she sat opposite him on a Chesterfield like a coal barge, she undid the top button of her blouse but he still couldn't see if she was wearing the locket. She caught the direction of his gaze and smiled. Unable to explain he wasn't ogling her tits, he flushed. She pushed the bottle and the glasses towards him.

'You pour,' she said.

He measured out equal amounts, generous but not excessive.

'Here's looking at you,' she said, drinking. 'So what about this feeling you've got, Joe? Still got it, have you, now you've seen me in the flesh?'

'Oh yes, it's still there,' he said. 'I can't explain it but there's something…I've had it from photos before… There was this guy and I got this feeling he was going to get killed in a plane crash, so I rang him up and told him.'

He paused as if bringing the incident back to mind. The real trouble was that invention wasn't his forte and he quickly ran out of steam.

'Go on,' she said, looking really interested.

'Well, it was like a sort of dream or a vision maybe, I saw him in a plane and I saw the plane coming down . . . it came low over a shoreline, there was this village and then there were some mountains, and the pilot had to make his mind up where to try to land . . .'

He thought he was doing rather well, having tapped some hidden spring of inspiration, but she was grinning broadly.

'You're having me on, aren't you, Joe Sixsmith? That's that old movie *The Night My Number Came Up*. I saw it on the box a few weeks back!'

So had he. He found himself wanting to return her grin and shamefacedly confess. Instead: 'Yes,' he said seriously. 'That's exactly what the man said. I felt really stupid. But I stopped feeling stupid when that Dutch Jumbo went down and I saw his name on the passenger list.'

Invention might not be his strong point but when it came to simple fact-based lying, he was no slouch.

He saw the smile leave her face.

Gotcha! he said to himself. Believe one stupid thing and you're a sitting target for every stupid thing going.

'So what's this feeling you've got about me?' she asked. 'I'm not mad about air travel anyway.'

'No, it's nothing like that. It was just when I saw the pic, I got this feeling first of all of, I don't know, tremendous relief.'

It was a long shot but not all that long. It was easy to see her as a wild freewheeling spirit who wouldn't hesitate to put a rival out of the way. But Sixsmith guessed there was a long gap between that and being willing to knock off a couple of innocent bystanders en route. It might have seemed a great idea in prospect to bring Gwen Baker's plane tumbling down, but when it actually happened and she came face to face with the reality of living bodies being twisted and mangled in the wreckage . . .

Hell's bells, I'm beginning to accept that she did it, he thought.

She was nodding her head.

'Yes,' she said. 'I was relieved. Mightily relieved. But anybody would be, when you see an accident and the people involved come out OK. You didn't come out of your way just to tell me that, surely?'

'No,' said Joe, seeking invention again and as usual falling back as far as possible on the truth. 'There was something else, a feeling like you were in danger, like someone had it in for you. A woman, I think. I don't know why and I don't know how, but it wasn't nice, something sort of pointed, like sticking a knife in you, but not really that...'

He saw he'd got to her now. But before she could respond there was a ringing at the front door, a dull truncated note like a cracked chapel bell. Perhaps there was a witches' mail-order company that supplied such things.

She went out, not bothering to close the door behind her, so Sixsmith didn't have to eavesdrop.

'Oh, it's you,' she said.

'Meg, I'm sorry, I got held up, bloody faculty meeting went on and on...'

'I'm glad there's one of your faculties that goes on and on. So I'm just to be left standing around, freezing my tits off, while you and the rest of those geriatrics plan how to be even more boring next term? Sod that, Jerry. Sod that to Sodom and Gomorrah!'

She was good, thought Sixsmith. Having little talent for vulgar abuse himself, he always appreciated it in others.

'Look, can I come in? I'm sure you don't want the whole street taking notes.'

'Come in, is it? Isn't this a hospital visiting night? Where's the grapes and flowers?'

'I don't have to go to the hospital. She discharged herself this morning.'

'Then she'll have been slaving over a hot stove for you all day. Better not let your dinner spoil, Jerry.'

Sixsmith, curious to have a glimpse of Gerald the Hyphen, rose and went into the bay window which gave him a side-on view of a tall, craggily handsome man who in normal circumstances probably had some of the presence of the late great John Wayne, but presently looked more like Norman Wisdom in retreat.

He was saying with an effort at insouciance, 'OK, Meg, you've made your point, but no need to labour it, eh? I'll give her a ring, say that the meeting's likely to drag on for another couple of hours...'

'A couple of hours?' she interrupted. 'Now what good's a couple of hours going to be to you? Way things have been lately, we could work on it for a couple of days and get nowhere.'

'Now that's not fair,' he said, growing angry. 'I've been under a lot of strain lately. These things happen. It's a temporary crisis. A little loving care, a little more patience...'

'So it's my fault, is it?' she cried.

'I'm not saying that, love, of course not. Though you do come on a bit strong...'

If this was an attempt at a scene-lightening joke, it failed miserably.

'Do I now?' she cried. 'Well, I wish I could say the same for you, boyo! Good night.'

The door slammed with a violence that made the sitting-room walls shake.

Sixsmith hastily resumed his seat. Meg Merchison came back into the room like the wild west wind. She was utterly gorgeous in her wrath.

'Did you hear that?' she said. 'The bastard can't get it up and he says it's my fault. Three weeks it's been, and I've sat here like patience on a daffodil, saying it doesn't matter, just take your time... And now it's my fault!'

Her eyes fixed on Joe Sixsmith's face. There was something of calculation in them, also something of something else, and Sixsmith felt a tremor of fear run through his flesh, also a tremor of something else.

'Do you think it could be my fault, Joe?' she asked in a softer, almost languid voice.

'I doubt it,' he said trying to keep his voice from trembling.

Her hand was at the second button of her blouse. She undid it and it was as if the movement released a spring which swept all her clothes off her. He had never seen a woman undress so quickly. He registered that her clothed body had made no claims you could get her for under the Trades Description Act. And he also registered she was wearing the locket, but only because it brushed his eyelashes as she stooped over him, impatient with the relative slowness of his disrobing.

'Careful,' she said, undoing the clasp and tossing it aside. 'Can't have you going blind, not just yet.'

She was as dextrous with his clothing as she'd been with her own.

'There,' she said, drawing back a little way. 'So that's what you mean by blood sympathy. I knew it couldn't be my fault.'

'Come here,' said Joe Sixsmith hoarsely.

HE STARTED getting dressed again about midnight.

She opened one eye and said languidly. 'Where're you going?'

'I've got a hungry cat in the car,' said Sixsmith.

'Oh yes. OK. Keep in touch, Joe. Especially if you get any more funny feelings about me.'

'Oh I will, I will,' promised Joe.

She went back to sleep. She lay so relaxed with her limbs sprawled in an attitude of such abandonment that he almost went back to her. But a little voice at the top of his head whispered, 'Don't push your luck, Joe boy. OK, so there's no knotted string out on you, but you're not in training for this kind of thing and how're you going to feel if it turns out your eyes are greedier than your belly?'

At the door he took one last look back.

Oh shoot! he thought. Why am I such a reasonable man?

Then he left.

As he fumbled in his pocket for the car key, his fingers touched what felt like a fine metal chain. He drew it out, and saw the ruby cameo locket dangling in his hand. It must have landed on his jacket when Meg threw it aside, and then slipped into the pocket as he picked it up. Or could it have found its way in with a little help from an enemy?

No, I'm not going to start believing that garbage!

But what was he going to do with the locket?

He got into his car to check on Whitey while he thought things through.

The cat, seemingly untroubled by his unexpectedly long absence, crawled on to his knee, yawning and purring at the same time.

'So what to do, Whitey?' said Sixsmith. 'I feel a real rat stealing that lady's locket after what she's just done for me. So should I just push it back through the letter-box and go home feeling noble?'

Whitey gave one last huge yawn, then sat upright looking fully awake.

'Yeah, but when I wake up tomorrow, will I feel so noble then, is that what you're saying?' asked Sixsmith. 'I mean, what I've got here is what I was hired to get, and if Ms Baker was telling the truth, I'm just recovering property her husband reported stolen. And unless I believe all that other garbage, which I don't, losing it ain't going to harm Meg Merchison, who incidentally took advantage of me only because Jerry the Hyphen is having this personal problem.'

Whitey burped gently.

'You're right,' said Sixsmith. 'A man's got to eat. And a cat too. Tell you what, why don't we sleep on it?'

He switched on the car radio, turned the key in the ignition and drove slowly away.

TEN

THE RADIO WAS tuned to a music station which was playing the kind of music disc jockeys think suitable for insomniacs and night workers. The streets were quiet. On weekdays Luton died at midnight, except for a couple of clubs where those with too much energy could find various ways of burning it off.

Some big band was playing a nice swinging version of *Lazy River* which Sixsmith on the whole liked, though he didn't think the background bells altogether worked.

In fact they were getting downright cacophonous. Then the headlights of the fire engine exploded the darkness behind him and the mighty machine went rushing past in a glory of light and noise.

'There's always some poor sod worse off than we are, Whitey,' mused Sixsmith.

A few minutes later as he turned into Greco Street, he realized that this time the poor sod was Mr Nayyar.

'Sorry, Whitey,' said Sixsmith, parking the car and getting out.

At least the family seemed to be all right. He could see Mrs Nayyar and her children outlined in a neighbour's doorway while Mr Nayyar was having an animated conversation with two firemen playing a hose through the smoke-blackened entrance to his shop.

'Please,' Mr Nayyar was crying as Sixsmith approached, 'the fire is out, you are ruining my stock with all this water.'

'Better safe than sorry,' yelled one of the firemen.

Mr Nayyar looked ready to give him an argument. Then he spotted Sixsmith and a new anxiety flitted across his face.

He came towards him and said, 'Mr Sixsmith, hello to you. Can you perhaps persuade these fellows to stop drenching my shop.'

'What happened, Mr Nayyar?' said Sixsmith, ducking the opportunity to test his natural authority.

'Someone poured paraffin through the letter-box, then set it alight,' said Mr Nayyar. 'I had put the fire out with my own extinguisher by the time these people arrived, but they do not seem to want to listen to me.'

'Did you see anyone outside?' asked Sixsmith.

'No. No one.' Nayyar hesitated then went on, 'Please, Mr Sixsmith, that trouble this morning. I would prefer you did not mention it to anyone. To make accusation without proof will just make things more of a problem for me.'

'If that's what you want, Mr Nayyar,' said Sixsmith. 'But I think you're wrong.'

The shopkeeper shrugged then, attracted by a crash from inside the store as the powerful waterjet brought something down, he rushed back to the firemen.

By now the police had arrived and were urging spectators to retreat with assurances that there was nothing to see. Presumably if there *was* something to see, they'd be selling tickets. Most of the hopeful onlookers looked like neighbours, curious, even concerned, but there was a group of kids with motorbikes obviously just having a good time. They were wearing True-Brits T-shirts. Among them Joe spotted the shoplifting couple he'd clashed with that morning. At the same time, the girl, Suzie, spotted him and pointed him out to her companion, Glen.

'So it's you again, Sherlock,' said a voice. 'Always popping up where there's trouble, aren't you?'

Joe sighed. It was Dean Forton, the fat young copper. Over his shoulder he saw the Brit couple, not wanting to see what came of his contact with the police, retreat into the dark.

He said, 'I know Mr Nayyar. I just stopped to see if I could help.'

'Is that right?' said Forton sceptically. He'd probably read a *Readers' Digest* article telling him that arsonists often turn up at their fires, offering help.

'That's right. If I were you, I'd be more interested in talking to those bikers from Hermsprong.'

'That's your professional advice, is it?' sneered Forton.

A voice from the Brits cried, 'When's the fire sale, then, Pakki?' and there was a jeering laugh.

'Of course, there are a lot of them,' said Joe sympathetically.

Forton glowered at him, then turned and headed aggressively towards the youngsters.

'And the best of British,' said Joe, getting back into his car.

It was with great relief that he got home. It had been a long, long day, and in more ways than he could have forecast demanding. All he wanted was a mug of strong tea, then a long, long sleep and Whitey on his shoulder purred his agreement.

But when he saw the tell-tale marks round the lock on his door, his heart sank. You didn't need to be a detective in these parts to know what they meant.

He'd been done over.

At least it had been by a pro. There was vast confusion but no deliberate fouling, though that was small consolation as he viewed the wasteland of tipped-out drawers and slashed upholstery. He went into the kitchen and found himself paddling in water. The doors of the fridge freezer hung open. It had needed defrosting for weeks and now it had got it.

At least that showed there was no urgency about calling for help, thought Sixsmith. Such a complete defrosting took at least a couple of hours so the sod who'd done it was long gone.

He felt quite pleased with his reasoning. This was real detection. He put the kettle on and went back into the living-room. Whitey had decided that the flat had been rearranged purely for his benefit and was curled up quite happily in the depths of the eviscerated sofa. Sixsmith would have given much for such a religious response to disaster, but, knackered though he was, he could not so philosophically accept the assault on his home. He owned nothing very valuable, but what he did own was precious to him.

And, curiously, it began to dawn on him as he looked around that in fact he continued to own most of it. The obvious targets for your modern hi-tec thief, like radio, tapedeck, VCR—were still here. As were a few things that might have appealed to your arty-farty connoisseur—the candle clock, the shell painting and the little soapstone menagerie, which were his heirlooms. He went into the bedroom. His genuine gold-plated cufflinks and cultured pearl tie-pin had been tipped out of the dressing-table drawer along with the cash card he didn't use because he'd forgotten the PIN number and the two fivers he kept as a reserve against finding himself moneyless on a bank holiday.

What the hell was this guy looking for?

What kind of nut broke into a hard-up PI's pad and started searching like he was expecting to find Imelda Marcos's pension fund?

He went back into the living-room and found out.

'Hello, Joe,' said Mr Blue. 'Who's a dirty stop-out, then?'

'Dirty stop-out, then?' echoed Mr Grey who was working at his fingernails with implements from a manicure set. It was like cleaning a chain-saw with Brasso. Vanity was a cuckoo, it nested anywhere. But this was no time for such philosophical musings. This was time for complete cooperation between nations.

Sixsmith said, 'Whatever you're looking for, I don't think I've got it, but if I have, it's yours, no hassle, OK?'

'Yeah, that sounds OK,' said Blue. 'What we want, Joe, is what that Indian slag left here last night. That's all. Then we'll be off.'

'That Indian…oh, you mean Mrs Bannerjee? Listen, she left nothing. Honest. She came with her suitcase, true, but she never opened it. I mean, think about it, friend, if she *had* left anything, you'd have found it!'

He gestured at the surrounding chaos. It seemed to him a clinching argument, but neither Blue nor Grey looked persuaded.

'What do you reckon?' said Blue. 'Kill the cat?'

'Yeah,' Grey said. 'Kill the cat.'

Whether they meant Whitey or were talking hip, Sixsmith didn't know. Either way, he didn't doubt they were serious.

'Listen,' he pleaded. 'There's no need to get heavy. I want to help. Truly. Maybe if you just told me what it is you're looking for…'

'Jog your memory, you mean?' said Blue.

'Knock his black head off, that'll jog his memory,' said Grey in a sudden flood of verbosity.

'That's true,' said Blue. 'But give him a last chance, eh? All right, Joe. Here it is. Mr Bannerjee was contracted to bring a small present home with him, by way of a sample as it were. Scag. Couple of kilos. Pure. Only the useless article got himself picked up, didn't he?'

Sixsmith looked at him aghast. Two kilos of pure heroin. Cut, and on the street, that must be worth hundreds of thousands. And this was a sample? These were truly very heavy people.

'Surely Customs must have got it,' he said.

'That's not what we hear, Joe. We hear they found nothing. But Mrs Bannerjee got let loose and she headed straight round here. That's what set us wondering, Joe. Did Bannerjee have some clever fail-safe plan?'

'No, listen, I don't know anything about this. I never heard of the Bannerjees before last night…'

'No? Just a coincidence, was it, that an old mate of yours was waiting to pick her up? Just the goodness of your heart that made you arrange a brief for her old man? No, we reckon there's something naughty going on, Joe. But just you tell us where the stuff is and all will be forgiven, except maybe my oppo here will want to smack your bottie for you. But that's better than your head, you'd better believe me.'

Sixsmith believed him. His mind was racing; well, not exactly racing; like his old Morris Oxford, you had to lean into the accelerator a long time before it picked up speed, but once it got some momentum going, there was plenty of weight there.

He had to think of something to get them out of the flat. Outside there might be a chance. In here, he was dead meat. He summoned up all his power of invention.

Then he realized he didn't need to fall back on that desperate device.

He said, 'Oh, shoot!'

'Yeah?'

'She did leave something. Not her, the kid, the boy. He left a toy bull.'

'How big?' demanded Blue.

Sixsmith made an outline with his hands. It was certainly big enough.

'So where is it, this bull?' demanded Grey, examining his fingernails critically as if in anticipation of pulling up floorboards.

'It's in my car,' said Sixsmith.

'You'd better not be pulling our plonkers, Joe,' said Blue.

'Do I look like I'm trying it on?' said Sixsmith indignantly. There's nothing a self-confessed coward hates more than being suspected of closet courage.

'Maybe not. Right, let's go.'

They ushered him out of the flat and into the lift. They saw no one else and it probably wouldn't have done much good if they had. Even Major Sholto's regime hadn't yet persuaded most people that after midnight good neighbourliness went beyond not pissing in the lift in mixed company.

Outside Sixsmith led them across the draughty hinterland of the tower block into Lykers Lane where he parked the Morris Oxford. There were several cars there, but they knew his without being told. Blue went ahead and tried the door.

To Joe's surprise, it opened.

'Trusting sod, aren't you?' said the man. 'All right, where's this bull?'

'In the back,' said Sixsmith.

'I can't see it.'

Grey made a noise at the back of his throat which gave Sixsmith courage to shoulder Blue aside and climb into the car.

There was no sign of the bull on the rear seat.

He searched the floor, got down on his knees and looked under the seats. There was no bull.

'Joe,' said Blue warningly, 'I'm starting to get bad feelings.'

'It was here, I swear,' said Sixsmith desperately. 'Hang about. Maybe I put it in the boot.'

He went to the rear of the car and unlocked the boot. It was empty, but he cried triumphantly, 'There it is!' The two men craned their necks to see, and Sixsmith stepped back between them, spun round and set off running.

He realized his mistake at once. He was running towards the dead end of Lykers Yard. Here there was no escape route, only the fortified double doors of the lock-ups, high, smooth and unscaleable.

He glanced back. His explosive start had opened up a gap, but the terrible twins knew their geography and weren't hurrying. He hesitated in the orange glow of the old sodium lamp which, suspended from a bracket high up on the angle of the last building on Lykers Lane, sent just enough light into the Yard to make the blackness of its corners look liquid. Once in there, he was completely out of touch with the world of lights and cars and people...

But there was someone in that darkness. His straining eyes glimpsed a movement, the figure of a man, raincoated, wearing a slouch hat, his hand up to the brim as if holding it on in a high wind...something familiar about him...but it didn't matter who he was...it could be Old Nick himself, just now he was a better bet than Blue and Grey who were almost upon him...

Joe threw his head back and screamed, 'Help!'

The figure paused, half turned, stepped back into the darkness, and vanished. He must have gone into one of the lock-ups. Not that it mattered.

Sixsmith had a strong suspicion that whoever it was, he wasn't about to offer assistance.

But it isn't only the devil's ear that picks up human cries for help. Somewhere out there in the dark after-reaches of the Universe, the Divine Ear twitched, the Divine Mouth opened, the Divine Voice spoke.

What He said was, 'Whee-whee-whee-whee.'

And He was saying it louder and louder.

Blue and Grey had stopped at the first note of the approaching siren.

'Let it not fade,' prayed Joe Sixsmith. 'Let it not fade.'

And it didn't. Nearer and nearer it came.

And Grey and Blue, realizing that the cul-de-sac which had been Sixsmith's trap was now their own, turned and ran for the open end.

Sixsmith, exhilaratingly changed from prey to hunter, went in pursuit. As the lights of the police car swept into Lykers Lane, he saw Blue and Grey fling themselves into a doorway. The car shot by them. Sixsmith ran towards it, screaming, 'You've passed them! There they are! Don't let them get away!'

The car stopped. Two policemen got out and came towards him. He was now so out of breath with his exertions that he couldn't express his gratitude.

But before he could embrace them to show how he felt, they did a funny thing. Or rather two not so funny things.

One kicked his legs from under him. The other knelt on his back and handcuffed his arms behind him.

'No use running, Sixsmith,' said the kicking cop. 'There's nowhere to go.'

He was wrong. There were plenty of places to go and from his worm's eye viewpoint, Sixsmith could see Blue and Grey slipping round the corner in their haste to reach them.

'Thought you'd give the car a bit of a spring clean, did you,' said the cuffing cop, pulling him to his feet and pushing him towards the Morris Oxford which with its doors spread wide and its boot lid gaping stood like a dodo vainly hoping for flight.

'What's going on?' gasped Sixsmith. 'You can't do this to me.'

'Quite right, you've got your rights like the rest of us. Here's what they are. Joseph Sixsmith, I'm arresting you. You don't have to say anything but anything you do say will be taken down and may be used in evidence. Understand, do you, sunshine?'

'Arresting me? On what charge?'

'You name it, Joe? For starters, how about rape?'

Which knocked the breath out of him again.

ELEVEN

IF ANYONE EVER published *The Wit and Wisdom of Joe Sixsmith*, they could get away with a single sentence.

Doubts may sometimes drop you in it, but for guaranteed total immersion, you can't beat certainties.

So convinced was he that Meg Merchison was the complainant that instead of exercising his right to say nothing, he started protesting, 'This is crazy. She wanted it as much as me. More! If anyone got raped it was me. I couldn't keep her off me, man. I tell you she was rampant!'

'Changed her mind later, did she?' said the kicking cop not unsympathetically. 'It happens. Without a witness and an affidavit, it's hard to be safe these days.'

He was still protesting his innocence when they took his clothes from him, but at least by then he'd had the sense to ring Butcher at home. She was ex-directory but in a moment of weakness had let him have her number.

'Jesus, Sixsmith, is someone paying you to stop me from sleeping?' she sighed.

Sixsmith, who thought he detected another voice in the background, said nastily, 'No, it sounds like you're paying someone else to do that.'

A weary doctor came and examined him, then, clad only in a scratchy blanket, he was dumped in an interview room.

After a while the door opened and Dildo Doberley came in.

'What the hell are you playing at, Joe?' he said.

'Red Indians,' said Sixsmith, pulling the blanket closer round his shoulders. 'What's it look like?'

'It looks like you're in deep dog shit,' said Dildo. 'Time of the month for you, is it? Lots of mentions in despatches for you today, Joe. Annoying a girl in Dartle Street. Then chatting up a jogger at the university—she took your car number. Acting suspiciously at the scene of a fire...'

'Come off it, Dildo. All that lot got sorted out,' protested Sixsmith.

'That's true,' agreed Doberley, looking at his sheet of paper. 'Explanations noted in each case. Plausible too. Pity you ran out of plausible explanations in this last one.'

'I tell you, she said yes.'

'So you did penetrate?'

'Penetrate?' exclaimed Sixsmith. 'Hey, man, she took me in so deep, I thought I was going to come out of the other side.'

Sexual boasting was not his bag, but if it helped him get off this ludicrous rape charge, he'd brag like a soldier back off leave.

'Then, willing or not, you're snookered, Joe. She's only fifteen.'

'Fifteen?' He thought of Meg Merchison's mature charms and began to laugh. 'You must be joking...or she must be joking...I mean, you *have* seen her, have you?'

'Oh yes, I've seen her. Fifteen's pushing it, I'd say. Looks more like twelve to me. We'll know exactly when we track her mother down.'

Before he could react to this new lunacy, the door opened, and a constable was half way through announcing that the prisoner's brief was here when Butcher shouldered him aside.

'What's going on here?' she demanded.

'A legal interrogation,' said Dildo indignantly. 'I must ask that—'

'Legal? Interrogating a man who's naked in an ice-box except for a dirty blanket, and you call that legal? I'd like a thermometer in here straightaway. I bet you'll need to shove it up his ass to get the mercury rising. Joe, have you been offered any refreshment?'

'Look, I don't want refreshment, all I want is...'

'No refreshment. Have you seen a doctor?'

'Yes, some guy took a look at me...'

Butcher, ready to be indignant if no doctor had been in attendance, switched tack easily.

'*Some guy?* Not your own doctor? You're entitled to access to your own doctor. Did this *guy* examine you?'

'He poked around a bit...'

'Poked around? With your permission?'

'No one asked for permission...'

'Which makes it assault.' She turned to Doberley. 'I think we can safely strike off as inadmissible anything my client may have said up to this point...'

'Butcher!' yelled Sixsmith. 'Stop acting like this is *LA Law.* This is so simple it's stupid. I went to bed with a thirty-year-old woman who was ready, willing and able, and Dildo here is trying to tell me she's under age and didn't want it! All you've got to do is look at her...'

'Yes, I'd like to do that? What do you say, Detective-Constable? Any chance of a quick glance at this—' she looked down at the sheet of paper she was holding—'Suzie Sickert?'

'Come off it. The girl's in shock. I can't just parade her around like a show dog,' protested Doberley.

'Who the hell's Suzie Sickert?' said Joe Sixsmith.

Butcher said, 'What?'

'I said who the hell—'

'I heard you. You mean this thirty-year-old you made it with isn't called Suzie Sickert?'

'No. Her name's—'

'Shut up, Joe. Mr Doberley, can I have a word with you outside?'

They went out. After about ten minutes, Butcher returned.

'What's going on?' said Sixsmith wearily.

Butcher sat down and said, 'About an hour and a half ago, a girl, Suzie Sickert, was brought in by her boyfriend, Glen Lewis. She claimed that some time last night she was walking along near Canal Street when a car pulled up alongside her, a man reached out and dragged her in, then drove off to a dark side street where he assaulted her. Eventually she managed to struggle free and went home in a distressed condition. There was no one there; she lives on Hermsprong with her mother who's in the entertainment business and works nights. The boyfriend called on the girl later. After some time he got the story out of her and finally persuaded her that she had to tell the police.'

'It's all crap!' exclaimed Sixsmith. 'What made them pick on me?'

'She said you were black and going bald. She described the car and she'd got most of the number. And she said that when you tore her pants off in your mad passion, you must have broken a silver bracelet she wears round her left ankle.'

'So?'

'So they've found the bracelet under the seat of your car, Joe. Also some bits of thread which match her torn clothing. Also some traces of her make-up on the upholstery.'

Sixsmith shook his head in bewilderment.

'This is crazy.'

'Crazy perhaps. Not so crazy as you shouting off your mouth that she was willing.'

'But I thought they were talking about—'

'Try to stop thinking, Sixsmith,' she said kindly. 'It could seriously damage both our healths. Just tell me about your lady friend.'

Sixsmith told her everything that had happened since they parted in the Tea-Room.

She said, 'Wow. So we've got an alibi for all yesterday evening. Great.'

Sixsmith said, 'I don't know...'

'You're not going to go chivalrous on me?' she said in alarm. 'Protecting the lady's good name, that sort of thing?'

'Don't be stupid,' said Sixsmith. 'All I meant was, I'm not sure she'll be all that keen on letting it be generally known she was screwing me last night. Not on such short acquaintance.'

'She will after I talk to her,' said Butcher with certainty. 'Now this other business with the two heavies, have you told the police about that?'

'Not yet. I didn't want to complicate matters,' said Sixsmith.

'Then keep quiet, could you? At least about the missing heroin. The *alleged* missing heroin.'

Sixsmith said, 'But why...? Hey, Butcher, I'm with you. You don't want me giving the Customs anything to hit your client, Mr Bannerjee, with! You're not trying to pervert the course of justice, are you? Or do you just not want to offend nice Mr Herringshaw from Birmingham who's paying your fee?'

It was just his fatigue and general irritation talking, but she gave him another of her funny looks.

Then she said, 'All I mean is, Bannerjee's got a nice wife and family. I don't want to see them suffering. Just keep quiet till I have the chance of talking to him again, OK?'

'OK,' said Sixsmith reluctantly. 'But I don't like the idea of that Spanish bull wandering round with a bellyful of scag maybe. That could cause serious environmental damage.'

The door opened and Doberley came in.

'We're not quite finished,' said Butcher coolly.

'No? Well here's something else you and your client might like to talk about.'

Doberley dropped Meg Merchison's cameo locket on to the table.

'Perhaps you'd like to tell us where you got that, Mr Sixsmith,' he said.

Butcher said, 'Perhaps you'd like to tell us why you're asking.'

'Certainly,' said Doberley. 'It was found in your client's pocket when he was searched on arrival here. It rang a bell with the duty sergeant, and soon as he had a moment, he checked it out. This locket was in a list of items stolen from the home of a Mr Collister-Cook about three months ago. Got another plausible explanation, Joe? Yes, Miss Butcher, I know. You'd like to talk to your client.'

Smiling, he left.

Sixsmith said, 'Oh hell, I forgot to tell you about the locket.'

Butcher listened in silence. Then she sighed and said, 'Oh, Sixsmith, why didn't I tell you to stick your redundancy money in the building society?'

'Too late now,' said Sixsmith. 'So what do I say? If I tell them the whole truth, they'll really think I'm mad. If I tell them simply that I picked it up by accident at Meg's house, they'll stir things up between her and the Hyphen, not to mention pulling him in for attempted insurance fraud. And I don't expect your mate, Baker, would be too pleased, which could mean she won't pay me. Which would mean, incidentally, I shouldn't be able to pay you.'

'Takes you a long time to get to the real crux, doesn't it, Sixsmith?' said Butcher.

She frowned and went on, 'Wouldn't it be nice to have a system where the law was so humane and citizen centred, you could afford to tell the police everything?'

'It would put me out of business,' said Sixsmith.

Her face crinkled into an incredulous smile.

'You think you're in business, Sixsmith?'

'At least if someone's paying for my advice, I give it to them.'

'All right. Tell them you found the locket in the public library and forgot to hand it in. They won't believe you, but so what? They won't believe you when you tell the truth either.'

'But Baker and the Hyphen—'

'Gerald can react any which way he likes, up to him. As for Gwen, it's not the locket, it's what it contains she's after, right?'

She prised the locket open with her thumbnail.

'Yuk,' she said, tipping what looked like a lump of putty with various scraps of hair and material embedded in it. 'If this is what she wants, this is what she shall have.'

She wrapped it in a tissue and placed it in the belt pouch she used in lieu of a handbag.

'You can collect it from me when you get out of here.'

'When's that going to be?'

'That depends. This other business, this kid's trying to fit you up. Why should she do that?'

'I don't know,' said Sixsmith. 'Unless she's about five foot three, with blonde hair razored off except for a narrow crest, and probably with a bit of sticking plaster on her arm.'

'Oh God. You *do* know her. Amaze me some more, Sixsmith.'

Sixsmith told her about Mr Nayyar's fire.

'So Suzie and her boyfriend saw me talking to the cops outside Nayyar's shop, reckoned I'd be pointing the finger their way and decided to get their retaliation in first,' he concluded.

'By fitting you up on a rape charge?'

'By doing anything that would make it look like *I* was trying to fit *them* up on an arson charge. Black man, under-age white girl. Racist cop. It's a powerful mixture, isn't it?'

'Come on, Sixsmith,' protested Butcher. 'This is Luton, not Alabama.'

'How many pubs you think you'd need to advertise in round here to get yourself a nice little lynch mob?' retorted Sixsmith.

'All right, point taken. So we tell Doberley, he checks with Mr Nayyar, the arson team take a close look at these kids...'

'Pointless,' said Sixsmith, who was having a bad attack of the three a.m. blues. 'Nayyar's probably too scared to say anything. And show me a cop who's going to bother about a white arsonist in the bush when he's got a black rapist in the nick.'

The door opened and Doberley came in. He was carrying a large plastic bag in one hand and a cup of tea in the other.

'OK, Joe?' he said. 'I've brought you some char. Also your bits and pieces. Sorry we had to take them just to eliminate you. Good of you to cooperate. So get yourself dressed soon as you like, then maybe we can all go home and get some sleep.'

He let out a rather stagey laugh as Butcher and Sixsmith exchanged glances.

'What about the charges?'

'What charges? You haven't been charged with any thing, have you, Joe? Just helping with inquiries.'

'Come on, Dildo, what's going on?' demanded Joe.

'Just normal good police work, nothing to get your knickers in a twist about, begging your pardon, ma'am,' said Dildo. 'One of our car lads, the one who talked to you at the fire...'

'Forton, you mean?' interrupted Joe. 'Short fat fellow? Acts like he was a supervisor on a plantation?'

'He's not very house-trained,' admitted Doberley. 'But you're lucky it was him who was there. Seems he leaned on this Brit biker he knows who owes him a favour. Got a whisper that some kid called Glen Lewis might be in the frame for firing Nayyar's shop. He goes looking for Lewis but can't find him. Then he hears that the lad is down here at the nick holding his girlfriend Suzie Sickert's hand, while she cries rape against you. Now he mayn't be Einstein, Dean Forton, but he's not daft. He goes back to see Nayyar who's still drying out his premises and twists his arm till he comes clean about the trouble this morning. He keeps it vague as he can, but the descriptions fit, and when the lad working on your car reported the lock had been forced—'

'I knew I'd locked it,' interrupted Sixsmith.

'—so I got to wondering about that anklet and the threads we found inside. Also the doc who looked at Suzie Sickert said there was no sign of forced entry, so to speak. Also nothing under her nails to match them scratches on your back and bum which in any case looked more likely to be the result of enthusiastic cooperation rather than resistance...'

'That was another expert opinion, was it, Constable?' said Butcher.

'You could call it that,' said Doberley, grinning. 'Must be hot stuff this lady friend of yours, Joe. What did you say her name was?'

'He didn't,' said Butcher. 'And he won't. So, you're admitting this has all been a mistake, that my client should never have been arrested?'

'Arrested?' said Doberley innocently. 'I don't think he was actually arrested as such...'

'Arrested,' said Butcher firmly. 'And cautioned. It'll be in the arresting officer's notes, I'm sure. So: false arrest, personal humiliation and inconvenience; professional reputation damaged...'

She was laying it on just a touch thick, thought Sixsmith. But Doberley was up to dealing with the situation.

'Any official complaint will of course be noted,' he said. 'Meanwhile the possibility of other charges is still under consideration.'

'Other charges?'

'Failure to report a crime; to wit shoplifting. Possession of stolen property—'

'This locket, you mean. Mr Sixsmith found it in the public library and was of course going to hand it in at the earliest opportunity.'

'Only he forgot? An honest mistake, eh, Joe? We can all live with each other's honest mistakes, can't we?'

The two men looked at each other for a moment, then Sixsmith said, 'Yeah, sure, I'm the local expert on honest mistakes. Now if you'll both excuse me, I'd like to get my clothes on so I can go home and get them off.'

Outside, he said to Butcher, 'Thanks for turning out.'

She shrugged and said, 'What did I do? It's your racist cop and terrified Pakky shopkeeper you should be thanking. By the way, I noticed you didn't mention the break-in at your flat.'

'And be kept hanging around here another two hours? No, thanks. My home may be a wreck but that's where I want to be.'

'What about the heavies? I think you really ought to tell the police—'

'You weren't so keen when you first heard, in case it dropped your client in deeper trouble.'

Butcher frowned and said, 'That was in there with the lights on. I just don't like the thought of you wandering around with a pair of thugs like that gunning for you.'

Sixsmith said, 'I could come home with you, I suppose,' then laughed when he saw her face. 'It's all right, Butcher. I've got Whitey to take care of me. And anyway, I think those guys are long gone. They still think the cops were coming to my rescue, remember? I'll be in touch.'

He waved a cheerful good night and headed round to the police car pound to collect the Morris.

As he re-entered his dark flat he felt less cheerful. But there was no one there but Whitey to greet him.

The devastation didn't look any less devastated but at least it was home.

He bolted the door, dragged a table and a bureau across it, took the phone off the hook, thrust as much of the stuffing as possible back into his mattress, crawled on top of it and plunged into deep black sleep.

He surfaced briefly, thinking a light had shone in his eyes, then realized it was just a rare flash of logic.

The Spanish bull stuffed with heroin had vanished from his car.

The terrible teenies, Suzie and Glen, had broken into his car to plant the rape evidence.

So it was probably one of them who'd nicked the bull.

'Sixsmith, you're a genius,' he said.

And fell back into sleep.

TWELVE

NEXT MORNING, late, Sixsmith got down to some serious tidying.

His radio was tuned to the local channel and as he worked he got an update on both the fire and the Casa Mia case.

A local youth was helping police with their inquiries into the arson. And the police were investigating about five thousand reports of sightings of Carlo Rocca and/or the blue Fiesta. This reminded Sixsmith that one good effect of his long hard night had been that he'd slept without being disturbed by the Casa Mia dream. Which in turn reminded him that he *had* been woken by his deduction that either Sickert or Lewis had stolen the bull.

Unlike most nocturnal inspirations, this one stood the test of daylight. The girl seemed the most likely culprit. OK, she was a thief, an arsonist and an embryonic slag, but mostly she was a kid, and the tawdry gaiety of a cuddly toy could still appeal. But getting it back without involving the law wasn't going to be easy.

He asked himself why he didn't want to involve the law but his question fell on deaf ears.

He was finding it hard to tidy up and think at the same time. One of them had to go. He tossed a mental double-headed coin, and took Whitey down to the Glit for a drink and a think.

Mr Nayyar's shop was open for business as usual, but Joe still felt some residual resentment that the shopkeeper had needed his arm twisted to bail him out of the Hermsprong kids' rape charge, so he didn't stop.

In the Glit, the eponymous Gary was singing *Frontier of Style*. The barman, who had neither the panache nor the figure to carry off tight trousers and a lurex shirt, said, 'Hello, Joe, how've you been?'

His name was Eric. At the age of sixteen he'd started as an office boy at Robco Engineering. Instead of the promotion he'd been promised on his eighteenth birthday, he'd been made redundant. There followed a year on the dole till he got an office management diploma course at the Tech, which was fine except that his grant blocked his dole, despite coming to less. It was Joe Sixsmith who'd got him the job at the Glit to help make ends meet. Who Eric told about his cash-in-hand wages was his own business. The only advice Joe felt he had to give him was to conceal his distaste for most music later than Beethoven's late quartets.

Sixsmith replied, 'How've I been? Terrible. Usual.'

Eric drew a pint of Guinness and filled a clean ashtray for Whitey.

'Merv's in the lounge. He was asking after you,' he said.

'Was he?' said Sixsmith, recalling that it was Merv's attempt at a good deed that had dumped the Bannerjees and all their attendant crap on his doorstep. 'I expect he wants to apologize.'

But it was accusation not apology that greeted him when he joined the philanthropic cabbie.

'You been hiding or what, Joe?' he cried. 'Not that you ain't got good reason. What you been doing?'

Mervyn Golightly, six foot six and stringy as a stick of ancient celery, was the most irrepressibly cheerful man Joe had ever met. Neither funerals nor failure, personal tragedy nor national disaster, could depress him for long. Cheerfulness would come bubbling through. On the day the news of the Robco redundancies broke, Merv's response had been to organize a fork-lift truck relay race around the plant.

'Always wanted to do that,' he declared. 'Only I never dared in case the buggers sacked me.'

'The buggers *have* sacked you!' retorted Joe angrily.

'No! This way round, they've just given me an opportunity!'

Today in the Glit, he sounded almost serious.

'What have I been doing?' said Sixsmith. 'Cleaning up after you, like always.'

'Oh, yeah? Then how come it's me the police have been hassling, not to mention your two little friends with gable-end faces.'

Sixsmith had no difficulty recognizing Grey and Blue.

'What did they want?' he asked anxiously.

'Cops wanted to know why I took the dusky lass to you. Was it planned? Did we have some special arrangement, nudge, nudge.'

'And the other two?'

'Same. 'Cepting they came on like extras in a Mafia movie. They even made the fuzz sound polite.'

'Oh hell. You all right?' asked Sixsmith, feeling guilty that his danger should have overspilled to include his friend.

'Fine,' grinned Merv. 'They were in the back of the cab. I stopped on the Airport Roundabout, opened the rear door, showed them Percy and invited them to piss off out. Then I drove off and left them standing on the island. Shouldn't be surprised if they were still there, all that holiday traffic!'

Sixsmith laughed. *Percy* was the biggest wrench he'd ever seen. Merv had kept it under his seat ever since an attempted mugging shortly after he started cabbying. It was a fearsome sight to see him spinning it like a cheer leader's baton. It was nice to know that Blue and Grey were also human.

'You take care, Merv,' he admonished nevertheless. 'These are not nice men.'

'So tell me about them, Joe,' invited Merv. 'I reckon I'm entitled.'

It was hard to argue, so Sixsmith gave a potted version of the story.

Merv looked at him with a new respect.

'Sounds like you're in deep, my son,' he said. 'And here's me thinking it was all divorce and lost dogs. If I'd known this earlier, I'd have kneecapped them jokers with Percy while I had the chance.'

'Steer clear,' said Sixsmith flatly.

'Like you?'

'It's my job. Anyway, all I want to do in this case is get that bull back and hand it over to Butcher.'

'And you suss it could be at this kid Suzie's place?'

'Could be. But I don't fancy going round there. First she lives on Hermsprong. Second, she's cried rape once. God knows what she'd yell if I turned up on the doorstep!'

'She lives on Hermsprong, you say? What's her second name?'

'Sickert, I think. Why?'

Merv's face had split in one of his sunrise grins.

'Joe Sixsmith, I always said that your fairy godmother turned up too late to stop you being short, bald and ugly, but to compensate she stuck this note in your nappy saying you were going to get more luck than a big black cat. You recall that dancer I was rushing off to collect the night I delivered the Indian lady? One of my regulars, from Hermsprong? Well, her name just happens to be Maisie Sickert, and I've heard her talk about her troublesome little daughter, Suzie, though I've never met the girl.'

He sat back in his chair, shaking his head as though he'd just discovered Joe was heir to a vast fortune.

'And that makes me lucky?' said Sixsmith. 'Just because you ferry some tart around the clubs? Forgive me if I don't order champagne.'

'Not a tart. An exotic dancer,' said Merv sternly. 'You're slower on the uptake than a Hermsprong lift, and none of them work. Listen, the point is this. If I turn up a bit early for Maisie, she always says, Come in, why don't you? Make yourself comfy, have a drink, while she's completing the camouflage.'

'So?'

'Joe, wake up, my boy! So if there's a Spanish Bull lying around in that apartment, I'll have it before you can say Speedy Gonzalez! End of problem.'

Sixsmith considered, then said grudgingly, 'You do that, I'll owe you.'

'And you'll pay. Starting now,' said Merv, laughing.

'You don't want any more to drink, not when you're driving that cab.'

'No, but I gotta eat. Mine's a cheeseburger with lots and lots of onions but go easy on the Glitter sauce.'

FORTIFIED BY Guinness and monosodium glutamate, Joe felt able to face clearing up the flat once more. He thought of looking in at his office but dismissed the idea. He didn't anticipate there'd be queues on the stairs, and if anyone did call, it would do them good to think he was busy out on a case.

After a couple of hours' hard slog, something like normality had been restored and he felt able to reward himself with a cup of tea and his daily reconstruction of *The Times* crossword. Tea was easy, but when he came to look for the paper he recalled that he hadn't bothered to pick one up. Recalling his reasons, he felt slightly guilty.

'We've all got troubles, Whitey,' he said. 'But that Mr Nayyar, he's got a wife and kids to worry about too, while I've only got myself.'

The cat opened one outraged eye.

'And you too,' added Joe hastily. He glanced at his watch. Just gone four. He was due at choir practice at five-thirty. Time to call at Nayyar's shop, pick up his paper, exchange words of mutual comfort before getting to grip with Haydn's *Creation*.

It was a dark, dank day. The low cloud cover would be forcing the big jets at the airport to rely on electronics till the very last moment, when the lights of the runway came into view and you knew whether or not you'd got it right. Detection was like that, mused Joe Sixsmith. At least it was to him. Flying blind till you saw the lights, and hoping that the lights you saw weren't running down the central reservation of the by-pass.

He was aware of a figure ahead of him as he turned into Lykers Lane, aware too that it was walking very slowly as if unsure of its direction but it wasn't till he came alongside and the man turned to look at him that he recognized Stephen Andover.

Surprise made both of them tongue-tied. Andover recovered first.

'There you are,' he said accusingly. 'How the hell does anyone find their way round this Godforsaken maze?'

'Mr Andover, how're you doing?' said Joe. 'Can I help you? What is it you're looking for?'

'You!' snarled Andover. 'I want a word with you, Sixsmith.'

'Oh yes?' said Joe taking a cautious step sideways. He'd started their acquaintance by wanting to keep space between him and this man, and first impressions weren't always wrong. 'You got a problem?'

'What the hell do you mean by molesting my secretary?' demanded Andover, matching Joe's step with one of his own which brought his face up very close.

Sixsmith put in another step, backwards this time. Andover followed. It must look like we're dancing, thought Joe. Except there was no one for it to look like anything to. He was beginning to have bad feelings about Lykers Lane.

He said, 'Look, Mr Andover, I'm sorry about that, but I got it sorted with the police. It was a silly misunderstanding, is all. Just a daft coincidence.'

'That's what they told me when I complained,' said Andover cynically. 'Well, that might be good enough for the police, Sixsmith, but in my line of business, you soon learn to distrust coincidence.'

Joe looked at him with interest. It wasn't every day you met someone who thought the cops were too trusting.

He said, 'You mean, like if you insured an old banger and it rolled over a cliff next day?'

'That sort of thing, yes.'

'How about a man has a dream of murder and it comes true, Mr Andover? Is that a coincidence too?'

'What the hell are you trying to say?' asked Andover furiously.

Sixsmith wasn't really trying to say anything, just trying to keep things verbal rather than physical. But he knew from experience it was possible to say clever things by accident, which was why not so clever people should be listened to just as carefully as clever ones. Especially by themselves.

'Nothing, I'm sorry, they're not the same, are they?' he said with a conciliatory smile. 'One makes people suspicious; the other, if it does anything...'

He paused, feeling himself teetering on the edge of cleverness once more. The wind suddenly gusted, driving a tornado of dust and litter into the open maw of Lykers Yard.

'Look,' he said. 'This is no place to talk. Why don't you call in at the office some time...'

'Why don't you?' said Andover accusingly. 'Why do you think I'm wandering round this awful bloody place?'

'We can't all live in Coningsby Rise,' snapped Joe defensively, realizing even before the words were out that it wasn't the most sensitive thing to say. Interestingly, though, it seemed, to have a soothing rather than incendiary effect on Andover.

'No,' he said reflectively. 'You're right. An Englishman's home is his castle, no matter how humble.'

Preferring greetings card sentiment to any kind of aggression, Joe said, 'Well, got to get on. Can I give you a lift back to where you left your car?'

The man said disbelievingly, 'Are you taking the piss, Sixsmith? Or have you just forgotten that I don't have a car because my brother-in-law drove away in it after murdering my wife?'

Oh shoot! thought Joe. Me and my big mouth.

He said, 'Sorry. Let me give you a lift then, I'm driving into town.'

The man hesitated, then a force ten blast down the funnel of Lykers Lane convinced him this was not a place he wanted to be.

'All right,' he said grudgingly.

In the car, Joe said, 'Any news about Rocca yet?'

'Nothing. The police seem baffled. But a man can't just disappear.'

'No, but he can lie low. You able to give them any pointers there, Mr Andover?' said Joe.

'What do you mean?' demanded Andover, looking ready to be angry again.

'Nothing. Believe me, Mr Andover. There's no need to be so negative about me. I've done you no harm, have I? In fact, the opposite. If I hadn't happened to be along when you found the bodies, that's when you'd have found out just how distrustful the cops can really be!'

Again he heard that distant echo of divine applause at some unconscious bit of cleverness.

He went on, 'What I meant by pointers was, you might know the kind of place he'd hole up. Holiday spots, that kind of thing. Or what about his old house? Could he still have a key to that?'

'Very clever,' said Andover nastily. 'Except he didn't have a house, he leased a flat, and when his electrical business went bust he had to give it up, which is why he came to live with us, remember? So he'd hand back his keys, and even if he kept one, I think the new tenant might notice a strange Italian with a big moustache hanging around her living-room, don't you? This'll do. I'll get out here.'

They weren't anywhere in particular, but Sixsmith wasn't arguing.

Before he closed the door, Andover leaned into the car and said, 'Just remember, Sixsmith, keep away from Debbie Stipplewhite. In fact, keep your nose right out. I want the police to find Carlo and bring him to justice, and I doubt if it will speed things up if they've got an incompetent amateur under their feet!'

He slammed the door with a force that made the car shudder.

'And thank me for the lift,' said Joe as he drove away.

He realized he had driven past Mr Nayyar's shop. No matter. He could see the man any time and he no longer wanted *The Times*. You didn't need a crossword puzzle to play the game of putting solution before clues. For instance, suppose he tried the interesting solution that maybe after all it hadn't been simple coincidence that put him with Andover while the murders were being committed and when the bodies were discovered. Suppose Andover had wanted to make sure he had an alibi?

He tossed this idea around in his mind as he drove rather erratically down the High Street. It was certainly clever enough, but it might as well be a five-letter word with three zeds when it came to devising clues to fit it. It implied some kind of conspiracy between Andover and his brother-in-law, and that made little sense unless Rocca was such a thickie he agreed to join a conspiracy in which he did all the dirty work and then took all the blame!

Forget theories, stick to facts, Joe reproached himself. When you were coming down through low cloud you had to trust your bleeping screen, not strain your eyes for the runway lights below or the distant stars above.

Fact: Andover had got really shirty at the mention of Rocca's old pad. What was it Mirabelle liked to say about sarcasm? 'Don't you get sarcastic with me, Joseph Sixsmith. Man who can't talk straight must have something to hide.'

'What do you think, Whitey?' said Joe.

The cat, who had scrambled over into his customary front seat as soon as Andover got out, yawned as if to say Joe would be better advised to mind his own business, but Joe was not deceived. Whitey loved a new scent above all things, and the more disgusting, the better.

He parked illegally alongside a telephone-box. It contained a tattered and out-of-date directory but that was exactly what he wanted. There was only one entry under ROCCA. It read Flat 22, Samgarth House.

They liked to live well, these guys who married the Tomassetti girls, thought Joe. Not that he'd ever been inside a Samgarth House flat, but he had seen the ads in the *Bugle* when the purpose-built apartment block had been opened a few years back. He tried without success to recall the name of the managing agents. Then he had another inspiration. On the corner a few yards away an old man was selling *Bugles* with a melancholy cry of 'Nominnyliff.'

Joe brought one and opened it in the car.

He'd been right. Again. If he went on like this, he might just go in for the Open University.

Rare opportunity to acquire remaining three years of seven-year lease in Luton's most prestigious apartment building.

The management firm was Cornelian Estates of Oldmaid Row. Which was scarcely a hop, step, and jump away for a clever dick on a hot scent.

He glanced at his watch. Did he have time? Choir practice at five-thirty. Occasionally he dared be late for the Rev. Pot, just as occasionally he dared be late for Auntie Mirabelle. But to be late for both of them at the same time...

Whitey howled a warning. He looked up to see the chunky traffic warden who'd fled from Blue and Grey approaching purposefully. Clearly she'd licked her wounds and re-emerged, determined to wipe out the shaming memory.

Joe dropped his paper on his lap and drove away as fast as he could.

Oldmaid Row was one of the loveliest bits of Luton, a Regency terrace facing on to a tiny elliptical park full of lime trees which had survived everything the polluters and the vandals could throw at them. Now entirely corporate, the terrace wore the medals of long and distinguished domestic service in the shape of several royal blue plaques which ad-

there was a

FIND OUT INSTANTLY THE G
ABSOLUTELY FRI

▼ SCRATCH-OFF GAME!

Scratch Off All 3 gold areas

LOSER

WINNER

LOSER

PLAY THE

CARNIVAL WHEEL

GAME...

GET YOUR FOUR GIFTS FREE!

PLAY FOR FREE! NO PURCHASE NECESSARY!

YES! I have scratched off the 3 Gold Areas above. Plea
gifts to which I am entitled. I understand I am under no o
any books, as explained on the back and on the opposite

NAME

ADDRESS

CITY STATE

◀ DETACH AND MAIL CARD TODAY! ▼

HOW

1. With a co
the 3 gold are
Wheel. By do
to receive eve
books and a s
ABSOLUTELY

2. Send bac
get brand-new
Mystery Libra
have a cover p
THEY ARE TO
shipping will

3. There's n
obligation to I
nothing—ZEF
shipment. And
any minimum
not even one!

4. The fact i
enjoy receivin
Mystery Libra
like the conve
and they love

5. We hope
free books you
subscriber. Bu
to continue or
why not take u
with no risk of
you did.

No Cost

© 1993 Worldwid

vertised to
resided here

If offer card is missing write to: The Mystery Library Reader Service™, 3010 Walden Ave., P.O. Box 1867, Buffalo, NY 14240-1867

BUSINESS REPLY MAIL
FIRST-CLASS MAIL   PERMIT NO 717   BUFFALO, NY

POSTAGE WILL BE PAID BY ADDRESSEE

MYSTERY LIBRARY READER SERVICE
3010 WALDEN AVE
PO BOX 1867
BUFFALO NY 14240-9952

NO POSTAGE
NECESSARY
IF MAILED
IN THE
UNITED STATES

...ables who had ...ded ...e, though what the world probably wondered was who the hell were Theobald Blacktooth, Inventor; Simeon Littlehorn, Poet; Daphne Margrave Podd, Missionary; Dr Oswald Polidor, Chirurgeon: and many others.

The offices of Cornelian Estates had once housed Marcus Astribe, Banker, and his spirit obviously lived on in the young receptionist whose steely blue eyes unabashedly totted up the cost of Sixsmith's cracked slip-ons, baggy trousers, balding corduroy jacket and round-collared shirt, multiplied it by his lack of rings, bracelets and gold neck ingots, and came up with nothing.

'Can I help you, sir?' she said in a tone which dripped doubt, but at least tagged the *sir* on.

'You got a flat in Samgarth House,' said Sixsmith.

'That's right, sir. An *apartment*. It's the remainder of a short lease. The vendor is looking for a premium of somewhere in the region of forty thousand.'

'Oh yes? Discount for cash, is there?' said Sixsmith. 'You do all the Samgarth flats, do you?'

'Yes, sir. We've looked after all the Samgarth *apartments* from the start.'

There followed a pause as Sixsmith racked his brain to think of where to go from here. It was all right being a fast-thinking, fast-talking PI when you had some movie scriptwriter smoothing the way for you. His own experience was that while it was easy enough to get in this kind of potentially useful situation, making progress was almost impossible.

He said, 'I got a friend lives there, is why I'm interested.'

'Oh yes. Then you'll probably know about the ground rent. And the management fee, which is quite heavy, but it has to be to cover the kind of services such a prestigious development requires.'

No inviting gap there. And if once he mentioned Rocca's name, then her alarm button already half depressed would surely make full contact.

As if translating ~~~~~~~~~~~~~~~~~~
peremptory buzz from her intercom.

'Miranda, can you step in here for a mo?'

'Right away, Mr Stornaway,' she said, pressing a switch.
'I'm just finishing with a client.'

She had the grace to flicker what might have been an
apologetic smile at Sixsmith as she said, 'Look, why don't
I give you the details and you can think it over?'

She went to a rosewood filing cabinet, pulled open a
drawer and extracted some sheets of paper which she then
placed in an ornate folder and presented to Sixsmith.

'You'll find everything there,' she said. 'Including the
general house rules contract which is of course binding even
when the apartment is sub-let.'

He recognized a fail-safe in case he was fronting for a
Heavy Metal group with a couple of Dobermans.

'If you're still interested, after reading it,' she concluded, 'we can make an appointment for our Mr Stornaway to show you round.'

'Great,' he said. 'I'll be in touch.'

He waved at her from the doorway. She didn't wave back.

He stood outside in the foyer and counted to twenty. Then
he slowly re-opened the door.

The reception area was empty.

He moved swiftly to the rosewood filing cabinet. The
drawer she'd used slid silently open. Thank God for expensive furniture.

Right at the front was what he wanted, a general index to
Samgarth House. He took it out and ran his eye down the
list.

Bingo.

No. 22. The name of Rocca was carefully crossed out with
a date some six months earlier alongside, followed by the
name of the new tenant.

Mr Stephen Andover.

THIRTEEN

HERE WAS ANOTHER ONE for the Sixsmith book of wit and wisdom: finding things out is easy compared with deciding what to do with them once they're found.

Tell the cops was the obvious move. Except they'd probably either sneer 'cos they knew already, or be dismissive 'cos they didn't want to know anyway.

Alternatively, he could keep sticking his nose into business for which no one was paying him and off which he'd been specifically warned.

That would be really stupid, but he hadn't got where he was today by being afraid of being really stupid.

He still hadn't made up his mind when he arrived at Boyling Corner Chapel just before five-thirty.

The Reverend Percy Potemkin, known throughout Luton as Rev. Pot, believed in catching his choristers on their way home, 'before they get food in their bellies to coarsen the voice and telly in their eyes to depress the soul'.

Joe, after an alienating diet of enforced attendance throughout his youth, now only rarely showed up at Sunday service. Rev. Pot didn't waste words admonishing him. 'Your soul's between you and the Lord, Joe,' he said. 'But your voice belongs to me. I've put too many years into that reedy baritone to let it go without slitting your throat.' So Joe still sang in the choir, not the Sunday service choir which consisted of a few old faithfuls led by the vibrant contralto of Auntie Mirabelle, but the famous Boyling Corner Concert Choir, twice winners of the Laurel Wreath at the Luton Terpsichorean Festival. The choir was ecumenical if not eclectic. Voice was all that mattered, virtue didn't come into it. 'I make them sing unto the Lord,' said Rev. Pot. 'It's up to Him to hand out prizes.'

Thus it didn't bother him that Detective-Constable Dildo Doberley had joined only because he had immoral longings for the well-developed chest of Deirdre Carnell, pride of the mezzos. Dildo was that rarest of beasts in the amateur vocal world, a genuine *basso profundo,* and this would have got him in even if he'd been dragging a forked tail behind him.

Joe bumped into Dildo in the doorway and this almost made up his mind for him. Here was a chance to offload what he'd found out about Rocca's former flat with minimum hassle. But before he could speak Dildo said, 'Hello, Joe. She's a bit sharp, that brief of yours. You should keep her on a leash.'

'Still giving you bother, is she?' said Sixsmith, not displeased.

'You'd have thought we'd had you over a slow fire all night,' grumbled Dildo.

'That's all right. I'm not going to sue,' said Joe magnanimously. 'And at least you got a result out of it.'

'Result?'

'Yeah. Those two Brits. Torching Mr Nayyar's shop and trying to fit me up for rape. That must be worth a slap on the wrist and five minutes' community service at least.'

As he spoke he saw an uncharacteristically shifty look come over the detective's face and he said, 'Dildo, they *are* being charged, aren't they?'

'Sorry, Joe,' said Dildo. 'They got a brief too, one of your Ms Butcher's mates from the Law Centre. It works both ways, see? Everything points to them doing the shop, but without either a clear sighting or firm forensic, there's no case.'

'All right, but they tried to fit me up on a rape charge, didn't they? Surely you can do them for that?'

''Fraid not, old son. Little Miss Sickert's withdrawn the accusation. Says she may have been mistaken about the car number and she was certainly mistaken about the anklet.

Now she's had a closer look, it wasn't hers after all. She's got the cheek to say CID pressurized her into identifying it! So it was some other black man in some other car who assaulted her, and her mother's shouting the odds about how bloody useless the police are.'

'She's not far wrong,' snapped Joe.

They went inside. Mirabelle was there with the nurse, Beryl Boddington. Fortunately she was introducing her prodigy to Rev. Pot and could only fix Joe with a gaze like a Star Trek tractor beam, but his irritation with Dildo protected him like a force-field. At least the exchange had made his mind up about the Samgarth House information. Why waste it on incompetents like the cops?

'You were *what?*' Rev. Pot's voice rose above the general hubbub and stilled it so that Beryl Boddington's reply was clearly audible.

'I was once a fairy in *Patience,*' she said.

Joe grinned broadly. In Rev. Pot's musical league, Gilbert and Sullivan came somewhere under Heavy Metal.

His lightening of spirits was shortlived. Rev. Pot said, 'Well, I see Joe Sixsmith's here, so we must be late. Let's make a start.' And for the next hour and a half as they grappled with Haydn's *Creation,* Joe found himself singled out with what felt like a malicious frequency.

Afterwards when, inevitably, Mirabelle got to him, he said, 'Rev. Pot's in a bad mood tonight, isn't he?'

'No, Joseph. You're in bad voice. Something on your mind, is there? It always shows. You gotta give this music everything!'

'Oh yes? That why Dildo gets told he's singing so well, when all he's got on his mind is getting into Deirdre Carnell's underwear!'

'Remember where you are!' exclaimed Mirablle. 'You not so big I can't still wash your mouth out with soap.'

He caught Beryl's amused gaze upon him and flushed. It wasn't helped by memories of occasions when his aunt actually had washed his mouth out. In fairness, though, he had to admit the brutal tactic had worked. It was only very rarely that he swore and when he did, his mouth tasted of Palmolive.

'Sorry, Auntie,' he said. 'Look, I've got to rush.'

'You're always rushing. That car of yours mended, is it?'

'What?' he said, puzzled, then remembered his lie at the Residents' Meeting. 'Oh yes. All fixed.'

Again he felt the nurse's gaze upon him, quizzical this time. He was convinced she'd spotted him as he drove by her in the rain.

'Then nothing to stop you giving this young lady a lift tonight, is there?'

He said, because there was nothing else to say, 'Well, OK, I suppose so. If she's ready now, straightaway...'

'No, thanks,' said Beryl Boddington coolly. 'I don't start my shift for a while yet, and there're a couple of things I need to do. Good night, Mirabelle. Mr. Sixsmith.'

'See what you've done?' said Mirabelle, watching her go. 'Last night she was calling you Joseph.'

'Then we're moving in the right direction,' said Sixsmith. 'Good night, Auntie.'

In the car Whitey gave the pathetic mew which meant, 'My stomach thinks my throat's cut.' Joe drove to Lucky Luciano's chippy on Gripewater Lane where he got haddock and double chips. He'd have preferred the plaice, but Whitey liked haddock and Joe was feeling guilty at the way he was messing up the cat's routine. At least they agreed that Lucky made the best chips in Luton.

They ate these parked up against the ten-foot brick wall which was the only physical remnant of Sir William Samgarth's estate. Sir William was an eighteenth-century entrepreneur, knighted for services to commerce and 'the King's friends'. His business acumen proved to be non-communicable, but its quality can be judged by the fact that it took his feckless descendants the best part of two centuries to spend what he had got. Bit by bit, however, the rolling acres were sold off till all that remained was the original Samgarth House which burnt to the ground with the last Samgarth in 1974. The story was that, having drunkenly decided to subsidize his remaining years by means of the fire insurance, the pie-eyed knight had forgotten to make sure the doors of his escape route were left unlocked.

During the loadsamoney 'eighties, the new gold and blue Samgarth House had risen out of the ashes, and its upper storeys looked down scornfully upon the dilapidated villas which lined one side of Chestnut Avenue where Joe was parked.

There were no buildings on the side of the avenue nearest the wall, just a line of ancient chestnut trees, a favourite resort of the kerb-crawling cars which infested the old Victorian suburb. Despite the earliness of the hour, the area looked like Tesco's car park already. Choir practice wasn't the only activity which got Luton folk home late.

'I bet,' said Joe in a tone midway between self-righteous and regretful, 'I'm the only fellow here who's got his trousers on.'

It didn't seem a profitable line of speculation, so he turned his mind to strategy. As usual, nothing better than the obvious suggested itself.

He'd just walk in and see what happened.

He spread the chip paper on the floor of the car.

'OK, you finish them off,' he said to Whitey. 'But don't chew the paper. You know the *Star* makes you sick.'

Fifty yards ahead there was a hole in the wall which had once held a small gate, presumably the tradesmen's entrance to the estate. Sixsmith went through. It was like stepping through a time warp. Behind, the shabby gentility of the last century and shadowy sub-life of this; ahead, the pastel blue concrete and if-you've-got-it-flaunt-it glitz of the next God knows how long.

He licked his fatty fingers, hitched his pants and went inside. He found himself in a small but nicely appointed vestibule that wouldn't have shamed a first-class hotel. There was a lift but the wall around it was freer of buttons than a hook'n'eye Baptist. High in a corner something blinked redly like the eye of a hungover God. Then a still small voice said politely, 'Can I help you, sir?'

'Er, yes. I hope so,' said Sixsmith, casting round for some form of assistance that wouldn't get him the immediate elbow. 'I've come to look at an apartment.'

He remembered the details he'd got from Cornelian. They were still in his inside pocket. He pulled them out and waved them vaguely in the air, his still greasy fingers leaving prints all over the pristine white paper. Rather to his surprise, the tactic worked.

'That'd be No. 18, would it, sir?'

'That's right.'

'Mr Stornaway is already up there. Please go ahead.'

The lift door opened. Sixsmith entered. Stornaway was the cool Miranda's boss at Cornelian, he recollected. It had fallen nicely that he was actually planning to show someone round this evening. Bit of luck. Or something. No point speculating. If you've got it, ride it!

He got out on the first floor in case the Eye was still on him and walked along the corridor till he saw a door marked Fire Stairs. He went swiftly through it and ran up to the next floor where he found that the stair door opened on to the corridor almost opposite No. 22.

Once more he cast around for inspiration. This was the danger zone. When he rang that doorbell he had no idea what was likely to appear but there was a reasonable possibility it could be a homicidal Italian with a stiletto in his hand. So he decided to do what he hadn't done since a little boy, ring the bell and run.

He pressed the button firmly and stepped back immediately through the door to the staircase, holding it open just a crack so that he could see without, he hoped, being seen.

There was a long pause, so long he began to think that possibly the flat was empty.

Then the handle turned and the door opened. A woman stood there, looking lovely, puzzled, and very familiar.

She was wearing a bathrobe, and the shower had dampened her hair from yellow to bronze, but he had no difficulty in recognizing Debbie Stipplewhite.

While his mind was still trying to accommodate this new factor, his ears were registering two noises.

One was the lift door opening at the far end of the corridor, the other was steel-toed footsteps coming quickly up the stairs.

Debbie had heard the former. She looked along the corridor, then her face broke into a smile which made her look even more attractive and she said, 'Stephen, darling.'

Next moment she was in Andover's arms and he was kissing her with a passion which looked so whole-hearted it threatened to become whole-bodied too.

The girl, conventional enough not to want to be taken on the corridor floor, began to pull him inside. The footsteps were at the half-landing. One more turn would bring the footstepper in sight of the lurking PI.

It could be that some energetic inmate of Samgarth House preferred to use the fire stairs and happened to think steel toecaps were 'in' this year, but Sixsmith guessed it meant Security. Or maybe even Blue and Grey.

The thought was like a match to blue touch-paper. He shot forward, shoving Andover's slowly retreating back with such force that he and the girl collapsed to the floor; then, stepping over the closely bonded couple, he kicked the door shut behind him.

The girl, eyes firmly closed, clearly took this sudden collapse to the horizontal as evidence that her lover's passion had reached explosion point, and was desperately wrestling with his trouser belt.

Andover, not so far gone that he couldn't distinguish a premature knee tremble from a push in the back, was equally desperately trying to disengage himself.

Sixsmith, while suspecting that what he had here was in every sense a whole new ball game, couldn't easily shed the suspicion that somewhere close lurked a mad Italian knifeman, so with the courage born of insupportable fear he went quickly through the apartment and found to his relief that it was empty.

Except, of course, for the lovers.

At last the girl had caught on that Andover's violence of movement had something more than passion in it. She opened her eyes and found herself looking up at Joe Sixsmith. Now she unglued her lips and began to scream.

Andover, with a speed of thought that made Sixsmith sigh with admiration and envy, immediately worked out that the last thing he wanted was a crowd of curious rescuers, and shut the girl up by slapping his mouth back on hers.

Debbie, mistaking this for an exhibitionistic attempt to resume their interrupted coupling, now began to fight him off with a ferocity outstripping his own previous efforts to break the embrace, while he confirmed her fears by grappling her to him with all his strength.

Only Sixsmith remained a free agent.

He said, 'Look, I'm sorry if this is an awkward time, but I'd like a chat, so can't we all sit down and talk things over? I could murder a cup of tea.'

Perhaps it was the word murder which was the Open Sesame.

Their lips separated. The girl didn't scream. The man's grip relaxed. They both scrambled to their feet. Andover's trousers fell down.

Sixsmith said, 'I'll put the kettle on, shall I?'

While the girl got dressed and Andover pulled up his pants, Joe made a pot of tea. The others ignored it with scorn, preferring a schooner of sweet sherry and a tumbler of straight vodka respectively.

With his trousers fastened, Andover had recovered his aplomb.

He said bitterly, 'So I was right, Sixsmith. You were watching Debbie.'

Sixsmith smiled enigmatically. Despite Auntie Mirabelle's asseverations, the truth was not always his friend. There was still a chance that Andover and Rocca had conspired to kill the Tomassettis, but, right or wrong, he didn't want to show his cards in this place at this time, particularly as he was still batting blind.

The girl said, 'Why don't you ring the police, Steve, and get him thrown out?'

Sixsmith said, 'Yes, Steve. Why don't you do that?'

Andover emptied his glass and said peremptorily, 'I'd like a coffee now, Debbie love, would you mind?'

Debbie looked as if she'd mind very much, but after a brief eye battle she stood up and flounced into the kitchen, slamming the door.

Sixsmith did not doubt her ear would be flattened against it, and Andover clearly felt the same for he dropped his voice a decibel or two as she said, 'OK, Sixsmith, what's your game?'

It was a good question. Not having any matching answer, Sixsmith thought he might as well recycle it.

'Never mind that,' he said authoritatively. 'More to the point, what's your game, Mr Andover?'

'I don't have to answer to you,' retorted Andover.

'That's true. Look, why don't we take your girlfriend's advice, ring the police and get me arrested? Trespass or something. Yeah, that would be it. Trespass. Hey, in court I could say, forgive us our trespasses, couldn't I? You know how the Press love a good quote. And when my lawyer asks what I was doing here, I could say I saw you in the doorway and I thought you were attacking this young lady, and if I'd realized you were only getting ready to hump her, I'd have naturally looked the other way and passed on by.'

He paused.

Andover said, 'I could sue you for slander.'

'Not for anything I said on the witness stand, you couldn't. Anyway I'd plead truth. Shoot, Mr Andover, no one's going to think any the worse of you. Man can't be expected to mourn for ever. It must be all of forty-eight hours since your wife had her throat slit.'

He thought he'd overcooked it and that Andover was going to explode into violence. But the moment passed and the insurance man shrivelled into his chain store suit.

'I suppose it must look pretty terrible,' he said in a low voice.

'I'm not bothered how it looks,' said Sixsmith, though to tell the truth he did think it was a pretty shitty way for a man to behave, even if he was in insurance.

Andover seemed to catch the disapproval behind the denial for he went on insistently, 'Look, to all intents and purposes it was over, our marriage, I mean. In fact it hardly ever got started, really. After the first flush of romance it was downhill all the way, a complete clash of cultures, I can't imagine how I ever thought... Well, you don't want to hear about that. All you need to know, Mr Sixsmith, is I'm sorry my wife had to die the way she did, but I'd be a hypocrite to say that I miss her. Debbie has been a great comfort to me during the past year. Why should I be expected to deny myself that comfort just now when I need it most?'

'That's not for me to judge,' said Sixsmith rather pompously. 'So you set her up in this flat...'

'Apartment,' said Andover. 'No, it wasn't like that. You make it sound like I'm some dirty old man setting up his fancy woman. She was looking for a place just about the time Carlo went bankrupt. The management company, Cornelian Estates, were about to retake possession, Carlo was way behind in his ground rent and his management fees, and they were entitled. So I got in quick, took over the lease on reasonable terms, which meant that Carlo got a bit of money...'

'And you got a place for Debbie,' completed Sixsmith. 'You must pay her very well if she can afford a pad like this.'

'OK, so she doesn't pay an economic rent. But she doesn't know that. All I told her was that my brother-in-law's flat was coming vacant and because of his unfortunate circumstances, I could put in a word with the managers who were looking for a new tenant for the rest of the lease. She's no idea I'm subletting it to her. I know Debbie. Any hint of being a kept woman and she'd be out of here without a second thought!'

Sixsmith regarded him with the weary cynicism of one who had been pulled into bed by a passionate witch only the night before and said, 'I dare say you're right, Mr Andover. I doubt if she'd need more than one thought either.'

It was a good line but now he was stuck. Whatever he thought about Debbie Stipplewhite's understanding of her situation, he couldn't really see either love or money persuading her to share her flat with a randy Italian who'd just butchered his family.

On the other hand, Andover had just admitted to a pretty good motive for joining in a conspiracy to kill his wife. But why bother with the others? Maybe Rocca had his own motives for killing them and had offered to throw in Gina in return for Andover's cooperation? Not that he had been all that cooperative. He'd gone out of his way to give himself an alibi, but as for covering his brother-in-law's tracks, nothing.

It was all beginning to make his head ache. He needed a clear mind for this sort of heavy traffic, and the only clear mind he knew belonged to Butcher.

The girl with yellow hair came back into the room with a mug of coffee. How much had she heard? wondered Sixsmith. And how much of what she heard had she known already?

He stood up and said, 'I'll be going now. We'll be in touch, Mr Andover.'

'About what?' said Andover with an attempt at aggression, but he couldn't keep the relief out of his face.

Joe gave them his enigmatic smile and got out quick.

He didn't fancy the stairway in case old Steelcap was still wandering around, so he walked to the lift. It stopped at the first floor in its descent and a young man in a sharp suit with a carnation buttonhole and a fifty quid hair-do ushered a middle-aged couple in, or would have done if they hadn't snapped to a halt at sight of Joe.

'Going down?' he said, smiling.

The young man's eyes had glazed for a second, then he said, 'Foyer,' in a commanding voice before resuming his half-moon smile and saying as he urged the couple forward, 'Service with discretion is our watchword. Security

without obtrusiveness. People who can afford this quality
of accommodation deserve to feel they belong to a community that is safe in every sense and that's what we at
Cornelian Estates aim to provide.'

This is young Mr Stornaway, thought Sixsmith. And the
sod's trying to make out like I'm the lift man!

The lift hit the ground floor. The doors opened to reveal
a bit of unobtrusive security in the shape of a uniformed
man whose toecaps glinted.

Sixsmith put his arm across the middle-aged couple's
shoulders and urging them out of the lift before him said,
'So maybe we're going to be neighbours here at Samgarth?
Now that will be truly great. You like music? I got a heap of
friends thinking of moving in here too and when they hear
from me what nice folks they'll be sharing with, they're going to be truly keen. Like Stornaway here says, we'll make
this a real community!'

The words carried him across the foyer and out of the
door.

He said to the dumbfounded trio, 'Good night now.
Don't want to be late for my shift at the canning factory.
Good jobs is hard to find these days!'

He was still laughing at their expressions as he slid into
the driving seat of his car. Whitey raised his head and gave him
a pained look which said loud and clear, You've been
drinking!

'Not yet,' said Joe Sixsmith. 'But that's not such a bad
idea either. Let's see what our friend Ms Butcher's got in her
drawer, shall we?'

FOURTEEN

BUTCHER SAID, 'Just the man I want to see.'

Sixsmith looked behind him to see if someone else had come in.

'Ha ha,' said Butcher.

She was at her desk, her small frame concealed by the piles of files before her, her head wreathed in cheroot smoke like a grumbling volcano. Theoretically the Law Centre shut at six, but it was rare that Butcher got away before eight and often it was even later.

'You'll kill yourself,' said Sixsmith.

'Working late, you mean? Well, if even my friends take advantage, why should I expect strangers to show more consideration?'

Abashed, Sixsmith said, 'Look, I'll give you a ring tomorrow...'

'Don't be coy, Sixsmith. Didn't I say I wanted to see you? Listen, have you got that heroin back yet?'

'I'm working on it,' said Sixsmith. 'You admit it does exist now?'

'Not till I see it,' she said. 'Like a drink?'

'Sole purpose of visit,' said Sixsmith. 'Whitey!'

The cat had dropped off his shoulder on to the desk and rubbed its bum against a stack of files which toppled slowly to the floor. Much taken by the phenomenon, Whitey moved on to the next pile. Joe snatched him up and said, 'Sorry. Were they in order?'

'Sort of,' said Butcher. 'But not necessarily in the best order. That cat may know something we don't.'

She produced a bottle of slivovitz and poured it into plastic cups.

'Present from a grateful client. Funny how rarely gratitude expresses itself in cash.'

'I paid for your lunch at the Tea-Room.'

She looked at him over her cup and said, 'My, we are defensive. Must be something really heavy you want to see me about.'

'No, I just need someone to organize my thoughts. What do *you* want?'

'Same thing, oddly enough. More gratitude?'

She held up the bottle.

'I'm driving. But the cat...'

With a sigh, Butcher, who reckoned there was something psychologically deviant about Sixsmith's relationship with his cat, poured some plum brandy in a clean ashtray and put it on the floor. After a cautious sniff, Whitey sucked it up like a Hoover.

'It's this Bannerjee thing,' said Butcher. 'I've talked to him again. I told him what had been happening with you and those thugs...'

'Was that wise?' interrupted Sixsmith.

'Listen,' she said acerbically. 'My clients are often in the habit of lying to me, but one thing I make sure is, I never lie to them. He got very agitated indeed. He says it's on account of his wife and kids.'

'That's reasonable,' said Sixsmith.

'Reasonable and true aren't the same, not in Luton,' said Butcher. 'Thing is, he's got so worried, he's changed his story. He says he's scared he might in fact have got mixed up with some drug traffickers. Inadvertently.'

'Inadvertently.' Sixsmith savoured the word. 'Go on.'

'He says now that one day when he was wandering around Marbella, he bumped into a Spaniard he knew vaguely through his job. Herringshaw's are like most British firms at the moment, reaching out to Europe with one hand while the other's trying to beat off the mugging they're getting from the recession at home. This Spaniard gets very friendly, takes the Bannerjees out to lunch. They meet again a couple of times and on the day they're flying back home, he turns up at the hotel and presents Bannerjee with a couple of litre bottles of Spanish brandy as a farewell gift.'

'Must be a really likeable guy, your client,' said Sixsmith. 'People go out of their way to be nice to him.'

'I wish you'd come right out with it and say you didn't like the sound of Charley Herringshaw from the start,' said Butcher irritably. 'No one likes a smart-arse.'

Sixsmith, who had no awareness that he had ever indicated, or was now indicating, that he didn't like the sound of Herringshaw, looked blank, which was evidently the same as looking like a smart-arse, for Butcher rolled her eyes and said, 'OK, so it's much more likely this Spaniard said the bottles were a prezzie for Herringshaw, but that's not the way Bannerjee's telling it. Can you blame him? The man's his boss and these are hard times for redundant middle-aged business executives, even if you've got all the best qualifications and your face is white.'

'So what happened to the bottles?' inquired Joe, trying to keep his eye on the main object.

'Bannerjee's no innocent abroad. He's heard all the warnings about carrying stuff you haven't packed yourself. So he opened one of the bottles and found it wasn't liquid flowing out, but powder. Now Spanish brandy may not be the smoothest drink on earth, but at least it's wet. It was too late to try to get hold of the Spaniard and Bannerjee didn't want to leave the stuff lying around. So last thing he did before leaving the hotel was pour all the powder down the loo and flush it away.'

Joe considered, then said, 'How's this leave him in law?'

'Out of reach,' said Butcher. 'There's been no offence committed, and he's not even certain it was drugs.'

'Is that how DI Yarrop sees it?'

'He says it's a step in the right direction and he'd like to hang on to Bannerjee in case he takes any more steps.'

'Naturally, you objected.'

'A little,' grinned Butcher. 'Only it wasn't any use.'

'Yarrop too smart for you?'

'No. Bannerjee said he was happy to continue helping with inquiries. It seems to me like he reckons he's safer in custody than he would be out in the big world with your friends Blue and Grey looking for him.'

'But it's OK them looking for me, is it?' complained Joe. 'I don't think I'll join his fan club. You ask him about the bull?'

'Of course. He said it is just a bull, a kid's toy, nothing in it.'

'You believe him?'

'I believe, either way, that's all he could say,' said Butcher. 'Oh, take that look off your face, Sixsmith. Yes, I believe him, but I'm just a gullible woman, as witness my association with you. But it would be very much simpler if you could prove us both right by finding that damn bull and cutting it open. You are working on it, I hope?'

'It's all in hand,' said Sixsmith with airy confidence.

He would have liked to ask her advice as to how he might do this as Merv's recovery scheme seemed far too vague. But sometimes he got pissed off with the way Butcher switched from treating him like he was some kind of genius, which he knew he wasn't, to treating him like some kind of moron, which he didn't think he was either.

And besides he needed to consult her about the Casa Mia case, didn't he, and one thing at a time is quite enough even for a bright lawyer.

He said, 'Oh, there is something you might be able to help with...'

She listened intently, only rolling her eyes heavenward a couple of times.

When he finished she said, 'You know, I think there's a really good case here.'

'You do?' he said hopefully.

'Yes. Trouble is, it's for invasion of privacy and Andover could make it against you.'

'You don't think he's got anything to do with the killings, then?'

She gave herself another snort of slivovitz. Sixsmith envied her double. First she didn't drive, and second she seemed able to put alcohol away like she had a tube to her own private cellar.

'I think from what you say he's probably not too grief-stricken to be rid of his wife and his in-laws, but that's a long way short of conspiring to knock them off.'

'I've proved he had a motive.'

'You've proved he had a bit on the side, all very nicely set up for his delectation both during working hours and after. All the sex, none of the household chores—most men's idea of heaven. And what about Rocca? He did the killing, right? So what's his motive? To help his brother-in-law out? I doubt it. No, you'd need something which would tie them in together.'

'Like what?'

'Like money. We know Rocca's in Queer Street. Bankrupt, relying on hand-outs. What about Andover?'

'How should I know? They don't let black PI's look at white men's bank accounts.'

She whistled softly and said, 'That's the first racist remark I've ever heard from you, Sixsmith. I hope you're not on the turn?'

'I'm sorry, it's just that one minute you're talking invasion of privacy, next you're implying I don't dig deep enough, even where it's illegal.'

'No, I'm not! I'm just asking if you use your eyes. What kind of clothes does he wear? What kind of car does he drive?'

'A Fiesta. We know that because it's all over the papers, that's what the cops are looking for,' said Sixsmith with an air of triumph. 'Clothes, just ordinary clothes, nothing flashy.'

'Do you mean Savile Row nothing flashy, or chain store nothing flashy?'

He said, 'Chain store off the peg. I recall thinking he's sort of between stock sizes. I get the same trouble with trousers sometimes. You see, I've got these long calves for my height . . .'

'Sixsmith, fascinating though the details of your anatomy are, let's stick to the point. So this fellow drives a small car and buys his clothes off the peg. He doesn't sound rolling in it, does he? Yet he lives on Coningsby Rise, and he's able to buy up the remaining term of Rocca's lease.'

'According to Mrs Rathbone, their neighbour, it's old Tomassetti who had the moneybags. He paid for the house, it seems and that must be worth a packet.'

'So whoever inherits will do OK. What about insurance? You say he's an insurance broker? With those guys, salesmanship begins at home. There could be big money there too. But only with the lot of them dead.'

'That's right,' said Sixsmith, getting quite excited. 'And as for buying up the lease on the Samgarth flat, Andover must have a lot of client money going through his hands and he could have dipped in there, which would make him desperate to get his hands on any inheritance coming his way.'

Butcher clapped.

'You see, Sixsmith, like the poet says, it's not what you know that matters, it's being able to *imagine* what you know.'

This sounded a bit *Times* crosswordish to Sixsmith, but he got the drift that she was saying something nice, albeit in her oblique satirical style.

He said, 'So where does this leave us?'

'Us? Hold on, Sixsmith. There's no *us* here, just you.'

Sixsmith's face dropped and Whitey, who had curled himself over his empty ashtray as if he had hopes it was a widow's cruse, let out a yell which was probably an appeal for more but came over like a sympathetic protest.

'Oh all right,' said Butcher. 'I'll do the legal bit and see what I can find out about the will. But tit-for-tat, Sixsmith, you get your black ass moving and bring me that bull, you hear me now?'

Her attempt at a Deep South accent was quite passable and she'd even managed to get her voice into a bass baritone register.

'That's good,' said Sixsmith. 'You ever thought of doing a drag show?'

'Sod off, Sixsmith,' said Butcher. 'No, hang about. I was almost forgetting. The other reason I wanted to see you, Gwen Baker rang a couple of hours ago. Seems that when she got home this evening she found a message on her answering machine asking her husband to pop in to the police station to identify a locket which matched the description of one stolen from their house. Naturally, being Gwen, she got down there tooty-sweety and claimed the thing. But when she got home she opened it and found it was empty. Next she tried to ring you, only you weren't to be rung. So in the end she contacted me. I told her I am not your social secretary, but I was able to reassure her that the contents of the locket were safe in my hands, which seemed to delight her very much. She told me to burn them, but I'm a bit chary about destroying other people's property. So here it is. You can give it to Gwen when you go to collect your wages.'

She took a matchbox out of a drawer and handed it over.

Sixsmith opened the box and looked at the contents.

'Funny,' he said. 'I read a bit about love charms and such down at the library, and they all seemed to work by being either fed to the person you were after, or buried outside his window or hidden under his pillow, something like that.'

'You're not starting to believe this crap?' said Butcher. 'If so, you can really sod off.'

'I'm sodding, I'm sodding,' said Sixsmith.

He always felt good after an encounter with Butcher and the feeling of mental alertness lasted till he was driving down the High Street and realized he had no real idea where he was going.

There was the quest for the Spanish bull, of course. He looked for a reason to postpone that and found it in Butcher's suggestion that he should collect from Baker while her gratitude was still lukewarm.

He dug her card out of his pocket, and turned the car towards Beacon Heights, which was where you lived if you were rich enough to look down on the inmates of Coningsby Rise. Not that physically speaking it was all that high. Around Luton 'heights' means anything above a hundred feet. But there was no doubt that the Baker house was the highest of the lot.

It took a long time for anyone to answer the doorbell and it was hardly worth waiting for.

'What the hell do you want?' snapped Gwen Baker.

Perhaps he'd disturbed her in the shower. She was certainly wearing what looked like a very exotic bathrobe in shot silk with a shimmering design of five-pointed stars and interlocking circles, but she didn't look damp. In fact she looked rather flushed and overheated.

'I want paid,' said Sixsmith who, though he sometimes fell short of matching finesse with finesse, never had any problem meeting bluntness with bluntness.

'What?' She scowled. 'You usually dun your clients at this time of night?'

'I could send you an invoice to your office,' said Sixsmith defiantly. If she wanted to turn him into an ant or something, let her go ahead. At least he wouldn't have to worry about the bull any more!

'Oh all right. I suppose you've done what I asked, though why the hell you had to involve the police, I don't know.'

'Keeps it legit, lost and found,' said Sixsmith. 'You wouldn't want me accused of theft, would you?'

He invented this justification without thought, but it made her look at him with a new respect.

'You may not be as dumb as you look,' she said. 'All right. Come in. But let's make it quick. I'm busy.'

Busy at what in that outfit? wondered Sixsmith.

She led him into a long airy lounge decorated with an eye for shape and colour which without being able to say why he felt reflected her taste rather than the Hyphen's. And her income too, he decided, taking in the quality of the furnishings. Unless teachers got a lot more money than they were always moaning about.

She left him there alone but returned too quickly for him to have a poke around. She was holding a bunch of twenties. She'd been so quick it couldn't even have been locked up, he thought enviously. There was probably more money down the sofa in this house than he had in the whole of his apartment.

As if to show how little it meant to her, a couple of notes fluttered loose. As she stooped to pick them up her robe fell open from the waist, revealing a pair of pastry-pale, tennis-ball breasts. She straightened up, saw the direction of his eyes and said, 'Don't get any ideas, Mr Sixsmith. This is purely a cash transaction.'

He almost said that a man who'd recently feasted on plum duff doesn't cross the street to eat cold cup cakes, but he didn't, (a) because he didn't think of it till later, and (b) because it wasn't the mini-mammaries he was really looking at but the yellow brooch she wore at the neck of her robe. He hadn't noticed it at first in the colourful and apparently random design, but now he recognized it as the same one she'd worn in his office, the one she boasted contained her protection against psychic attack.

He said, 'Is your husband home, Mrs Baker?'

'Why?' she asked sharply.

'Just thought we'd better have a story ready in case I bump into him.'

'No need to worry. Gerald's out. Probably enjoying himself in the company of his lady-love.'

A wicked smile played across her lips. Cats didn't smile, but something about her expression put him in mind of Whitey when he got himself a mouse.

And he thought: How come the Hyphen's still sniffing around Meg when I've got her love-charm in my pocket?

As if she'd caught the thought, Baker said, 'Why did you remove the charm from the locket?'

'I didn't want the police playing around with it,' he said. 'They can be very nosey.'

'And you gave it to Cherry?'

'What? Oh yes. Cherry.'

'I told her to burn it. She did that, did she?'

She was searching his face with a gaze like a laser. He filled his mind with an image of Butcher's flame-thrower lighter incinerating the end of another cheroot and said, 'Oh yes.'

'Fine,' she said, still with an edge of doubt. But her 'business' was clearly too urgent to be neglected further. 'Now if you don't mind...'

Perhaps she had a lover upstairs and she was scared he'd start without her, thought Sixsmith as he got into his car.

He drove away quickly, partly to put distance between himself and those penetrating eyes, partly because he felt a sudden urgent need to see Meg Merchison.

There were lights on in the tall terraced house but no one answered his repeated ringing. Then the door of the neighbouring house opened and a unisex head with large spectacles appeared.

'She's not there,' it said.

'Oh. Do you know where...'

'There was an ambulance. About an hour ago. Maybe more.'

'An ambulance? What was wrong? Where have they...'

But the head had said all it was going to say.

Sixsmith didn't waste time trying to resummon it. Even a non-crossword-solving detective knew where ambulances went.

FIFTEEN

OUTSIDE, the Royal Infirmary was Luton's answer to Buckingham Palace.

Inside, it channelled visitors along a maze of corridors that could have baffled an experimental psychologist's champion rat.

There were tests and rewards along the route. First test was to get someone to admit that Meg Merchison had been admitted. Reward was to be given directions to Ward 37.

Next test was to find a lift that wasn't marked STAFF ONLY or full of trolleyed corpses. Reward was to be crowded in with a bunch of fruit-and-flower-bearing visitors, most of whom looked so gloomy they'd have been better off bringing myrrh.

Final test was to attract the attention of an ill-tempered ward sister who was tearing a strip off a nurse.

'It's your job to keep them out, not let them in. This is a hospital, for God's sake, not a five star hotel! You got that, Nurse?'

'Yes, Sister,' said the nurse meekly.

'Then remember it.'

With a look of loathing at Sixsmith, the sister hurried away.

The nurse turned round. Only now did Joe recognize Beryl Boddington.

He said, 'Hi. Miss Boddington. Beryl...Look, excuse me, I need to talk to Sister...'

She blocked his way and said, 'I shouldn't bother. She's busy.'

'Not too busy to chew your head off,' said Joe. 'Look, maybe you can help.'

'That's what we're here for. If you can help somebody as
you pass along... or drive along, eh, Mr Sixsmith?'

So she had seen him. *Shoot.*

He said, 'Look, I'm sorry.'

'No need. If you wait here, Sister'll be back sooner or
later.'

She turned to go and he grabbed her arm. It felt firm and
muscular. She turned and fixed him with an unblinking
gaze. He let go of her arm.

He said, 'You've got a friend of mine in here. Merchison, Meg Merchison.'

Her expression became a professional blank.

'That's right. If you care to wait for Sister...'

'What's wrong with her, for God's sake?' he exclaimed.
'Or is there some law round here against anyone telling
anyone anything?'

The professional blank dissolved under the jet of his
emotion.

'Look,' she said in a lowered voice, 'I don't think anyone knows what's wrong. She's got severe abdominal pains
and that's all I can tell you. I'm sorry.'

'Like appendix?' he said hopefully.

'You a doctor as well as a detective?' she said. 'No, not
like appendix. These pains seem to move around, now here,
now there. And they come and go. About forty minutes ago
they stopped completely, and I was silly enough to let
someone in to see her... he was so insistent, so concerned.
Then suddenly it all started up again worse than ever. She
screamed, Sister came in and found this fellow there...that's
what she was bawling me out over. So I daren't let anyone
else near.'

Sixsmith groaned. The times fitted with his arrival at
Baker's house and his interruption of her 'urgent business'.
Beryl took his groan as evidence of straightforward emo-
tional distress and urged him through a nearby door.

'Sit in here for a bit,' she said. 'I'll see if I can get you a
cup of tea. And I'll check what's happening.'

He found himself in a small waiting-room full of jolly signs telling you what awful things smoking, drinking, eating, and having sex could do to your health. There was one other occupant, Gerald the Hyphen.

He had his elbows on his knees and his head clutched between his hands. He didn't look up as Sixsmith sat beside him.

'I'm a friend of Meg's,' said Joe. After the previous night he didn't feel fraudulent at making such a claim.

The Hyphen looked at him questioningly as though hoping he might be the bearer of good news, but what he saw in Sixsmith's face clearly answered his question.

'What happened?' demanded Joe urgently. 'Was it something she ate? Or drank?'

His mind was still seeking a simple solution.

Collister-Cook shook his head.

'We were just sitting talking,' he said desperately. 'Then she doubled up and started screaming. Oh God. It was terrible.'

'It must have been,' said Sixsmith. 'But what did they say when you got her here? They must have *some* idea.'

The Hyphen shook his head helplessly.

'Nothing. I saw her for a while. She seemed to be better. Then it started again worse than before. I think she's going to die.'

There were tears streaming down his face as though some bottomless pool had been tapped.

He loves her, thought Joe. Nothing to do with charms or philtres or any of that stuff. He just loves her.

Which meant that matchbox in his pocket meant nothing.

Or meant something other than what Gwen Baker had told him.

And before his eyes again flashed those tiny pale breasts and the yellow brooch pinned on the open robe.

He stood up and went out.

Beryl was coming towards him with two cups of tea.

'I brought one for him as well,' she said.

'Never mind that,' said Joe impatiently, taking them from her and setting them on the floor. 'What's the news.'

She examined this new piece of unmannerliness and decided it could be put down to his distress.

'They're going to do tests,' she said.

'Like X-rays, you mean?'

She shook her head.

'They've done X-rays. There's nothing.'

'Christ, you mean they're going to open her up?'

'Look, they've got to do something,' she protested. 'They've pumped her full of dope but it doesn't seem to have any effect.'

At heart every doctor's Mack the Knife, thought Sixsmith.

He found his hand, not obeying any conscious command from his brain, had pulled the matchbox out of his pocket.

'Give her this,' he said.

'What? Look, she can't take anything that's not prescribed by the doctor...'

'I don't mean she's got to eat it,' said Joe in exasperation. 'Just give it to her. Put it into her hand. Or under her pillow if she can't hold anything. Somewhere close, preferably touching. Please.'

She looked at him like he was mad, which he agreed she was clearly entitled to do. Next time he saw himself in the mirror, he guessed he'd have much the same expression on his face. But that didn't matter. When straws were all you had, that was what you clutched at.

She took the box and peered fearfully inside.

'What is *that?*' she demanded.

'I don't know. Probably nothing. But it's all I've got. Don't ask questions, don't tell anyone else, eh? Just give it to Meg. Look, I know you think I'm just an ill-mannered yob. I'm sorry. It's nothing to do with you personally, it's just Auntie Mirabelle keeps on producing these eligible girls. I mean, she's crazy, who'd want an ill-mannered old yob anyway? But sometimes I get irritated with her...nothing to do with you, which is no excuse I know, only don't let it stop you helping me now. Please.'

She closed the box and slipped it into the pocket of her uniform.

'Your tea's going cold,' she said.

He picked up the cups and took them into the waiting-room.

Collister-Cook seemed to have passed through the storm of despair into a Dead Sea of hopelessness.

'How long did you know Meg?' he asked as he took the tea.

Sixsmith noted the tense.

'Not long. And you?'

'Long enough.'

'For what?'

'To get like this.' He looked at his free hand as if it belonged to a stranger. 'I'm married, you know. It's a funny thing. While Meg was living I could never quite bring myself to leave my wife. But now that she's dead, I shan't stay. Crazy, eh?'

'Sure it's crazy. She's not dead, that's what's crazy!'

The Hyphen looked at Sixsmith with calm compassion.

'Don't punish yourself with hope, friend. There is none. I know. I get an almost supernatural feeling about such things.'

Joe couldn't stand any more of this. He finished his tea and made for the door.

'I'll see if I can get another cup,' he said. 'You like one?'

'No. Not for me,' said Collister-Cook.

Joe went out. He walked along the corridor and stood by the big window at its end. All of downtown Luton lay spread below him, like a patient on a table. Andover was down there. And Blue and Grey, Butcher and Bannerjee, Suzie Sickert and DS Chivers, all of them. And none of them seemed important. It was a good corrective viewpoint once in a while, a high window in a hospital.

'Mr Sixsmith. Mr Sixsmith!'

He turned. Beryl was hurrying towards him, her face alight with joyful amazement.

'It's incredible,' she said breathlessly. 'I gave her that matchbox, slipped it into her hand underneath the sheet and closed her fingers round it. And thirty seconds later it was gone, the pain was gone, you could tell just by looking at her! She stopped moving, her colour came back, she sat up in bed and said she'd like a drink! It's beyond belief! Isn't it marvellous!'

'Indeed it is,' said Joe Sixsmith, a huge smile splitting his face.

It seemed perfectly natural to seize the nurse in his arms and give her a long, lingering kiss. She tasted delicious, sort of honey and coriander. And she took her time pushing him away.

'You'll get me fired,' she said. 'Are you going to tell Mr Cook?'

He liked the way she just dumped the hyphen.

'No,' he said. 'You tell him. It's you who gets to break the bad news. Only fair you should get the chance to announce the good. I'll see you around maybe.'

'Aren't you going to wait to see your friend? Once the doctor's finished checking her over, she should be able to have visitors.'

Sixsmith shook his head.

'I got things to do,' he said. 'Besides, two's company. It's him she'll want to see.'

Also there would be explaining to do, and he had a feeling that some things were better left unexplained.

He was glad to leave the Infirmary behind, even though the usual after-impression of cold corridors, antiseptic smells and carnal decay was overlaid this time by a powerful tactile image of the warm wet softness of Nurse Boddington's lips and the yielding softness of her full body under that starchy uniform . . .

He shook his head free of the thoughts. Beryl was one of Mirabelle's anointed. He hadn't found out yet what was wrong with her, but he'd be a mug to forget that something certainly was.

'You know what, Whitey,' he said. 'I got money in my pocket, I've been working hard all day and most of the evening too. Time for a bit of pleasure. How about we look for a slice of the high life.'

Whitey looked at him doubtfully, then peered through the windscreen.

'I see what you mean,' said Joe.

His Nurse Boddington reverie must have distracted him so much he'd taken a wrong turn, for now he realized he was heading away from the centre of town where, if anywhere, the high life was surely to be found.

He glanced in his mirror, checked that the only other vehicle in sight, a small white job about twenty yards behind him, wasn't a police car, and did a nifty and strictly illegal U-turn.

The small white car followed suit.

As he headed back into town, Joe's mind puzzled on this. Could be a coincidence, of course. Luton drivers were notoriously creatures of impulse, going about their business with a Latin impetuosity.

On the other hand, Mr Blue and Mr Grey travelled round in a small white car...

He slowed in an attempt to get a glimpse of the inmates, but the white car slowed too and all he could make out was that there was a double silhouette...

They were near the centre now.

He hit the gas and pulled away. Within seconds the white car was back on terms. Without signalling he turned right into the narrow lane running between the old Gaiety Theatre and the new Sikh temple.

The headlights swung after him.

'Oh hell,' said Sixsmith.

He reached a T-junction where the lane cut into the service road running behind the Palladian Shopping Mall. Left would take him to the High Street, right to Ondine Place.

He heard a high-pitched peep-peep-peep. It was the reversing warning of a lorry and he could see it now to his left, backing out of the loading bay behind the Starbright Freezer Store. It was either a late delivery or an early robbery. None of his business, but maybe his salvation.

He swung the wheel hard over and hit the accelerator.

It was a close thing. His wing actually brushed the tailgate of the reversing truck. But he got through and had the satisfaction of seeing the road behind him completely blocked as he burst into the High Street.

Whitey must have been holding his breath, for now he let it out in a cry of outrage in which to the finely tuned ear the words 'Bloody maniac...not fit to be in charge of a pram...' were clearly audible.

'OK, so you need a drink? You think you're the only one?' said Sixsmith.

Thoughts of the high life were sponged from his mind. What he needed was the security of the familiar.

He found a spot on the crowded car park of the Glit and went inside.

The pub was packed and he recalled it was Golden Oldie Karaoke Nite. Whitey on his shoulder was purring like a Roller. He dearly loved a crowded pub. The sight of a cat drinking beer usually created such admiration that his ashtray would be foaming over, not to mention the crisps and pork scratchings which a generous public pushed his way also.

Sixsmith was less enthusiastic, claiming that a night with a drunk cat followed by a day with a hungover one was not his idea of happiness. But Whitey put it down to jealousy. Tonight, though, the cat was out of luck. If there was one thing the patrons of the Glit found more entertaining than an alcoholic cat it was the sight of their nearest and dearest making prats of themselves and Karaoke Nite gave full measure of that. He was already feeling grievously neglected when Dick Hull, the manager, refulgent in full Gary Glitter fig, came up to Joe and said, 'Glad you made it, son. We're badly in need of a bit of class. I don't mind a laugh but they'll be throwing things soon. Just look at that mate of yours!'

Sixsmith looked. On the stage a lanky figure made even taller by an ill-fitting tophat was belting out 'Oh Sweet Mystery of Life', undeterred by the cat-calls from the audience and the fact that he had to keep his hand over his mouth to retain his Groucho Marx moustache. It was Merv Golightly.

'You'll give us Sammy Davis, *"That Ol' Black Magic"*, won't you, Joe?' pleaded Hull.

'Oh, all right,' said Sixsmith. 'But let me enjoy my drink first.'

Whitey, his nose now quite out of joint, retired under the table to sulk.

Merv finished to a tumult of laughter and applause. He spotted Joe and came across to his table.

'That went down well,' he said complacently.

'Like a barometer,' said Joe. 'Who were you supposed to be? Groucho Marx?'

'Ha ha. I was Webster Booth. Or maybe Richard Tauber. What's it matter as long as they love me? Listen, I was hoping I'd catch you in here tonight. I've just ferried Maisie Sickert to her first show.' He glanced at his watch. 'Blimey, that time already. She'll be finishing at the Blue Lamp soon and looking for me to take her on to the Sundowner.'

'What about the bull?' said Joe hopefully.

'Well, I got there early, like I said, and I sat around waiting and I spotted it, stuck on top of her cocktail cabinet.'

'Great,' said Joe. 'Did you manage to get it?'

'Sorry, mate, but Maisie came in just then and there was no way. It's a bit big to tuck up my jumper anyway.'

'Well, thanks,' said Sixsmith. 'At least we know it's there.'

'Hang on,' said Merv. 'I'm not finished. I'd noticed that Maisie keeps a spare key to the flat in a saucer on the table by the front door. I palmed this as I passed. Here it is.'

He dropped a Yale key on the table in front of Joe, who said, 'What am I supposed to do with that?'

'Do? You can stick it up your arse for me, my son, as long as it's back in the saucer by the time I get Maisie home round three a.m. And the only way you're going to get it there is by going round and unlocking her door.'

'And stealing the bull, you mean?'

'Now what a good idea! Why didn't I think of that? Of course I mean stealing the bull, only it's not stealing as the kid lifted it from you in the first place, right? Tell you what, Joe, I sometimes think you'd be better off driving a cab except you'd be stopping off to ask a bobby the way all the time. What's up with that mog of yours?'

'Sulking 'cos Dick asked me to sing.'

'Is that right? Sammy Davis? Hey, you can borrow my hat and tash if you like.'

'I don't think so,' said Joe.

'Please yourself. See you, Joe. Make sure you get the key back, won't you? I think you're on. Good luck, mon capitaine!'

Dick Hull was at the microphone.

'And now, folks, a special treat: the late great Sammy Davis Junior's golden hit version of *That Ol' Black Magic* sung by your friend and mine, Joe Sixsmith.'

In fact Joe's voice was as unlike Sammy Davis's as Merv's was unlike Webster Booth's, but at least all those years under the eagle eye, and ear, of Rev. Pot had taught him how to hold a tune and he returned to his table to warm applause.

It felt good, and safe, sitting there with beer in his belly and friendly chatter all around. He stayed till closing time, then found, as many before, that the longer you stay in the nice warm pub, the darker and colder the night outside.

'You gonna sulk forever?' he said as he placed Whitey on the passenger seat.

The cat gave him his long-suffering why-don't-we-just-go-home look, and Joe would have been more than happy to accede. But he could feel Maisie Sickert's spare key burning in his pocket.

He looked around the car park almost hoping he'd see Blue and Grey's car lurking there, but even that excuse for no action was missing.

'Look,' he said to Whitey. 'There's something I've got to do. It won't take long but it can't wait, OK?'

The cat closed his eyes and feigned sleep.

Slowly, reluctantly, Joe began to drive towards the Hermsprong Estate.

SIXTEEN

LUTONIANS TALK ABOUT Hermsprong with a muted horror which is almost pride. Here is the original urban black hole into which all social subsidy and welfare work is sucked without trace. Perhaps the best account of the estate was given by its senior social worker on Radio Luton shortly before her breakdown.

'Hermsprong is a truly organic community,' she said in a very quiet, very restrained voice. 'Here everyone has a place and a function. Here there are none so poor they cannot be robbed, none so insignificant they cannot be reviled, none so inoffensive they cannot be hated. This is the far end of Thatcherism. On Hermsprong they need no nanny state, they already take care of each other.'

Compared with this, Rasselas was a health resort.

Joe parked in front of Carey House, the block where the Sickerts lived. No point in trying to hide the car. Speed was of the essence. Armed with nothing but a torch, he took a deep breath and went through the entrance doors.

He was glad he'd brought his own illumination. Compared with the fetid gloom inside the building, the diesel-stained night outside seemed like the countryside at noon. It was at times like this he realized how much the Major had achieved on Rasselas. He'd waged a long campaign to get unbreakable light fitments. Nothing had happened till one winter's night someone with a high-powered air rifle and a very good eye had shot out all the porch and security lights on the housing chairman's suburban villa. Now there was light almost everywhere on Rasselas. Here there was only darkness visible.

Joe ignored the lift, guessing that even if it worked, it would be like travelling in Whitey's litter tray after a heavy night at the Glit. Fortunately the Sickert flat was only on the third floor, though that was quite high enough for a man to climb who was out of condition and trying to hold his breath.

He inserted the stolen key and turned it gently. The door swung open with barely a sound and he stepped into the living-room.

The thin beam of his torch sketched the furniture till it found a cocktail cabinet. Slowly it ran up the shelves, crowded with multi-coloured bottles like an apothecary's shop, till it touched the top.

And there, on its side and looking suitably tipsy in such a situation, was the Bannerjee bull.

He reached up and grasped it. The imminence of the bottles tempted him for a moment, but amid their many-coloured delights he couldn't see anything that looked like a simple scotch.

Besides, at the moment he was merely reclaiming lost property. Open one of those bottles and he was into theft.

He turned to leave.

And heard a noise.

It wasn't in itself a frightening noise, nothing much more than a kind of gurgling sigh, but in this place at this time, any sort of noise was enough to turn his legs to tubes of toothpaste.

The noise came again. It was time to leave. Yet he was finding it difficult. Some stupid little insignificant bit of him, as useless as an appendix but always ready to nag if it sensed someone in trouble, was tracking that noise to possible sources and coming up with a gagged mouth. Suppose Maisie Sickert had come back early and been assaulted? Or her daughter, Suzie? Suppose one or both of them lay in a bedroom, bound and gagged, desperately trying to cry for help...?

Self-interest wasn't going to take this bleeding heart blather lying down.

Suppose their assailant was still in there with them, weapon poised to strike if any foolish intruder came through the door?

Sixsmith, you're not cut out for this business, he told himself for the hundredth time.

But he had no choice. Cut out or not, he couldn't leave without knowing.

He took a deep breath and tried to focus his ears through the roaring of his own blood as his heart pounded in panic.

There it was again. He shone his light at the door beyond which lay the source of the noise. It was slightly ajar.

Saying a comprehensive prayer which took in most of the deities of East and West, none of which he actively believed in but there was no harm in being careful, he pushed open the door.

The point of light arrowed in, struck, then gently flowered and spread over the naked bodies of Suzie Sickert and Glen Ellis. They lay together, limbs entwined, her head resting on his chest, his lips buried in her short hair. It was a tableau strangely unerotic. It spoke more of primal innocence than mature experience. So might a sculptor have depicted Adam and Eve before the fall. Sleep had smoothed all the macho aggressiveness from the boy's face and replaced the streetwise knowingness of the girl with a childish wonder. She breathed out, shallowly, hardly enough to stir the immature breasts, but just enough to produce the soft bubbling sigh which had caught Sixsmith's ear. It was the kind of noise a baby might make as it slumbered in its cradle.

Then she opened her eyes.

Joe froze, every nerve in his body knotted tight as he waited for the scream.

Instead the girl's eyes fixed on him with unalarmed curiosity, a smile touched her lips, then her eyes closed again.

She thinks it's part of some dream, thought Joe. But she won't think that again.

Quietly he pulled the door shut. Quietly he made for the exit, pausing only to slip the key back into the saucer. Quietly he slipped out into the urine-scented gloom. His stealth was no longer the stealth of a burglar but more like that of a parent. For the moment these two were children. They would wake soon enough into a world which pressurized them into being something else.

Outside he took a deep breath and began to let triumph trickle into his veins. He'd done it. He'd got the bull. Butcher would be proud of him. He could be proud of himself!

Except that something which had bothered him as he talked to Butcher was bothering him even more now that he actually had the toy in his possession. It was tantalizingly close, right on the tip of his mind, only he couldn't quite reach it. It must be something so subtle that it took the trained professional eye to detect it. He strained every fibre of his intellectual being to make the last connection and it came to him as he reached the car.

Blue and Grey had said they were expecting two kilos of heroin.

However much this bull weighed, it was a long way short of two kilos.

He got in the car and said, 'Whitey, you're living with one dumb detective!'

Whitey did not reply. Not even the offended snort which indicated he was pissed off and sulking.

He wasn't on his usual spot on the passenger seat. Sixsmith twisted round and peered in the back. He wasn't there either. His stomach beginning to tighten like a knot of wet leather, he stooped down to look under the seats, calling, 'Whitey, hey, Whitey, are you down there?' and prayed to the God he didn't believe in for an answer.

The great Ironist in the Sky wasn't going to miss a chance like this.

The car door opened and a mocking voice said, 'Hey, black boy, you looking for Whitey? Well, here I am!'

A hand seized his shoulder and next moment he was dragged out of the car like a gaffed fish and dumped face down on the pavement. At eye level he could see three pairs of eighty-pound trainers. He twisted round and looked up. Three pairs of eyes looked down at him, three mouths stretched in toothily expectant smiles.

They were white, in their mid-teens, all wearing the same Union Jack T-shirts.

They were Hermsprong Brits, and he was as good as dead.

'This is a private parking area, friend, didn't you know that?' said the tallest of the three in a rough approximation of an American accent. 'You're parked illegally, ain't that right, boys?'

'That's right,' echoed the other two.

'So what we're going to do is impound your car. But first you gotta pay your parking fee. And after that we're gonna kick shit out of you. That's nothing to do with your parking, that's just because we don't like black bastards stinking up our turf. Ain't that right, boys?'

'That's right.'

They would have been comic in their imported menace if they hadn't been so menacing in their own home-grown right.

And he would have been terrified speechless if it hadn't been for Whitey.

As it was, he was still terrified, but the thought of his little cat helpless in the hands of these thugs, while it didn't give him courage, at least gave him speech.

He pushed himself up to his knees and said, 'Where's Whitey?'

The response at least surprised the Yankee pastiche out of his interlocutor.

'What's all this Whitey stuff, then?' he demanded in the authentic accent of left-bank Luton. 'You tryin' to take the piss, or what?'

'My cat. What have you done with my cat?'

'Cat? What cat? You trying to talk hip? We don't speak nigger-speak round here.'

'I mean my cat!' yelled Joe, standing upright. 'Even a brain dead moron like you must have got to know what a cat was before they kicked you out of kindergarten.'

Both the yelling and the standing were tactical errors.

The first provoked; the second presented a target.

An expensive trainer caught him in the crutch. And as he doubled up, a rocky knee smashed into his face.

He went over backwards and once more found himself with a pavement-eye view of their feet.

'Maybe he's talking about a real cat,' said one of the others thoughtfully. He must be the group intellectual.

'A real cat? And he's called it Whitey? For that he gets his balls stamped flat!'

And presumably in preparation for this operation, both the speaker's expensive feet left the ground.

Now something really interesting happened. Instead of descending with all the weight of the youth's muscular frame on Sixsmith's already pancaked testicles, the feet remained in the air.

Perhaps, thought Joe, the youth has achieved a new religious level and is levitating.

Or perhaps time has been suspended.

He raised his eyes in search of an answer to this metaphysical puzzle and found an instant solution.

It wasn't time that was suspended, but the young man himself.

Mr Blue (or it may have been Mr Grey—Joe's eyes were still watering copiously) had seized him from behind by his belt and was holding him in the air one-handed. Meanwhile the other half of the couple was addressing the remaining pair of the trio.

'You look like likely lads,' he was saying, 'and normally we wouldn't dream of interfering in your little hobbies.'

This was definitely Mr Blue. Joe recognized the style.

'Only Mr Sixsmith here is helping us with a little problem we got, and until we're done, no one gets to lay a foot on him. Except us, savvy?'

The likely lads did not reply. Blue nodded to Grey, who let go of the belt and the boss youth fell to the ground beside Sixsmith.

'So run along,' said Blue. 'We'll clear up here.'

The pair still on their feet looked as if they might think this was a good idea.

Joe was not a vindictive man but it struck him they were all getting off a touch lightly. He had recovered sufficiently to sit upright and he gasped in the boss youth's ear. 'Won't Mummy let you play with the big boys, then?'

It was playground stuff, but it was enough. The youth's hand went into his jacket and came out with a blade. He launched himself at Grey's knees.

What happened then was too simple to be dramatic. Grey caught his wrist, drew his arm vertical and twisted. The knife flew loose. Something snapped. The youth screamed.

Blue meanwhile stepped between the other two, swung his fists wide like a man using a chest expander, and caught them perfectly synchronized blows right on the ear. They reeled to left and right, like a pair of drunk formation dancers, keeping the wrong time but keeping it in unison.

The really terrifying thing about the performance was its simple economy, and the way the two big men now totally disregarded the injured youths as if there were no earthly possibility of counter-attack.

And they were right, Joe could see that. The trio no longer offered any nationality of menace. Love and sleep had reduced Glen and Suzie to children. Now pain and humiliation had done the same for these boys.

Blue pulled him to his feet.

'You OK, Mr Sixsmith?' he asked.

'I'll survive,' Joe gasped.

'Not unless you get yourself another lady love, you won't,' said Blue.

He thinks I've been getting my end away, thought Joe indignantly.

'This is no place for someone like you,' Blue went on. 'My advice is get home, have a good sleep. You don't want to be late for your appointment in the morning.'

'No, you don't want to be late,' said Grey, who was busy combing his hair though his recent exertions hadn't noticeably disturbed its oily contours.

'What appointment?' asked Joe, bewildered.

'With us,' said Blue. 'Ten o'clock in your office. You're going to bring us that stuff we talked about. So off you go. Drive carefully.'

It was the mention of driving that brought Whitey back to Sixsmith's mind. The pain in his crutch had made him temporarily forget. It was a reasonable excuse, but it didn't stop him flushing with shame.

'Whitey, they've got Whitey!' he said looking after the teenagers who were staggering off into the dark. 'Don't let them go! They've got my cat.'

'No, they haven't,' said Blue. 'You really are slow on the uptake, aren't you? *We've* got your cat, friend, and you'll get him back when we get what belongs to us. OK? See you at ten sharp.'

They began to move away. Sixsmith, sick at the thought of Whitey in their brutal hands, cried, 'Wait!'

They could have anything they asked. What was a couple of kilos of heroin by comparison with the tons of the stuff pouring into the country every year? He reached into the car for the bull.

Then he remembered his great if rather late deduction.

Even if the bull held some of the drug, it was far too light to hold all of it, and these two weren't going to settle for less than all.

Blue had stopped and was looking at him expectantly.

'Make sure he's got some water, will you?' said Joe. 'He doesn't care for milk, but he eats most things. Take care of him, please.'

'You take care, we'll take care,' said Blue. 'Ten sharp.'

They vanished into the night, and the Hermsprong Estate seemed to heave a sigh of relief.

Sixsmith got in his car. In the mirror he saw that his face was a mess, with blood oozing from both nose and mouth. His upper lip was split open but nothing seemed to be broken. The pain in his crutch had eased to within groaning distance of bearable. But this was no place to wait for improvement or administer first aid. He could sense Hermsprong refocusing its attention on the wounded animal in its midst now that the two deadly predators had gone.

He turned the key and drove away.

He headed for home. There was nowhere else to go, or rather no one else to go to. When you fell in deep doo-doo, you cleaned yourself up, you didn't go tracking it into your friends' houses.

His mind was spinning with what had happened, what was going to happen, and as he turned into Canal Street, he thought that he'd spun totally out of control into time-slip. It was last night again!

There were the spectators in the street, the police cars, the fire-engines outside Mr Nayyar's shop. There was Mr Nayyar standing looking helplessly at the fire.

But things weren't quite the same. The fire-raisers had done a real job tonight. The flames were leaping high out of the shop window and even as he watched, they blossomed upstairs in the living quarters.

Joe Sixsmith slowed, but he didn't stop. Not tonight. Tonight the world could take care of itself. Tonight the Great Detective had troubles of his own.

In his flat he took the bull into the kitchen and ripped it open with a carving knife. Kapok floated out of it. Nothing but kapok. He sniffed it and it smelt only of kapok. He tasted it and it tasted only of kapok. He soaked the remains in warm water in case they'd devised some method of transporting the stuff in solution, but the water tasted and smelled of nothing but kapok.

He poured himself a large whisky. The spirit burned into his cut lip but he paid it no heed. Pain had made him forget Whitey once tonight. Perhaps pain would help him forget again.

He drank himself into a troubled sleep. Dreams came. Dreams of Whitey, of Butcher trapped beneath a heap of files, of Bannerjee's bull, grown life size and scattering the Chapel Choir. Then he was into the Casa Mia dream, only this time the bodies round the tea-table, still with their heads up to their faces, rose up like zombies and rearranged themselves as he'd actually found them. From their pale lips came a dull moaning sound, like an attempt at singing though he couldn't pick out the tune as he followed Gina Andover out into the entrance hall and watched her insert the knife in her throat before lying down at the foot of the stairs. Then he heard a scream and looked up to see smoke billowing down the stairway. Out of it staggered Auntie Mirabelle leaning heavily on the shoulder of Beryl Boddington, and scolding her, and scolding him, and scolding everyone, till behind the escaping pair, huge flames erupted, and he found he was looking up at Mr Nayyar's bedroom window, and there on the sill yelling his fear and anger and indignation was Whitey...

He awoke. He was slumped in an armchair in his sitting-room. The whisky had spilled over the carpet. Its stench filled the room. So did daylight. He looked at the clock on the mantelpiece.

It was coming up to seven. Three hours to go.

SEVENTEEN

HE WAS SITTING on the step of the Bullpat Square Law Centre when Butcher arrived just before eight.

'Sixsmith, you're no advertisement for early rising,' she said. 'What the hell are you doing here? You look like you should be queuing up at Casualty.'

'I rang you at home,' said Sixsmith. 'Your *friend* said you'd left for work.'

'I don't like the way you say *friend,* Sixsmith. Was it speaking that way that got your mouth needing stitches?'

'No,' said Sixsmith. 'It was listening to you.'

'You'd better come inside and explain.'

He told his story. Her reaction was not what he was looking for.

She said, '*Great!* That really puts Bannerjee in the clear. I couldn't see any way the Customs boys were going to let a toy stuffed with smack through their hands anyway.'

'Well, I'm pleased you're pleased,' said Sixsmith angrily. 'You're getting job satisfaction while all I'm getting is a bleeding face. Plus they've got Whitey.'

'I'm sorry about that, Sixsmith. But people are more important than pets, right?'

Sixsmith's instinct was to shove her head into her waste bin for mouthing such a smug generalization, but his natural courtesy and pacifism plus doubt whether he could actually hold her down in a direct physical struggle, gave him pause.

He said with tight restraint, 'I'm not arguing theory, I'm arguing reality. What's important is what churns you up. I dreamt I saw Whitey in a burning house last night. According to you, if I had the choice between rescuing him or any human being from the fire, the human should always come first. I'm not sure I could promise that. In fact I could give you a short list of humans who wouldn't even come second.'

'Then you've got a problem, Sixsmith,' she said.

'You mean generally or specifically?'

'I mean both. Listen, these people aren't going to hurt your cat. Why should they? It's a threat, that's all. The more you show them you care, the more effective the threat will be.'

'So what are you saying, Butcher? I should go along and tell them that Bannerjee's brief is convinced he flushed their dope down the lavvy, and I'm not all that bothered about my cat anyway, so hard luck, boys.'

'Something like that,' she said. 'Better still, why not tell the police? It's their job to protect the citizenry, after all.'

Sixsmith shook his head in painful wonder.

'I don't believe this,' he said. 'When I wanted to go to the cops in the first place, you said no, don't do it, because you were scared there really was some heroin floating around and it would incriminate your client. Now we're pretty sure there isn't, suddenly our corrupt and inefficient police force are just the boys to see.'

'Sixsmith,' she said, 'you're almost eloquent when you're angry. Listen, I'm sorry for your troubles, I really am. And where I can help you, I will. Like this Andover business you were telling me about. First chance I get this morning. I'm going to check out the inheritance situation, I promise. But when it comes to protecting you against thugs who have stolen your cat and are making demands with menaces, that's not my domain. No, I don't believe the police are perfect, but they're all we've got, and this is their line of country.'

Sixsmith made for the door.

'Thanks a bunch, lady,' he said, pausing. 'You feel pretty superior to that old school chum of yours, Baker, don't you? Well, let me tell you this, for all her love of money and her daft magic, she's still got time for a bit of direct action when there's a threat to something she values, someone she loves. Next time I talk to your *friend* on the phone, I'll maybe ask when was the last time you even let friendship make you a few moments late for work.'

The door was too ill fitting to slam properly, but at least he had the satisfaction of hearing one of the joints go.

Reason told him he was being unfair, but what did reason have to do with it? He'd wanted someone to share his gut-wrenching anxiety about Whitey, and Butcher had been the best, perhaps the only candidate.

She was right about one thing, though. His lip needed a stitch, perhaps two. If he let it heal up the way it was, he was going to end up with a cleft he could wedge a silver spoon in.

He drove to the infirmary. As he locked the car he heard his name being called. He turned round and saw Beryl Boddington coming out of the Casualty door. She must have been up all night and she looked better than he did.

'I thought it was you,' she said. 'Hey, what happened to your face?'

'Accident,' he said briefly. 'I've come to get it stitched up. So long as I don't have to wait for ever, that is.'

'You should be in luck. This is usually the quiet time in Casualty, before the going-to-work accidents start coming in. Listen, I just wanted to tell you that your friend's going home this morning. No more problems, she's as good as new. They finally worked out what it was.'

'They did?' said Sixsmith.

'That's right. Simple, really. A kidney stone. Got stuck in the ureter, then moved along a bit and got stuck again before it finally got flushed clear. That was why the pain kept coming and going.'

'But isn't that fairly common?' said Sixsmith. 'I mean, you people were running around like this was weirder than a priest with a phantom pregnancy.'

'The duty doc was very young and he'd been on for fifty hours,' she said defensively. 'What's the matter anyway? You still think it's down to your major matchbox?'

'No,' he said. 'You don't know how glad I am to hear she's OK. Thanks for taking the trouble to tell me. Now I'd better get in and see what the stitching's like in this place.'

'Look, I'll come with you, maybe help you jump the queue if there is one.'

He didn't argue. To tell the truth he was beginning to feel a bit weak at the knees. He hadn't had anything to eat since Whitey's haddock, twelve hours ago, since when he'd been knocked about and consumed half a bottle of Scotch.

He wasn't certain whether she jumped a queue or not, but in what seemed remarkably little time he was gingerly fingering two very neat stitches in his upper lip.

Beryl was still there.

'You OK now,' she asked. 'If I were you, I'd get home and have a day in bed, you look like you could use it.'

'I could use it but I can't afford it,' he said grimly.

'Why? What you got to do that's so important?'

'I've got to get you home, that's the first thing. No, I insist. I've made you late already. And I reckon I owe you a lift.'

He urged her into the car and they headed off back to the Rasselas Estate. On the way they passed Mr Nayyar's shop. It looked like a burnt-out shell. Inside he glimpsed firemen picking over the ashes.

Beryl said, 'That looks bad. I hope no one got hurt.'

'What? Oh yes. I hope so too.'

'You sure you're all right, Mr Sixsmith?'

'Fine. I've just got worries. Like everyone else. And why're you Mistering me again? I feel old enough today without that. The name's Joe.'

'OK, Joe,' she said. 'And I'm sorry you've got worries.'

'Yeah? No need,' he said irritably. 'It's nothing important. Just a cat, that's all. Nothing that anyone concerned with real human troubles in their work is going to think worth worrying about.'

The shaft was aimed at Butcher. He spotted too late that it might sound like he was having a go at Beryl too.

She said equably, 'A cat? Oh yes, Mirabelle told me about your cat. Whitey, isn't it? He got lost or something?'

'No, he hasn't got lost, he's got stolen, and the people who stole him aren't nice people, and they're going to do something not very nice to him unless I give them something I ain't got.'

It came out explosively, and he felt instant shame at unloading his worry and irritation on someone who'd gone out of her way to help him.

'Sorry,' he began, but she was saying with real concern, 'Joe, that's terrible. These people must be sick. No wonder you're so snarled up.'

He said, 'I know it's just a cat, and—'

'No need to explain to me, Joe,' she said. 'There was an old tabby hung around where I lived. Didn't belong to me, but she came to eat with us couple of times a day. Once I came across a couple of the local kids giving her a hard time. The way I whaled into them I really surprised myself! After that she more or less moved in, then a while back she just jumped on my lap, went to sleep, and didn't wake up no more. When I realized what had happened, I sat there and held her and cried. So I know how they can tear you up. What are you going to do? Tell the police?'

'There's no proof,' said Joe wretchedly. 'Except catching them with Whitey, of course. I'm scared if I bring the cops in, they'll just destroy the evidence.'

'But what else can you do?'

'I don't know. I guess I'll have to persuade them I'm telling the truth. If I can do that, maybe they'll just dump Whitey. If he gets loose, he'll find his way home, no bother.'

He didn't even sound convincing to himself.

Beryl said, 'Next left.'

It was a street of small neat red brick semis, part of the old estate which, like Lykers Yard, had survived the birth of the high rises, though unlike the Lykers area, this had an air of being very well cared for.

'This is nice,' said Joe, 'but I thought you had a flat in the same block as Mirabelle?'

'That's right. This is where my sister, Lucy, lives. She takes care of my boy Desmond while I'm working.'

'You've got a kid?'

It came out all wrong and she turned to him with a hostile, challenging expression.

'That's right. Four and a half. Just started school. You got some objection?'

'No, of course not, I'm sorry...'

He couldn't tell her that recent events and her kindness had quite put out of his head that she was one of Mirabelle's menaces and his tone was merely the surprise of being reminded that for once he'd been right. She wasn't ancient and she wasn't homely, and she showed no sign of inherited lunacy or a drug habit, therefore she had to have some other built-in marital impediment like a ready made family.

'Look,' he said. 'My head's not really together at the moment. Anything new's hard to take in. I like kids, I really do. I'd just got you placed in a slot and suddenly you're out of it, that's all. Sorry.'

She considered this, then nodded.

'You mean, you'd temporarily forgotten there's always some catch with the females Mirabelle pushes at you, and suddenly you've spotted mine. That's OK, Joe. I understand.'

He looked at her aghast. Old-fashioned witchcraft was one thing but this kind of mind-reading was pure sorcery!

Beryl threw back her head and laughed joyously.

'Come on, Joe,' she said. 'You don't imagine the old girls in the block don't gossip? First thing they told me was that if I was looking for a daddy for my little Desmond, Mirabelle Valentine would be serving up her nephew, Joseph, on a plate. Only he didn't seem to want to be served. And I got a list of all the others who'd been paraded before you.'

'Oh shoot. Look, I'm really sorry—'

'For what? Look, I like Mirabelle, so that's OK. And my boy's got one daddy, and that's one more than enough,' she added rather grimly. 'So you can uncross your legs, Joe Sixsmith. I'm not after getting in your Y-fronts. So there's one trouble for you to cross off your list. As for the others, I really hope you get them sorted. Best of luck. Keep me posted, huh?'

She got out and walked away with a wave.

Joe drove away feeling irrationally comforted, but it didn't last for long. He had an hour to come up with something brilliant. No problem to the legendary PIs of old. But legends didn't live in Luton. He was down to his own resources and the cupboard was bare. The Sixsmith serendipity was out of stock. Which left only the last resort of the honest citizen.

He went to the police.

At the station they told him that DS Chivers was busy and he'd have to wait. He sat on a bench and watched a wall clock with a sweep hand making circuits like Seb Coe. He heard a familiar voice and looked round just in time to see Dildo Doberley escorting Mr Nayyar out of the door. A moment later the door opened again and Dildo came back in.

'Hello, Joe,' he said. 'Thought it was you in spite of the plastic surgery. What can we do for you, mate?'

'I was hoping to see Chivers,' said Joe. 'Dildo, I need help badly.'

'You must do if you've come asking for it from Chivers,' said Dildo. 'Still, the way you look, maybe it'll melt his heart or something. Come and wait through here, I'll see if I can rustle you up a mug of tea.'

He led Joe through the swing doors out of the public area.

Here, sitting on a chair with a uniformed constable in attendance, he was surprised to see Glen Ellis. The boy looked at him with unconcealed hate and bared his teeth in the snarl Joe remembered from Nayyar's shop.

'What's he doing here?' he asked Doberley in a low voice.

'Shortage of space. All the cells jammed with remand prisoners, and we've even got a waiting list for interview rooms.'

'No, I mean, why's he been brought in.'

'You've not heard, then? Mr Nayyar's shop got done again last night and this time they made a real job of it. Fortunately Nayyar had decided to send his family off to stay with relatives after the previous do.'

'And you've brought Ellis in on suss?'

Doberley grinned, not unlike the boy's snarl.

'Better than that. Mr Nayyar got woken up by the noise they made breaking in and pouring petrol everywhere. He looked out of his window just in time to see them tossing matches into the doorway. Then *whoosh!*'

'Them!'

'Yeah. Ellis and his tart, Sickert, the one who tried to fit you up. Absolutely firm ident. No messing. Cast iron.'

A door opened and a WPC came out with Suzie Sickert in tow.

'You OK?' said Ellis, but he was pushed by her into the room before she could reply. The WPC forced Suzie to occupy her boyfriend's chair.

'Got a fag?' she demanded loudly. The WPC shook her head.

'What about you, Sambo?' she said. 'I'll have one of yours. I'm not proud.'

'Sorry, I don't smoke,' said Joe.

She was studying him with a frown on her face. She's remembering her 'dream', he thought.

He turned to Doberley and said, 'What time was it, the fire?'

'Just before midnight. Nayyar was just on his way to bed. He was dead lucky, managed to get down the stairs and out of the back before the fire took hold. After that, write-off.'

'And what do the kids say?' asked Joe.

'You'll love this. They were screwing round at her mum's flat! Great alibi, huh? Here, this'll slay you. Chivers looks them straight in the face and says, *Any witnesses?* Deadpan, not a flicker. *Any witnesses?* Hang about here and I'll see if I can get you that cuppa.'

He went away.

Joe went towards the seated girl. She looked up at him defiantly.

He said, 'Suzie, it'll be OK.'

'What?' She looked at him blankly. 'What you know about anything?'

'Please, sir, you shouldn't be talking to her,' said the WPC.

'I'm sorry. I just wanted her to know it'll be OK.'

The girl shook her head as if there was something there she was trying to dislodge.

'You wasn't really there...no, that's stupid...stupid...'

'Sixsmith, what the hell are you doing here?'

It was Chivers who'd just emerged from the room Ellis had been taken into.

'Wants to see you, Sarge,' said Doberley, returning with a cup of tea.

'That for me? Thanks,' said Chivers, taking the cup. 'Listen, Sixsmith, whatever it is, it had better be good and it had better be quick. I can spare two minutes, tops.'

That made Joe's mind up. Mr Nayyar's fire would have to go on the back burner, so to speak. It was going to be hard enough to persuade Chivers to offer assistance as it was, without the added disincentive of cocking up a nice cut and dried case.

To his credit, Chivers listened without interrupting. But when he did start speaking, it was clear he wasn't feeling very helpful.

'So you thought you had a quantity of smuggled smack in your possession and you didn't try to hand it in?' he said incredulously.

'Well, it was... I mean, I thought it was in the bull, and like I say, I mislaid it...'

'So now it's not even in your safekeeping, it's floating around God knows where, and still you told no one?'

'I told...' Sixsmith hesitated. Pissed off though he'd been with Butcher over her reaction to Whitey's disappearance, implicating her in ignoring the law was a poor return for all her past help.

'I told no one,' he concluded. 'Because I wasn't sure. And in fact when I found the bull again and ripped it open, I realized I'd been wrong. There is no heroin, Sergeant, that's the point. But there are two thugs who think there should be some and reckon I've got it.'

'So what do you want me to do?'

'They're criminals. Arrest them?'

'Criminals? What's their crime?'

'They're dope merchants, or at least they're employed by dope merchants,' cried Joe indignantly.

'But you've just told me there is no dope,' said Chivers. 'You want me to arrest two men for asking you to give them something that doesn't exist?'

'With menaces! They've asked with menaces.'

'To your cat, you say. You got any proof they've got your cat?'

'No, of course not.'

'Anything in writing which indicates they've got your cat?'

'No.'

'Any witnesses to anything to prove they've menaced you or your cat at all.'

'No, I haven't,' said Sixsmith. 'Look, they ransacked my flat...'

'You reported this?'

'Well, no...'

'Sixsmith,' said Chivers, 'you're wasting my time. Perhaps that's why God put you on earth, to waste my time, though I think it's more likely He looks down at you in that so called PI's office of yours and thinks that maybe He wasted His time in creating you at all.'

Sixsmith felt a great surge of rage sweeping up his body but he held it in check. He said very quietly, 'Please, Mr Chivers, whatever you think, they've got Whitey and they say they'll hurt him if I don't give them something I haven't got. They're coming to see me in twenty minutes. I'm asking for help. I'm asking for advice.'

Chivers shook his head in exasperation but for the first time there was a touch of sympathy in his voice as he replied, 'I'd like to help, even though you've brought most of this on yourself. But what do you want me to do? If I come along and talk to these guys, what do you expect me to say? They'll deny everything, natch. And with no evidence, they'll stroll away free as the air. And if they *have* got your cat and he hasn't just gone for a wander, what then? All I've done is give them good reason to put it in a bag and chuck it in the river.'

His analysis of the likely outcome of police involvement was so like Joe's own that all quarrel was knocked out of him.

He said, 'I've got to go.'

Chivers said, 'Play for time. I'll have a word with DI Yarrop in the Drug Squad, see if he knows anything about this pair. No names, you say?'

'I just think of them as Blue and Grey. Big men. Very broad, but they fit into some kind of white mini. One thing. You know that traffic wardress, the one with the jaw and the metal tooth? They frightened her off.'

'Good God,' said Chivers, looking impressed for the first time. 'In that case, you take good care of yourself.'

'I thought that was what we paid the police for,' said Joe Sixsmith accusingly.

EIGHTEEN

THEY WERE PROMPT.

And they were polite, knocking at the door before coming in.

Joe, who was beginning to feel quite expert on Mr Blue and Mr Grey, took little comfort from this initial courtesy. He got the impression the two thugs had been quarrelling about how they should deal with him, and Blue was asserting his ascendancy by this artificial politeness.

This was confirmed when Blue suspended his buttocks over the client chair and said brightly, 'All right if I take the weight off my feet, Mr Sixsmith?'

Grey sneered widely, broke wind noisily and noisomely, took out a pair of nail scissors and began manicuring his left hand.

Blue said, 'Sorry about him, Mr Sixsmith, but he can't help it. Now, you know what we've come about so let's not mess around . . . Jesus Christ!'

A shard of nail had flown off Grey's thumb and hit him in the eye.

'For God's sake,' snarled Blue, 'either stop that or sod off and do it in the bathroom. And if you can get rid of whatever's died in your gut at the same time, that'd be a bonus!'

For a moment Joe thought Grey was going to return the aggression and a small hope flickered that perhaps they would come to blows. But finally Grey satisfied himself with an obscene gesture with the scissors before lumbering into the tiny washroom like an angry bear into its cave.

'Right,' said Blue. 'While things is peaceful, where is it, Mr Sixsmith?'

If the brilliant idea was going to come it had to come now.

It didn't. So Joe fell back on his old stand-by, and told the truth.

'I found the bull,' he said. 'That's what I was doing on Hermsprong last night. But there wasn't any heroin in it. Nothing but kapok. I can show you the kapok.'

'No heroin? You're telling me there was no heroin? But that can't be, Mr Sixsmith. We know there was heroin.'

'Of course there was, in the beginning. I'm not arguing about that. But Bannerjee found it in the bottles and got scared and flushed it away down the lavatory.'

Blue nodded, and Joe began to hope he was at last getting through.

'Yeah, we know that too,' he said. 'Leastways, we know that's the line Bannerjee's pushing. He'd like us to think that all them rats and crocodiles and things that live down the sewers at Luton airport are swimming around high as a 707 on two kilos of top grade smack. It's a very good story, Mr Sixsmith. It's also a very sad story.'

'It's the truth,' said Joe, hope beginning to fade.

'Truth.' Mr Blue sucked the word like a slice of lemon. 'That's what makes it so sad. Funny thing, is truth. Me, I've had to ask a lot of people a lot of questions, and when they're lying and telling me things I don't want to hear, truth can be a door they can get out of. But when they're telling me the truth and I still don't want to hear it, then it's a bare corner in a narrow room, you understand what I'm saying, Mr Sixsmith?'

Joe understood. The truth wasn't going to set Whitey free. Only the heroin was going to do that. The heroin that, according to Butcher, was now polluting the Med, though according to what Blue seemed to have heard, it had probably just been recycled into Luton's domestic water supply.

As if to underline this rather odd disparity, a sound came from the washroom. Mr Grey was having a pee. This might be the best chance he had for flight. Except that without Whitey flight was pointless, the situation remained unchanged. Somehow he had to get Whitey here, grab him, then run like hell. It wasn't a very subtle plan, not even by Joe Sixsmith standards. On the other hand, he couldn't see anyone around selling a better one.

He laughed lightly. 'Ha ha.'

Mr Blue said sympathetically, 'Something stuck in your throat, Mr Sixsmith? Go take a drink of water when barrel-bladder's finished in there.'

Joe decided to abandon the light laugh and said, 'OK, you win. Let's stop messing around. I know where the dope is. Give me my cat back and I'll tell you.'

He listened to himself on that instant interior playback which is the source of all embarrassment and didn't blame Blue for looking unconvinced. Assertion wasn't going to be enough. He needed detail.

He said, 'What happened was this. Bannerjee did get scared, that was true. The thought of being caught with all that crack on him really snarled him up. He knew he didn't have the bottle to walk through Customs with it. But he's a businessman, he likes money, and the thought of just dumping something worth more than half a million snarled him up too.'

Inspiration dried. He hoped it might sound like a dramatic pause.

Mr Blue said pleasantly, 'So what did he do? Wrap it up in a parcel and post it?'

Joe looked at the man with admiration. They'd got this the wrong way round. It should be Blue doing the lying, he was so much better at it. On the other hand, never kick a gift horse in the teeth.

'Oh, you knew about that all the time,' said Joe, trying to sound both disappointed and puzzled. 'So what's all this in aid of, then?'

For the first time he saw uncertainty in Blue's eyes.

'You're losing me, Mr Sixsmith,' he said. 'Which is a good way to go about losing, first, your cat, and after that your teeth, bollocks, and toenails, not necessarily in that order. Know all about what?'

Joe added surprise to his range of inflections.

'About Bannerjee posting the stuff back to the UK, of course.'

'Are you pulling my plonker?' grated Blue, leaning forward and fixing Joe with a gut-liquefying glare.

'No!' cried Sixsmith, not having to dig deeper into his range of voices to find one which expressed sheer terror. 'I'm being straight, cross my heart and hope to die. He just parcelled it up and posted it back here. He reckoned that the Customs couldn't check on all incoming mail so there was a fair chance it would get by.'

Blue considered this, never taking his eyes off Joe, who was glad the man had given him an excuse to look terrified.

'So where'd he address it to?' asked Blue. 'Here, was it? Are you trying to tell me he posted it to you?'

'Oh no. Definitely not. He's not stupid. He chose somewhere nice and busy, lots of people, lots of mail, somewhere he could easily check out to see if there was anyone watching before he picked it up.'

This sounded so good to Joe, he couldn't believe Blue wouldn't buy it. But the man's face was still the same sceptical mask.

'Yeah? And where was that?' he asked.

Joe's inspiration ran dry beyond all hope of irrigation. Also, he might not be the world's greatest liar, but he knew better than to go beyond the point of checkability.

He said, 'No.'

'No what?' said Blue, like Auntie Mirabelle reminding him to mind his manners.

'No, I'm not telling you any more. Not till I see Whitey.'

'The cat's OK, Mr Sixsmith. You give us the goods, we give you the cat, that's the deal.'

'But I can't give you the goods,' exclaimed Joe. 'They're not here yet. You're going to have to watch and wait till the Spanish PO comes through. It might be days. So I want to check out Whitey, give him his vitamin tablets, see if his nails need clipped. There's a hundred and one things you got to do with a cat if you're keeping him shut up for any length of time. And I'm telling you, anything happens to Whitey, anything at all, and the deal's off. So when do I get to see him?'

Blue looked at him speculatively for a long moment, then said, 'OK. But if you're pissing me about, my son, I'll put that beast through the mincer and feed it to you in tea-spoons. You gonna stay in there all day?'

He rose and kicked open the washroom door. Grey was standing over the basin, combing his hair in the cracked mirror. How could such an unattractive creature be so vain? wondered Sixsmith. I bet even his mother reckoned he was homely!

'Get yourself out here,' said Blue. 'Keep a close eye on Mr Sixsmith. I'm going to the car to get the cat.'

'Oh yeah? Hey, bring me that tube of mints from the glove compartment. My gut isn't feeling so good.'

'You live on fried egg sarnies, what do you expect?' said Blue scornfully. 'I won't be long.'

He left. Grey collapsed into the vacated chair, rubbing his stomach. He belched explosively and said, 'Better out than in.' It was debatable, thought Joe. Not that he wanted to debate it. He wanted to work out a very clever plan for overpowering the two of them when Blue returned with Whitey, then escaping with the cat. But the sight of Grey slouching before him was not conducive to deep thought.

He said, 'I need to go to the lav.'

'Yeah?' Grey glanced into the washroom to confirm there was no window, no other door. 'OK. Go.'

Sixsmith went in and pushed the door shut behind him. He sat on the toilet and applied his mind to the problem, but found his new surroundings didn't exactly inspire deep thought either.

What he needed was a weapon. Or a miracle. He looked around but saw nothing to suggest the imminence of either. It would have been nice if Grey had left his Swiss Army knife, but all he'd left were nail clippings on the rim of the basin and black hairs floating around the grubby water he hadn't bothered to empty away.

Nail clippings. Hair. Water he'd washed in . . .

Sixsmith found he was thinking of the books he'd looked at in the reference library; of Gwendoline Baker and Gerald the Hyphen; of a light plane crashing and a raven-haired woman writing in agony. . .

He looked at himself and mouthed, 'That old black magic has me . . . Hey, Joe man, you must be going *crazy!*'

But why not when there was nowhere else to go?

He picked up the lozenge of soap, dipped it in the dirty water and began squeezing it till it was pliable as putty. Then he moulded it into the shape of a little fat man. He was good with his hands, it was only his head he sometimes had problems with, and while he couldn't claim any real resemblance between Grey and the poppet taking shape under his fingers, it at least had his proportions. Anyway, what was it that Gwen Baker had said? It's not the likeness that counts, not even the scraps of human matter, but the intensity of hatred you focus through the doll.

How much did he hate Grey? he wondered as he pressed the black hairs into the doll's head and the nail clippings into its arms.

He feared him, that was true, but hate? He let his mind slip from the thug sitting out there in his office to Whitey. Somewhere his cat was being kept a prisoner. Perhaps in the boot of a car. Perhaps with his head muffled so he couldn't make himself heard. He would be hungry, thirsty, frightened. He might have fouled himself, which was the ultimate degradation for a member of a race to whom cleanliness was next to catliness.

And this man and his mate were responsible for this. And if they didn't get what they wanted, they'd have no compunction about destroying Whitey as painfully as possible . . .

Hate him? 'Oh yes, you bastard,' breathed Joe Sixsmith. 'I really hate you!'

And he took a pin from his lapel and drove it into the poppet's gut.

Then he pressed his ear to the door and listened.

Nothing. What the hell do you expect? he asked himself mockingly. This old black magic ain't for you, Joe boy. Better just stick to singing about it . . .

At this moment the door burst open flinging him back against the wall, and Grey staggered in, his face the same colour as his suit, and collapsed on his knees before the toilet, groaning and retching.

'Oh shoot!' said Joe.

He didn't want to believe he was responsible for this, he didn't want to believe anything about it. He pulled the pin out of the poppet. Grey groaned. There was a hole in the soap. Joe squeezed it with his thumb to smooth it over. Grey doubled up and jetted vomit into the pan.

Sixsmith turned away. On his desk, the phone rang. He grabbed at it. This was a line to help for Grey. For himself. For Whitey.

'Hello!' he yelled.

'Sixsmith? Butcher. Now listen to this. Andover gets everything his wife left. And she shares with her sister everything their parents left, with the rider that if one of the sisters should die before the parents, the surviving sister kops the lot, all of which makes the order of all their deaths of the essence. Let's assume . . .'

'Get off the line!' screamed Sixsmith.

But it was too late, even if Butcher did get off the line immediately, which, being the bossy type, seemed most unlikely. He could hear footsteps on the stairs. Blue was returning. Sixsmith prayed he'd have Whitey. He grabbed the client chair and stood behind the door. He doubted if he had the strength or the skill to knock a man built like Blue unconscious but he could surely incommode him long enough to grab the cat and run like hell.

The door opened. He swung the chair up high. A voice said, 'Christ!' Another more familiar voice said, 'Miaow!'

and into the room rushed Whitey, skidding to a halt at Sixsmith's feet and stretching up to claw his knees in a one-cat chorus of outrage, delight, and hunger.

The chair was beginning to feel heavy. Sixsmith set it down and the cat used it as a springboard to reach his shoulder, where he continued his purring protest in Six-smith's ear.

'Well he seems glad to be back,' said Detective-Inspector Yarrop, sucking at a long scratch in the ball of his thumb.

Two uniformed constables pushed past the Drug Squad inspector and rushed to the washroom, skidding to a halt when they glimpsed the retching Grey.

'Bloody hell,' said one of them. 'He doesn't look too clever.'

'What's up with him?' said Yarrop to Sixsmith.

'I don't know,' said Joe. 'Something he ate, I think.'

He glanced fearfully at the doorway and said, 'Where's the other?'

'Helping with inquiries,' said Yarrop. 'I think this one better have an ambulance. Don't want talk of police brutal-ity, do we?'

One of the constables picked up the phone, listened, said, 'You too, lady,' depressed the rest and dialled 999.

Joe went to his filing cabinet and found an old packet of pork scratchings which he scattered on the floor. Whitey jumped down and began to Hoover them up.

'He'll give himself indigestion,' said Yarrop.

'How did you get here?' asked Sixsmith.

'You owe DS Chivers for that,' said Yarrop. 'He gave us a bell and told us what you'd told him. The descriptions put me in mind of a couple of old chums, so I set off to see you and got here just in time to see Big Phil taking a cat out of the boot of a car.'

'Big Phil?'

'Philip Froggat. The thinking crook's heavy. He's got the beginnings of a brain, which is more than you can say for Tiny here.'

'Tiny?' said Joe looking at the belly-clutching bulk of Mr Grey.

'Timothy Orrel. Tiny Tim. He dreamt a thought once but woke up and spat it out. Now, Mr Sixsmith, why don't you tell me the history of your relationship with these pleasant fellows?'

Joe coughed the lot, including what Butcher had told him. If she'd broken client confidentiality, that was her business. All he wanted was to contribute everything he could to the very worthy cause of getting Blue and Grey banged up as long as possible.

Yarrop was a good listener. When Joe finished he said, 'Could have saved yourself a lot of grief by coming to us sooner.'

'I got badly advised,' said Joe.

'Oh yes? Ms Butcher, I presume. That figures. But don't sulk for ever, Mr Sixsmith. She's a feisty lady. I'd rather have her with me than against.'

Joe looked at him in surprise.

'You on an incentive bonus for being nice, or what?' he asked.

Yarrop laughed.

'No. I just reckon if I make allowances when people go too far for what they believe, they might do the same for me.'

An ambulance bell had been growing louder. Whitey, who didn't care for loud noises, made one, and Joe opened his drawer. Still protesting, the cat got in.

'Hungry?' said Joe. 'Hang about.'

A quick search through the other drawers produced some boiled sweets and a soggy poppadom which he dropped in alongside the cat before closing the drawer.

'I reckon he was better off kidnapped,' said Yarrop.

Two ambulance officers, one male, one female, came into the room carrying a stretcher.

'This him?' said the man, looking down at the groaning Grey.

'Guess,' said Yarrop. He turned to one of the constables who'd brought Grey out of the washroom and said, 'I need a run-off. That place usable?'

'If you don't breathe, sir,' said the man.

Yarrop went in. The ambulance officers were checking Grey's pulse and respiration.

'Severe abdominal pains, is that right?' said the woman.

'That's what he complained of,' said Sixsmith. 'What do you think it is?'

'Ruptured appendix, burst ulcer, bad takeaway, anything,' said the woman. 'Ready, Sid?'

Expertly they manoeuvred Grey on to the stretcher. In the washroom the toilet flushed, water gurgled in the basin, then the toilet flushed again, and Yarrop came out drying his hands on his handkerchief.

'That place needs a Government health warning,' he said.

'I keep it clean,' protested Joe. 'This guy's just been sick in there.'

'Maybe. But it's you that's responsible for the soap. Now that was *really* disgusting. How's our boy doing? He don't look like he'll be a burden on the taxpayer long.'

His prognosis seemed well founded. Grey was convulsing and gasping for air, like a drowning man going down for the third time.

'Come on, Sid,' said the woman urgently. 'Let's get him out of here.'

Joe said, 'Inspector, what did you do with the soap?'

'The soap? Flushed it down the pan, didn't I? A man could catch beri-beri off something like that.'

'Oh shoot,' said Joe Sixsmith.

NINETEEN

TROUBLES ARE LIKE Alps, you get over one and there's another waiting. Joe Sixsmith had never climbed an Alp, but he knew where to go for his next bit of trouble.

Pausing only to buy Whitey a placatory takeaway from the Sun-Never-Sets Gourmet Emporium next to the abattoir on Twist Road, Sixsmith made his way to Mr Nayyar's shop.

The firemen had finished picking through the ashes but Nayyar was there now. He looked up as Joe appeared in the empty doorway.

'Please be careful,' he said. 'The firemen say pieces can still fall. They are coming back shortly with equipment to make all safe. I think I will take the chance to see if anything is worth saving, but there is nothing. See, the heat was so tremendous, all the cans have exploded.'

He thrust a burst and blackened can under Joe's nose.

'A bad business,' said Sixsmith.

'Very bad. Such wickedness, to come back again and finish off the job like this.'

'Still, you saw them this time,' said Sixsmith.

'Oh yes.'

'And you're sure it was the same pair, the ones shoplifting the other morning?'

'Definitely,' said Nayyar. 'I looked out of my window and there they were, clear as daylight.'

'You couldn't have been mistaken?' said Sixsmith.

'No! It was them, definitely. Why are you asking me these questions, Mr Sixsmith?'

Joe looked at the narrow lined face and sighed.

'You'll have to swear to it in court,' he said. 'On the Koran or whatever it is you lot swear on.'

'*Us lot,* as you call us, are as honest as any other lot, and our oath is just as binding. You think I cannot swear it was these two who set fire to my shop? Oh yes, believe me, Mr Sixsmith, I can swear that on any Holy Book you care to put before me!'

He spoke with such a persuasive vehemence that for a moment Joe almost doubted the evidence of his own eyes.

Then his mind caught the form of words. Jesuheretical, as that fine Baptist, Auntie Mirabelle, described all forms of Romish doubletalk.

'I believe you, Mr Nayyar,' he said. 'And I'd swear to it too. Those two definitely set fire to your shop. But not last night. The first time, but not the second.'

'Why do you say this?' demanded Nayyar.

'Because I saw them somewhere else at the time you say you saw them here. And I can swear to that too.'

Nayyar's face had smoothed into the blank of a market trader when the bargaining takes an unexpected turn. The bright brown eyes regarded Sixsmith with shrewd calculation. It was not what Joe had hoped to see. There'd been a chance Mr Nayyar was genuinely mistaken, that he really had seen a young white couple running away and mistaken them for Ellis and Sickert. It would have been a natural mistake. We see what we expect to see, what we want to see.

But the proper reaction now would have been bewilderment and indignation, not this cool assessment.

There was worse to follow.

The burst can fell from Nayyar's hand, sending up a puff of grey ash which clouded their feet and the facial blank began to fracture. Sixsmith saw what was coming and he didn't want this either. All he wanted was for Nayyar to back off from his positive identification far enough for it to be unlikely the police would proceed against the kids. He didn't want to be the shopkeeper's confidant. A trouble shared was a trouble too many for a man with cash flow problems.

There was no money in hearing confessions, not unless you were a priest. Who'd said that? He had! To Andover all those years ago; three days, to be precise, but it felt like years. His mind totted up all the other people's troubles he'd taken on board since then, and all of them freeloaders except for Gwen Baker. And he wouldn't be surprised if her money turned into frogspawn when she found out Meg Merchison was out of danger!

He said, 'Please, Mr Nayyar, all you have to—'

But it was too late. The man's eyes and voice were full of tears and his hands grasped Joe's arm as he said pleadingly, 'You must understand me. Mr Sixsmith, you are a kind-hearted man, I can see that, and you too know what it is to be treated as second-class citizen, I am sure. I try to make a living, give a service, harm no one. All I want is to look after my family. So I put up with many things, little things mainly, some not so little, but I put up with them, telling myself, these people are the few, the ones who make jokes, speak threats, scratch my car, scrawl insults on my door. They are drunk or feeble-minded. They yell, "Go home, Pakky, you do not belong here," but they are the true foreigners in this society. This is what I tell myself, my family.'

He paused and Joe tried to break away, saying, 'That's a good point of view, Mr Nayyar. Give and take's the best way forward.'

'Oh yes. Give your dignity, take all their crap!' blazed Nayyar, his grip tightening as his anger dried up his tears. 'You saw yourself how much I take, even letting them steal from me rather than cause trouble. But that does not stop them from trying to burn my shop. Even then, I say nothing. You were here, you saw I made no accusation. I think: I have no proof, and I think: The damage is not so great and I have good insurance. Yesterday morning I ring my insurance company and they send their assessor round. Later I hear that these two, the shop-lifters, have been taken into custody by the police, and I think: This is after all a good country. Then in the afternoon the insurance man rings me.

He says that they will pay for the door which is burnt, and the floor covering also, but not its full value as it is old. The rest, they say, that is water damage caused not by the fire but by the fire brigade, and I must pursue a claim with them!'

'That's bollocks,' said Sixsmith. 'They can't get away with that. They're trying it on!'

'Oh yes. Trying it on,' said Nayyar bitterly. 'I am their customer for more than ten years, no claims, prompt payments, and now they try it on. But listen to me. I go straight round to the insurance office and demand to see the manager. He tells me very politely, very reasonably, that I should realize that in the light of this attack, I must expect my premiums to go up. I say: Why? He says: You are very high risk, Mr Nayyar, this has now been proved. In fact, he says, you are lucky that we insure you at all! I grow very angry and I leave before I lose my temper. I think that nothing can be worse than what I have just heard, till later that same afternoon I heard that the police have let these two criminals go because they do not have enough evidence!'

It occurred to Sixsmith to suggest that if Nayyar had been willing to give evidence against them a day earlier for shoplifting, all of this might have been avoided. But he doubted if the man was in a listening mood. Also he was still hopeful of making a break before the confession—or rather self-justification—reached its forecastable climax.

'It's been a truly terrible experience for you, I can see that,' he said. 'But you'll think about what I said, won't you? Now I've got to rush, urgent appointment . . .'

But Nayyar had gone too far to let him go before he had administered absolution.

'So you see how things are, Mr Sixsmith?' he said, half aggressive, half pleading. 'I am in the right but I suffer. I pay my premiums but they will not pay me. We know who the criminals are, but they are set free. So I decide, if the law cannot help me, I must help the law. This time they will not be able to say the damage is not all caused by the fire. This time they will not be able to say there is no witness to the culprits. I sent my family away, I make my prep...'

'Mr Nayyar,' interrupted Joe urgently, 'I don't want to hear this. I can't afford to hear it. You can't afford to tell me it. In fact, I'm glad I'm a bit deaf in one ear, 'cos I think I've probably misheard most of what you're trying to tell me. Which means I've got nothing to tell the police, have I? Except that I know where Glen Ellis and Suzie Sickert were when your fire started, and it wasn't here. But I won't need to tell them that, will I? Not after you tell them you might have been mistaken, because you were naturally so upset at seeing *everything* you'd worked for, *everything* you possessed going up in flames. Thank God for insurance, eh, Mr Nayyar? They won't be able to get out of it this time, not unless there was any doubt about how it started.'

He broke free from the shopkeeper's grip.

Nayyar said softly, almost contemptuously, 'I thought you would believe in justice, Mr Sixsmith.'

'Oh I do,' said Joe sadly. 'That's always been my trouble. Goodbye, Mr Nayyar. And good luck.'

In the car Whitey had finished the takeaway and was chewing the polystyrene container.

'All right, smart ass,' said Sixsmith. 'You'd have let him fit up the kids *and* rip off the insurance company, right? Well, maybe you're right, the kids had it coming. But guilt ain't transferable, at least not in law. You start saying, "Well, he did it once, so no matter if it wasn't him this time, it'll come out even in the end," you stop having law. What you've got is Judgment Day when everything goes in the balance, and Luton's not ready for that yet, not by a long chalk.'

'What about the insurance company, don't they have rights too?' said Whitey, though to an insensitive auditor it may have sounded like a cross between a yawn and a burp.

'Companies don't have rights, they have responsibilities,' said Joe. 'They don't meet them, they're fair game. All they had to do was pay up and be nice. If an ignorant kid tells you you're rubbish, that's nothing. If a big insurance company does, that's official. So what's Mr Nayyar supposed to do?'

'Keep the peace and obey the law,' said Whitey.

'Pardon,' said Joe.

But this time all he heard was a yawn tailing off into a post-prandial snore.

Sleep seemed a good idea. There hadn't been much of it around the Sixsmith lifestyle in recent days. He thought of going back to the office, but even his wrecked flat would be more comfortable than his office chair and also there was less chance of being disturbed by clients. Not that there was much chance of that in the office either. The only real *client* he'd had recently was Gwen Baker and he still felt guilty about pocketing her money.

So home it was. Things hadn't got any better. The place was still a wreck, the council hadn't sent a man to mend the lock. He'd need to have a word with the Major about that. But his eviscerated bed looked inviting.

He pulled the phone plug out of the wall, stripped to his pants and singlet, and plunged into the ruined mattress.

Sleep swallowed him up. He felt its darkest depths washing around him, then he was into happy oblivion.

Some time later he floated up into the luminous level where the wrecks of reality decay into dreams, and was not surprised to find the dead Tomassettis waiting for him. Once more they rose from the table, their hands before their faces, singing in tuneful chorus as they rearranged themselves as he had found them.

Only this time he recognized the song. It was 'Sweet Mystery of Life,' and in his dream, he dreamt he knew the meaning of it all.

A voice said, 'If you're both dead, I hope the cat went first, otherwise we could have problems with the will.'

He opened his eyes. At the foot of the bed stood Butcher carrying a newspaper and a four-pack of Guinness. He pushed himself upright with a groan and realized that

Whitey was lying next to him, his legs sprawled wantonly, his head dangling over the side of the bed.

'Practising for the Death of Chatterton, is he?' said Butcher.

'Hey, man, don't go intellectual on me,' said Joe. 'What was that you said about wills?'

'I said that I hoped the cat died first...'

Whoomph! There it was again. That sudden flash of understanding which made him forget his embarrassment at being caught in his Y-fronts.

'That's it!' he cried, now wide awake. 'That's why the Tomassettis' bodies were arranged the way they were! When it came down to it, Andover realized it had to be made perfectly clear what order they'd died in. His wife had to die last so he could kop the lot!'

Butcher frowned and said, 'It's not so simple. I mean, who's to say if death was instantaneous in any case? You can get the same problem in car accidents. I'd need to look it up but I think the assumption is...'

'Andover's not a lawyer. He'd think like a normal person. No, I'm sure I'm right. And there's something else...'

At least there had been, but he now realized with some irritation that he'd quite forgotten the rest of the meaning of it all. His mind strained like Eddie the Eagle to make the leap, but he wasn't going to get within migrating distance of a medal.

He gave up and instead demanded rudely, 'What are you doing breaking in here anyway?'

'Wasting my time, quite clearly. I got worried about you after the strange response I got to my phone call. Finally I rang the police and Detective-Sergeant Chivers assured me everything was taken care of. That got me really worried. So soon as I could I got round to your office. Nothing. No one. Sick with anxiety, I checked that grisly place you drink in and they said no, they hadn't seen you this lunch-time but could I give you your second prize in the Karaoke competition which you forgot to collect last night?'

Joe seized the four-pack of draught Guinness from her and pulled the ring tab off one of them.

'Second prize?' he said indignantly. 'Who won? Oh shoot!'

The stout had ejaculated itself down his vest.

'Sorry, it must have got a bit shook up, as did I when finally I came round here and found your door lock broken and the flat in a state of chaos. But I see I needn't have worried. Thanks for wasting my time.'

'Hey, I'm deeply touched,' said Joe. 'I'd be even more touched if you didn't keep on putting down my theory about Andover. No conflict of interest, is there? I mean, he's not another of your crooked clients?'

'No, he is not. I simply cannot see Rocca, who by all accounts didn't even like his brother-in-law, letting himself be talked into a murder conspiracy in which he does all the dirty work and takes all the blame. But why be in such a hurry to rush from one load of trouble that's not your business into another? I presume you got yourself out of your last little bit of bother?'

'Why do you presume that?' asked Joe.

'Because that animal's still alive—I think. And because the police were reasonably polite when I mentioned your name. I was glad you took my advice and went to them after all.'

'Your advice?' snorted Joe indignantly. 'I'd have gone to them a lot earlier if it hadn't been for you trying to protect your client.'

'Innocence is its own protection, Sixsmith,' she said piously.

'Innocent? You mean he didn't have the bottle to be crooked, don't you?'

'Why not? If that makes him guilty, there's a lot of guilty people running around loose.'

'Listen, I reckon he thought seriously about getting into the dope-smuggling business, and anyone who needs to be scared of doing that is guilty as hell in my book.'

He realized to his surprise that Butcher was looking rather discomfited. Just for once, he thought not ungleefully, I've got the moral high ground and she doesn't like it!

'That's a lousy thing to say about someone you haven't even met,' she counter-attacked. 'He saw the powder, guessed what it was, and got rid of it. You say he was scared off. Well, I've met the man and I say he was principled, and I'd back my judgement against yours any time.'

Joe smiled but didn't let it show. This was Butcher's Achilles heel. You could stab her bleeding heart all day and get no change, but tap her ever so gently on her character judgement and watch her go tumbling.

'Maybe,' he said. 'Only if, say, he got as far as Luton baggage claim before he dumped the stuff, that would be pure terror wouldn't it?'

'Where did you dream that up from, Sixsmith?' she demanded.

'That's what Blue and his friends at this end heard,' he said. 'And the only possible source is Bannerjee himself when his boss, Charley Herringshaw, went to see him.'

Butcher thought a moment, then said, 'Well, that's what he would tell Herringshaw, isn't it? The man's got a grip on him. He's not going to tell the truth, is he? He needs to put himself in the best light possible. He'd probably say yes, he got as far as baggage reclaim, then something happened, maybe he spotted that his suitcase had been tampered with, so he got scared and headed for the loo with his flight bag, and dumped the dope, and wasn't he right to do so as the Customs had clearly been tipped off to look out for him.'

'Maybe he tipped them off himself,' mocked Joe.

'Maybe he did. In fact, that's very good thinking, Sixsmith. It would mean he must have decided he was going to get rid of the stuff as soon as he saw it.'

'Why's that?' said Joe, feeling lost.

'Because he must have done the tipping off before he left Spain, which means he never had any intention of trying to smuggle the stuff through,' she said triumphantly.

Joe gave up. It was no good. He never came out of an argument with Butcher anywhere but under. Not even when, as now, he felt there was something there he could club her into submission with, if only he could lay his hands on it.

He said obstinately, 'So what it comes down to is, despite you being so sure you were right and Bannerjee hadn't got the dope through in the kid's bull, you let me risk my butt chasing after it just in case you were wrong. Well, thanks. You won't be sending me a bill for your unbiased professional advice, I hope.'

'It was you and your mad cabbie mate who got us all into this, Sixsmith,' she pointed out. 'But OK. You know I can't resist that downtrodden minority look. Will a pint and a cheeseburger at the Glit buy your friendship again?'

'Hey, you think I'm that cheap? I want something classy. Like lunch at the Georgian Tea-Room.'

'You want to get me banned? Oh all right. But that's it, account clear.'

'Just one thing more,' said Joe. 'That *The Times* you've got there? You couldn't leave it? My newsagent just went out of business.'

She dropped the paper into his lap and said, 'Still doing the crossword back to front, are we? Let me know when you finish one. I'll buy you two lunches!'

'Don't be a lousy loser, Butcher,' he said, grinning.

'I haven't had your practice,' she replied. 'Incidentally, it might be wise to cover your naked frailties a bit more comprehensively before you start in on the puzzle. Your next visitor could be a little more strait-laced.'

'My next visitor?'

'That's right. Gwen Baker rang this morning. She didn't sound too pleased with you. I got the impression she was going to call at your office this afternoon.'

'You didn't give her my home address, did you?' asked Joe alarmed.

Butcher grinned evilly.

'As if I'd do that. Mind you, someone in her line of business shouldn't have too much difficulty tracking you down. Promise me one thing. When Gwen starts suing you for false accounting, and Andover starts suing for defamation, call some other solicitor.'

She left laughing. Sixsmith didn't bother to try a riposte. You could never have the last word with a lawyer. And besides, he was too busy dressing.

TWENTY

WITH ALL HIS clothes on and another can of Guinness in his belly, Joe felt a little more in control of his destiny. But not much.

He checked the phone was still unplugged and though he couldn't lock his door, he pushed a table against it to give the impression it was locked.

Then, opening a third can, he sat down to steady his nerves with *The Times* crossword.

Time passed. Outside the afternoon greyness gloomed towards night. But time and tide meant nothing to Joe Sixsmith. No thought of Gwen Baker troubled his mind, and it was as if Stephen Andover and Carlo Rocca, Mr Blue and Mr Grey, Suzie and Glen and Mr Nayyar, had never existed.

One of life's glittering prizes was within his grasp.

He'd almost completed a *Times* crossword puzzle.

He'd found real words to fit nearly all the spaces, and invented good clues to point to all the words. It was all going to hinge on a nine-letter word across the middle of the puzzle, six of whose letters were dictated by Down answers. Exercising all his ingenuity, he had avoided x's and z's and q's but still he ended up with the unpromising combination of P-TW-TR-P. He tried every possible vowel combination in the blanks, but soon had to acknowledge that a single word was impossible. But two words were permissible, even three, as long as you could come up with a decent clue. His first experiment produced PET WET RAP. He looked at Whitey, who sneered. He tried again and again, and eventually ended with PIT WIT RIP. Three real words, certainly, but could they be linked together? A pit was a mine... wit was a funny man, or his humour... and rip?

All kinds of things. He needed a connection. He reached for his tattered dictionary, opened it... and there it was, leaping out of the page. *Rip:* in coal-mining, the act of blasting a tunnel or 'gate' to the coal face; or the rock brought down by such a blast; or the roof space left by such a blast which it is then necessary for a specialist, called a ripper, to make safe.

And there it was too, the cryptic clue.

Underground comic brings the roof down.

He looked at it with ineffable satisfaction. Whether it was good enough to get another lunch out of Butcher remained to be seen, but it would do for him!

'Whitey,' he said, deciding maybe his satisfaction was effable after all, 'What's it feel like to be associated with Joseph Sixsmith, Private Investigator and Public Genius?'

'Like being ravished by a midget. You know someone's screwing you, but you can't see who,' said Gwen Baker.

Joe shot to his feet. It was a courtesy he'd been brought up to extend to a lady. Also it was a better position from which to start running.

How had she managed to get in without him hearing? And did he want to know?

He said, 'Mrs Baker...Ms Baker...nice to see you. Won't you sit down?'

She looked at the chairs on offer and said, 'I think not. This shouldn't take long. I just thought you might care to know that my husband has left me. His tart, it seems, was ill, but for reasons no one quite understands made what is described as a miraculous recovery. Gerald writes that this experience has forced him to face up to his true feelings. Don't you find that very moving, Mr Sixsmith?'

'He *writes?*' said Joe, focusing on what seemed the area of least provocation.

'You don't imagine Gerry had the balls to say such things to my face?' she said. 'He and she have taken the precaution of putting the Channel between them and me. She probably has the old-fashioned notion that moving water is a barrier.'

He knew better than to ask, to what? He said, 'And how can I help you now, Mrs . . . Ms Baker?'

'Help me *now*? As opposed to helping me *when,* Mr Sixsmith? Perhaps you'd like to tell me which of your services I've already paid for?'

It was time to be bold.

He said, 'Maybe for upholding the law.'

She gave him a look which with a little more effort could have turned a prince into a frog and he added hastily, 'Look, if it's a refund you're after, maybe we could come to an accommodation . . .'

'Money's not what I came here for,' she said.

'What, then?' he asked fearfully.

And suddenly she laughed, turning in an instant from a ticking bomb to a handsome sophisticated woman sharing a joke with the help.

'Just to look,' she said.

'You mean, you're not mad about the Hyphen . . . that is, your man . . .'

'The Hyphen? I like that. Listen, Joe, any woman's mad when another woman lifts her husband, no matter what kind of rat-fink he is. But the good news is my lawyer tells me he's got the legal tangle sorted and if old Meg Merrilees imagines she's going to see any of my money, she's in for a shock.'

'And what about, you know, the string thing . . . ?'

'This, you mean?' She pulled the knotted cord out of her bag. 'You don't mean to tell me you actually believe in any of this, do you, Joe?'

The cord was swinging like a pendulum. His eyes followed the hypnotic motion.

He said, 'All I know is, I'd feel better if you'd undo it.'

'That's what you want? OK.'

She twitched the cord in her hand and the knot unravelled.

'Thanks,' he said. 'About the money, now, maybe if I hung on to enough to cover expenses . . .'

'I told you, I don't care about the money. Like I said, all I came for was to look.'

'At what?' he asked bewildered.

'At nothing, that's the secret.' She smiled and offered her hand. 'We're parting friends, OK, Joe Sixsmith?'

'Yes, sure,' he said, taking the offered hand. It was cool and dry and the contact set up a small tingle like a minute electric shock which persisted as she held on and peered close into his face. Finally she said, 'You're not thinking of going somewhere dark and confined? A cellar, maybe. Somewhere there's a lot of boxes stored—and a nasty smell?'

'I'm sorry? A cellar? No, I don't think so. . .'

'If you do, take care.' Then she laughed again and released his hand. 'But why am I saying take care to a man who's taken care of? Cherry was right. You're not a man to mess with.'

'Butcher said that?' said Joe, now thoroughly bewildered. 'Why? What's she mean?'

'Better ask your cat,' she said. 'Be happy.'

Joe remained standing till he heard the downstairs door close behind her, then he sat down with a thump.

'Weird lady,' he said to Whitey. The cat gave him its takes-a-one-to-know-a-one lip-curl, then went into the kitchen to renew its five year project to find a way of breaking into the refrigerator.

'Shouldn't bother,' shouted Joe. 'We're out of everything again. Looks like another night on the junk. What's it to be? Luciano's? The Gourmet Emporium? Or the Glit?'

Whitey re-entered spitting out bits of rubber. Eventually he would pierce the air-tight door seal, thus rendering useless what he had won. There was a Radio Four Thought-for-the-Day in there somewhere.

Joe looked at the flakes of rubber and said, 'You fancy the Chinese chicken, then? OK, the Emporium it is. Let's go.'

In the hallway, he noticed the unplugged phone. It had probably been ringing all afternoon with Californian millionaires offering him employment in Beverly Hills.

'Let 'em ring,' he said with the devil-may-care indifference of a man who'd seen off a witch and *The Times* crossword in a single afternoon.

He turned to the door, which opened so suddenly, he stepped back, stumbled on Whitey, and sat down heavily.

'Joe, are you OK?' said Beryl Boddington anxiously.

'I was till you knocked me down,' he groaned.

She stood over him. She had nice legs.

'I've been trying to ring your office all day. And I got so worried I got your home number from Mirabelle and tried here and there's been no reply all afternoon, and I didn't want to worry Mirabelle no more so I thought I'd ...'

Her words, and her concern, dried to a trickle as her gaze drifted to the unplugged phone, then to Whitey who was rubbing himself against her legs and purring.

'I see I needn't have worried,' she resumed flatly. 'I'll let your aunt know you're OK.'

She turned to go. Joe scrambled to his feet.

'Yes, you should've been worried,' he called, hurrying after her. 'What are you saying? You'd have been happier to find me bleeding on the floor and Whitey dead?'

She stopped and said over her shoulder, 'OK, well, maybe, but at least you could have told Mirabelle you were OK.'

'Mirabelle didn't need told 'cos she'd no reason to think I mightn't be OK, not till you got her stirred up.'

He could sense her reluctantly admitting the justice of this.

She said, 'But I had reason, didn't I? Not that I was all that worried, you understand. But I bumped into the Major and he said he hadn't been able to get hold of you and could I give you what he calls this bumf seeing as I was in your section.'

She reached into her handbag but Joe said, 'No, hang on to it, will you? And wait here while I run back in and phone Mirabelle, OK?'

He didn't wait for an answer, but she was still there when he returned a minute later.

'That didn't take long,' she said doubtfully.

'To listen to one of Auntie's lectures you mean? You're right. Only I told her I was taking you out for a drink and you were waiting. After that, she couldn't get the phone down quick enough.'

'Who said you were taking me for a drink?' she demanded.

'You want to make me a liar to Auntie Mirabelle? Besides, you're on my team, remember? We need to talk tactics.'

She smiled and said, 'So long as it's business. Where're we going?'

'How about the Glit?' he said. Whitey wouldn't mind. Their chicken was even more rubbery than the Gourmet Emporium's.

'The Glit?' she echoed. 'I was told respectable girls don't go in there.'

'What you heard was, they don't come out. Come on.'

When they entered the bar, Gary was blasting away with *Rock'n'Roll Part 2*. Beryl winced in pain, though perhaps some of this was caused by the sight of Dick Hull's bespangled suit.

'Come early to get your seat for the Mastermind-of-Luton Quiz Nite, have you?' he yelled above the music.

Joe looked around the empty room.

'No, we've come early to miss it,' he said. 'Don't you ever have a Quiet-Drink-Nobody's-Going-To-Hassle-You Nite?'

'Where's the profit in that?' said Hull. 'So what can I get you?'

'Pint of the black stuff, bag of cheese-and-onion crisps to put Whitey on, and . . . ?'

'Gin and tonic. I'm not working tonight,' said Beryl.

They took their drinks to the quietest corner and sat down.

'So what happened, Joe?' she asked.

He meant to be non-committal, but he found himself giving a detailed account of nearly everything that had happened from the time Andover walked into his office. All he censored was the necromancy. He didn't mind her thinking he led an exciting life, but he didn't want her thinking he was a nut.

But even without the necromancy, that was how she was looking at him when he finished.

'This is like old Chicago!' she said.

'It's a tough old world out there,' he said complacently.

'Maybe. But you don't have to go looking for it,' she said. 'I mean, it's not like you're some macho kid, or some guy who's come out of the police or the army with a taste for action. You seem a nice ordinary man—I don't mean that as a put down, I think ordinary is great, it's what we get when we're settled with ourselves—so what I'm really asking is, why do you do it, Joe?'

He felt an upsurge of irritation but washed it back down with a draught of Guinness.

'OK, I'll tell you,' he said. 'But only if you promise to tell me how come a nice girl like you got so obsessed with other people's blood and crap.'

'That's not the same,' she flashed. 'I want to help people, make them feel better, help them deal with their pain. The blood and crap as you put it are incidental.'

'It *is* the same,' insisted Sixsmith mildly. 'Only if you're a PI or a man, you're not allowed to put it like that; at least, not in Luton.'

She snorted a disbelieving laugh and he said, 'See what I mean?' She sipped her drink thoughtfully, then shook her head.

'No, it won't do,' she said. 'You want to help the world, there's a lot better ways than bunking off from real work to spend your time peeping through bedroom keyholes.'

The phrase sounded familiar. It was one of Mirabelle's favourites.

He said abruptly, 'How old are you?'

'What?'

'And what happened to your kid's father?'

'None of your damned business.'

'Well, I'm sorry but I've gotta ask because I don't know your Auntie Mirabelle.'

'I haven't got an Aunt Mirabelle,' she said in bewilderment.

'But surely you must have? Everyone's got a Mirabelle. She's the one who saves folk the embarrassment of asking you stuff that's none of their damn business by filling them in with all the details of your life.'

For a moment she looked ready to give him an argument, then she began to grin, rather shamefacedly.

'OK,' she said. 'Point taken. But I never had to ask her anything. Once she took it in her mind to give me a rundown on her favourite nephew, there was no stopping her.'

'I bet there wasn't,' said Joe, smiling. 'So along with all this bedroom keyhole bit, what was the good stuff?'

'What makes you think that wasn't the good stuff?' she mocked.

'Because Auntie was selling,' he said. 'I bet you got what a cute kid I was, and would be again once I got this silly PI thing out of my system and settled down to a steady life once more. I bet you know more about me than I know about myself!'

'That wouldn't surprise me,' she said gently. 'OK, she did give a pretty comprehensive rundown.'

'Bet she didn't mention I was losing my hair,' he said.

'No, but I expected that,' she said. 'Bound to be a bare patch with that halo rubbing all the time.'

'It's the dunce's cap that does the damage,' said Joe gloomily. 'Look, you asked why I do this stuff, and you were right when you said I don't have the build or the speed for it.'

'I didn't say—'

'You implied. And you were right 'cos I implied I'm the kind who can handle himself. Well, I'm not. The only reason I got myself messed up like this is stupidity. My legs get me places before my mind catches up and says, Legs, this ain't where you want to be. But I'm learning. It's like being a nurse, I suppose. You want to be one, but that doesn't make you into one overnight. You've got to do the training. Only with PI-ing, the training's all on the job, the only manuals are what you see at the movies or read in the pulp paperbacks, and for every one pointer, you get half a dozen red herrings.'

He suddenly realized he was sounding very earnest, flushed and said, 'End of lecture. Bet Mirabelle didn't tell you I could bore the pants off you, did she?'

'That would certainly be a novel technique,' she said demurely.

Shoot! thought Joe. We're flirting. How did I get into this? How do I get out of it? Do I want to get out of it?

A voice cried, 'Well, there he is, my main man, the Sam Spade of sunny Luton, enjoying a drink with his little niece up from the country.'

It was Merv Golightly. He folded his lean length into the chair next to Beryl and grinned deep into her eyes.

She regarded him coldly and said, 'I'm not his niece.'

'I'm sorry to hear that, girl,' said Merv. 'Because this man is far too old for you and besides he has a wife and seventeen children back home in Bechuanaland. Me now, I'm twenty-nine and fancy free.'

'Merv, we were talking,' said Joe.

'At your age, that's very wise,' said Merv. 'I just wanted to ask how it went. I've called by your office a couple of times but you're never there. Hey, has someone beaten you up, or are you having that face job at last?'

'Beryl, meet Merv,' said Joe. 'He used to be a friend of mine.'

'Best friend he ever had,' said Merv. 'Sorry, cancel that. The only friend he ever had. Glad to meet you, Beryl. Take no heed of me. It's just I'm used to seeing Joe out with them old dogs his Auntie Mirabelle digs up from the RSPCA, so it knocks me back to see him sitting next to a real vision. You gotta be a client. This can't be social.'

'It's social,' said Beryl, refusing to thaw. 'And it was enjoyable till a moment ago.'

Merv whistled, unabashed. Joe who abashed very easily watched with envious admiration. Merv said, 'Sassy too. I like that. Any time you want to ride in my taxi, you're welcome, though I should warn you I charge extra after midnight. Joe, did you or did you not get the stuff?'

'Not,' said Sixsmith. 'It wasn't there. I mean, the bull was there, but the stuff wasn't in it.'

'So what about the stitched lip?'

'Bit of trouble with some Brits, but I sorted it.'

He saw Beryl's nose wrinkle in distaste at this macho modesty.

'Yeah, I see,' said Merv. 'Beat their fists to a pulp with your face, did you? So all that scag's still floating around?'

'Floating's the word,' said Joe. 'It went down the pan in the Med. Or at Luton Airport. Take your pick.'

'Is that right? Always thought the scampi they serve here must be on something. By the by, Joe, congrats on your second prize in the Karaoke comp.'

'Yeah, I meant to ask Dick, who got first.'

'Haven't you heard?' Merv took out a ballpoint and scribbled his name on a beer mat.

'Treasure that, kid,' he said handing it to Beryl. 'Ten years from now it could be worth millions.'

'You?' said Joe incredulously. 'But you had the punters chewing the carpet.'

'That's right. Made 'em thirsty. Haven't you sussed it out? Listening customers aren't buying customers. It's the turns that send them rushing to the bar that Dick rewards. Seriously though, I got this great idea as I was driving around after my triumph. How about we make it your theme song?'

'Make what?'

'*Sweet Mystery of Life.* Get it? I could put it on tape and feed it into your answerphone, so whenever anyone rang you and you weren't there, what they'd hear is... Are you listening to me, Joe?'

It was clear he wasn't. In fact he stood up so abruptly, the other two were momentarily united in surprise.

'Joe, are you all right?' said Beryl.

'Call of nature,' said Sixsmith. 'Excuse me.'

He headed for the Gents. It wasn't nature that was calling, not in the conventional sense. But something was calling. He was on the edge of another revelation and this time he wanted to see all the way before something happened to knock him off.

He locked himself in a cubicle and tried to let his thoughts drift in free association. The trigger was 'Sweet Mystery of Life'. Merv singing it... More importantly, in his dream the Casa Mia corpses had been singing it as they rearranged themselves in the order that would best suit Andover legally... His mind kept drifting from the corpses to Merv doing his turn in the Glit and he had to drag it back in search of the real answer, the true connection...

It was going, it was fading, he was losing it...

'Sixsmith, you're trying too hard!' he admonished himself.

He let go the reins again, and again with renewed irritation found himself back at Merv's performance when the real clue had to be somewhere in the words of the song...

'Oh, Sweet Mystery of Life,' he crooned, bringing an uneasy cough from the next cubicle. He stifled a giggle, and in the gap thus created in his thinking there popped up a woman, gleaming with gold like a pharaoh's tomb and almost as dusty.

Mrs Rathbone, Andover's nosey neighbour, accosting him in the Georgian Tea-Room... Mrs Rathbone telling Dildo Doberley, 'I saw him come running out of the house. Oh yes, it was definitely Rocca. He had his hand up to his face as if he was trying to hide in case anyone was watching, but I'd recognize that awful moustache and dreadful gangster's hat anywhere!'

The revelation exploded in his brain like frozen cod dropped into a pan of boiling fat.

It was after all the singer, not the song. It was Merv's performance, not Merv's material which had made the connection.

Merv with his hand to his face, trying to hold his false moustache on...

Rocca running out of the house, his hand to his face...

'Oh shoot,' said Joe Sixsmith.

He needed time to think this over. He also needed a drink. He pulled the chain and went back into the lounge.

'You OK?' said Merv.

'Fine,' said Joe, sinking the rest of his pint in one draught.

'No wonder nature calls so often,' said Merv. 'Same again?'

Without waiting for an answer, he gathered up the glasses and made for the bar.

Sixsmith said, 'Sorry about Merv. He's OK. In fact, he's great, only he sometimes gets carried away.'

'I've noticed,' smiled Beryl. 'No need to apologize. He was quite different while you were in the Gents. Really nice. I've often noticed that with men. You bring out the worst in each other.'

'Only when you women are egging us on,' said Joe. 'Look, I'm sorry, after this drink, I've really got to go, one or two things to sort out...'

'No sweat, Joe,' she said with a slightly hurtful indifference. 'We're not on a date, are we? If maybe you could give me a lift back home first ... It sounds like there might be a storm coming on ...'

There was a confirming rumble of thunder which filled the gap between *Hello, Hello, I'm Back Again* and *Shake It Up* on the tape.

'Sure,' said Joe.

'But one thing we should do while we've still got a moment is make some arrangement about this Watch thing. Like I said, I saw the Major—'

'Look, I'm sure you're better organized than me. Couldn't you sort it out?' said Joe rather irritably. He wanted to think and here she was distracting him with Major Sholto's daft vigilante schemes, not to mention her full soft lips, rounded figure and sweet perfume ...

'No way,' she said firmly. 'I'm just the messenger girl because you're so hard to get hold of. Here, captain, these are for you ...'

She produced a sheaf of papers from her bag and placed them before him.

He glanced down, uninterested. The topmost sheet was headed *Lykers Yard Lock-Ups. Key-holders and telephone contact nos. where known.*

'The Major really ought to leave this kind of thing to the cops,' he complained.

'Like you, you mean?' she laughed.

'Hey, come on! It's my job ...'

His voice died away, his gaze became fixed.

'Joe?' said Beryl.

'Gone again, has he?' said Merv returning. 'Not another call of nature? You need a good flush out, my son. Get that through your system.'

He banged a black pint on the Major's sheet. Joe picked it up. The name was still there. *Lock-up 5, Lykers Yard. Keyholder: S. Andover. No telephone number.*

This was the way it happened with him. Some people might give it that fancy name serendipity; he preferred to think of some jokey minor god having a laugh, nudge nudge, wink wink, let's get old Joe Sixsmith going. Sometimes it pissed him off, but no point in getting narked with a deity, even if he was only second team stuff.

His mind fitted things together. The vaguely familiar figure he'd seen in the Yard the night he ran from Blue and Grey. His encounter with Andover in Lykers Lane which the quick-thinking insurance man had explained by claiming he was on his way to see Sixsmith to warn him off harassing Debbie Stipplewhite.

He put the pint down untouched and stood up.

'I'm sorry, I've got to go,' he said.

'Crikey, Joe, you ought to see a quack about your prostate,' said Merv.

'I mean, go,' he said, scooping up Whitey who protested he hadn't had his chicken. 'Beryl, I don't want to rush you...'

'That's OK, Joe, I'll look after Beryl,' volunteered Merv. Beryl grinned at him.

'No, thanks, I can't afford the fare. Hey, Joe, wait for me.'

She grabbed the papers he'd left on the table and set off after him. Merv shook his head sadly, then drew the abandoned gin and tonic and pint of Guinness to flank his lager.

'Waste not, want not,' he said and began to drink.

TWENTY-ONE

THE STORM WAS getting nearer. Thunder rolled across the sky like the Jumbos in July, and from time to time lightning turned the eastern horizon into the Western Front.

Joe knew all about the First World War. In fact he'd been educated to the age of fifteen before he realized that history happened anywhere else but Europe. So now, as the moment approached when he would confront the cunningly concealed and deeply dug-in truth, it was natural for him to think of himself as going 'over the top'.

He would have preferred to be alone with his thoughts at such a time, but with Beryl beside him, burrowing for explanation, it seemed an acceptable compromise to shut her up by testing some of his theory in words.

'Here's how I see it now,' he said. 'Andover wasn't just a conspirator with Rocca, he was the main man. He did the lot! Came to see me to set up an alibi, provoked me into bringing Sergeant Chivers, watched his house till DC Doberley turned up, then put on a false moustache and Rocca's hat and "accidentally" bumped into Dildo as he was coming down the drive...'

'Hang on. You're saying it was Andover who actually did the killings? But what's Rocca doing while all this is going on?'

'Being seriously dead, is my guess. Andover probably killed him that same morning and hid the body. Now he does for the rest of the family, making sure his own wife is definitely last so that he'll inherit everything. Mrs Rathbone, the neighbour, sees him rushing to the car with his hand up to his face, not, like she thought, trying to shield his identity, but holding on to his moustache which probably came loose during the killings.'

'But he was back in your office by the time Sergeant Chivers rang to tell you it was all a load of nonsense,' Beryl objected.

'Dildo had to get back too, remember. And knowing Dildo, I wouldn't be surprised if he didn't stop off for a coffee or something on the way, though that wouldn't appear in his report.'

'But Andover's car...? There wouldn't be time to hide that surely?'

'No. He probably got out of it round the corner from my office, his partner got in and drove it away to a pre-arranged hiding spot.'

'His partner? But you said he'd probably killed Rocca...'

'Not Rocca,' said Joe impatiently. 'Debbie Stipplewhite. He actually rang her from my office, probably she had a mobile phone. His call let her know that everything was going OK and she could ring the police with a pre-recorded tape of Andover in his best Italian accent putting the finger on himself! I think he intended to turn up at the house after the police, but when he conned me into giving him a lift, it didn't matter that we made it before they did. He had his built-in witness.'

The towers of Rasselas loomed ahead, momentarily etched sharp against a sheet of lightning.

'So where do you think Rocca's body is? And the car? And where are you going in such a rush, Joe?'

This was where frankness had to falter to a stop. Joe Sixsmith didn't know much about women, but he knew that where a man can't command obedience, he'd better make very sure he contrived ignorance.

'Some stuff at the office I need to look at,' he said vaguely. 'Just to make sure I've got my ideas all sorted before I contact the cops.'

'So you *are* going to get in touch with the police?' she said uncertainly.

'Hey, what do you think I am? One of these gung-ho gumshoes who goes rushing in where the fuzz fears to tread? This is Luton, girl, and this is Joe Sixsmith speaking!'

He pulled up in front of her block. She opened the door but didn't move to get out. It was, he thought, his mind still dwelling on war imagery, like one of those old movies where the guy's going back to the front after leave and they both get this premonition of death, so she lets him have his way with her to make sure that some of his being remains . . .

Now this was really going over the top, in every sense, he mocked himself. But enough of the impulse remained to make him lean across and plant a substantial kiss on her lips which parted probably in surprise rather than welcome, but nevertheless giving him the full benefit of that warm moist mouth, tasting of honey and perfumed with coriander, or maybe it was just gin and tonic . . .

She moved away, not forcefully but firmly, and got out of the car. He reached over and pulled the door shut. As he drove away, he could see her in his mirror, still standing on the pavement, just like an old movie shot.

His macho mood lasted only for the short time it took him to drive down Lykers Lane. He parked right at the end of the Lane where it gaped into Lykers Yard. The storm was right overhead now, its lightning flashes so brilliant that the after-darkness seemed almost solid, despite the feeble glow of the bracketed sodium lamp above the car. At least it wasn't raining. Yet.

He opened the glove compartment and took out a pencil torch. Then he reached under his seat and probed his fingers through a slit in the upholstery till he found a wash-leather pouch. Whitey watched these preparations with interest and when Joe got out of the car, he prepared to follow.

'No,' said Joe. 'Generals don't get their bayonets dirty. They lounge around HQ signing casualty lists.'

Whitey yawned as if to acknowledge the justness of this as Joe closed and locked the door, waited for a lightning flash, and set off towards the lock-ups.

The return of darkness turned the worn but fairly even flagstones into a rock-strewn desert, and he stumbled several times. His torch beam did little more than scratch the surface of this blackness. When the lightning flickered again, the lock-ups seemed to be further away, as if they'd taken the opportunity to shuffle backwards. He pressed on, arms outstretched like a blind man. Suddenly he was there, and had to stop in mid-pace to avoid a painful collision with the wall.

He felt a sense of relief but not for long. Walking across the yard, he'd just been a guy walking across a yard, a bit odd maybe, seeing that it didn't actually lead anywhere, but strictly within the law.

Now he was on the brink of becoming a burglar.

Worse, if for once he'd got it right, he was on the brink of finding a car with a body in the boot and maybe a killer in the offing.

He took a deep breath and said to himself, 'Come on, Joe. Either do it or shog off home, watch a bit of cosy mayhem on the telly.'

Was it a real alternative? Not for a man with a mind-reading cat waiting to sneer at him.

He checked the flaking number on the wooden door. Fate or good judgement had brought him straight to No. 5. From his pocket he took the wash-leather pouch. It held a set of picklocks. A man as good with machines as he was hadn't had any problem making these out of a set of kitchen skewers. A man with friends like Butcher and Sergeant Brightman knew that mere possession of such implements could get him banged up for six months with desperate men like serial killers and poll tax defaulters, which was why he kept them hidden in the car seat.

Carefully he selected, gently he inserted, deftly he twisted ... There was a click, the door groaned at the release of pressure, Joe let out a sigh of relief and self-congratulation.

And a hand descended on his shoulder and a voice in his ear breathed, 'Hello hello hello.'

He recognized the honeyed breath even as he shrieked with shock and twisted round to defend himself, and he was able to stay his blow and even bring his voice down within an octave of normal as he said, 'Beryl, what the hell are you doing here?'

'Thought your auntie said you didn't swear, Joe?' she said.

'My auntie never frightened me half to death,' he replied. 'So what *are* you doing here?'

'You kissed me,' she said.

He shone his torch into her face to try to get some visual clue to her enigmatic meaning. All he saw was her big brown eyes regarding him with gentle seriousness.

'That mean you're compromised, or something?' he said. 'That mean we're going to be engaged maybe?'

'You kissed me twice,' she said. 'First time in the hospital was because you were all relieved and happy your friend was going to be all right. Second time, just now, it felt more like a soldier's farewell kiss, know what I mean?'

'I know you seem to be some kind of expert on kissing,' said Joe. 'You take a course, or what?'

She ignored his gibe and went on, 'So I got to thinking about what you'd been telling me in the car and wondering what crazy thing you must be considering to make such a shy bashful boy so bold.'

'My auntie told you I was bashful?' said Joe. 'Isn't that woman ever going to let me grow up?'

'Don't rush it, Joe,' said Beryl reprovingly. 'It'll happen. Anyway, it struck me that this sudden urgent need to get back to Rasselas came after I showed you the Major's list, so I took a good look at it, and know what came jumping out of the page? Lock-up No. 5 was let out to a party name of Andover. Now that's not a common name. So maybe it's this insurance man with the dead wife. In which case, what's he doing with a lock-up out here? Is that where Joe's gone, I asked myself. Only one way to find out. And here I am.'

Joe looked at her with the admiration he always felt for those whose minds moved with such microchip speed. Reverse the situation and with her limited information he might have got there, but a couple of hours, or maybe even a good night's sleep, later.

'OK. But that still don't explain why you've come,' he said.

'Joe, surely you know a soldier's farewell kiss gives a girl the right to know how long she's supposed to stay in mourning after she gets the bad news,' she said, her eyes bright with mischief now. 'Now are we going to take a look inside or just stand around out here spooning?'

She was mocking his fears of falling into one of Aunt Mirabelle's carefully baited traps, thought Joe. Which meant she really wasn't interested in being the bait. Which should have filled him with relief . . .

This was no time for trick-cycling.

He said, 'You wait here while I take a look, OK?' in his masterful voice.

Then he pushed open the door and stepped inside.

There are times when being right is almost a bigger disappointment than being wrong.

'Oh shoot,' said Joe as the narrow beam of his torch hit the bonnet of a blue Ford Fiesta.

He let the light slide down to the number plate just to be sure.

'Is it the one?' breathed Beryl in his ear.

'Yes,' he said. 'Hey, I told you to wait outside.'

'Have you got a royal warrant saying you can order me around?' she asked sweetly. 'What's all this stuff?'

Her eyes were better than his or maybe it was just her mind. The walls of the lock-up were lined with stacks of cardboard boxes. The torch picked out names like Sony, Panasonic, Phillips. If full, the boxes had to contain several thousand quids' worth of VCRs, tape-decks, CD players and so on.

This was a puzzle, but even a man who'd found a clue to fit PIT WIT RIP in *The Times* crossword couldn't be expected to deal with more than one problem at a time.

He said, 'Wait here. Please. I'm going to look around.'

Again her quick mind was with him and ahead of him with dazzling speed.

'You think if it was Andover did the killings, his brother-in-law could be in the boot,' she said. 'We'd better open it.'

'No,' he said sharply. 'Not you. I'll do that.'

She bubbled a laugh.

'Joe, don't go chivalrous on me. How many dead bodies have you seen? Me, I see them all the time.'

'You do? Remind me to stay clear of your hospital,' said Joe. But he could tell that argument was useless. The sooner he got this next bit over, the sooner they could get out of here and back to a telephone and a stiff Scotch.

He sniffed the air as he moved forward. There was a strong body smell here, pungent, faecal. The smell of decay? How quickly did a body begin to break down? In her line of business, Beryl probably knew. Just like in her line of business, Gwen Baker knew he was going to end up somewhere dark and smelly and it could be dangerous.

He pushed all these know-it-all women to the back of his mind and stooped over the boot with his picklocks.

Beryl took the torch from his hand and said, 'It'll be easier if I hold the light.'

She was right. In fact having her there made things easier in all kinds of ways. Put simply, her presence was a comfort to him. He examined the proposition, decided it held no danger, and admitted it gladly.

The picklock caught, held, turned again, then the lock snapped open.

He took a deep breath, held it, and raised the lid.

Beryl let the torch beam wander over the floor of the boot.

It contained an emergency triangle, a canister of oil, a windscreen scraper, and a thick paperback in a plastic cover. Beryl picked it up and looked at the title. *Cobbett's Actuarial Tables—1st Edition (Revised)*.

'I saw the movie,' she said. 'Joe, don't look so disappointed. Not finding bodies is a good thing, believe me. The car's enough to win you fame and fortune. I think that now would be a good time to go for the police and make it their problem.'

She was wrong, thought Joe looking over her shoulder. Five minutes ago would have been a good time. Now they definitely had a problem of their very own.

Beryl computed the focal point of his eyes, turned and saw it too.

Silhouetted against the paler darkness beyond the door was a figure. Medium height, overcoat, slouch hat.

'Oh shoot,' said Joe. 'Andover.'

He was less disturbed than he might have expected. Perhaps it was Beryl's presence again, making him feel macho, but he was pretty sure if it came to a struggle he could deal with Andover, and his mind had already slipped past fear to the prospect of triumph as he actually handed over the cringing killer to DS Chivers.

Lightning jagged across the invisible sky and suddenly the silhouetted figure looked bigger, solider, more formidable.

Joe took a step forward.

'It's over, Andover,' he said with an authority only slightly marred by the awkward assonance.

'Stand still,' said the man, his voice made low and sibilant by (Joe hoped) his fear.

Beryl flicked the torch beam towards him and he raised his right hand to ward it off but not before Joe had got a glimpse of his face.

What he saw made him laugh out loud. The stupid sod was wearing his big droopy false moustache. He'd actually disguised himself once more as the man police all over the country were looking for!

This swept away any residual fear. The fellow was a clown!

'OK, Stephen,' said Joe in his kindest tone. 'Let's go somewhere a bit more comfortable and sort this thing out.'

He advanced confidently. Lightning flashed, thunder rolled. It was all comically theatrical.

'Stand still,' said Andover, still putting on his comic Italian voice. He reached his hand beneath his coat.

'Got a gun, have you, Stephen?' mocked Joe. 'You been seeing too many movies.'

The hand came out. There was something in it. Certainly not a gun. A pen maybe? Perhaps he was hoping to sell some insurance. Suddenly irritated, Joe leapt forward to bring an end to this farce, and seized the false moustache with both hands to rip it off.

The man shrieked like a mating peacock as his head was dragged down against Joe's chest.

It is strange how strongly the mind clings to its misconceptions. Almost as strongly as these hairs were clinging to this lip.

He must have used superglue, thought Joe as he tugged and tugged with no result except a leap of an octave in the screaming.

And it wasn't till the man's thumb found the button in the object he'd pulled out of his coat, and a long thin blade snapped into the air that he admitted he'd got it wrong.

Interestingly his mind was at last working at computer speed, though not in any useful direction. Somehow in the split second before the blade reached his throat, he had time to think, PIT WIT RIP was wrong.

Clue: epitaph for a dumb dick.

Answer: PI twit. RIP.

The knife point struck.

Joe fell sideways, feeling more like he'd been hit with a blunt instrument than stabbed with a pointed one. Perhaps that's how the death blow always felt. Difficult to know, of course, as first hand accounts were hard to come by. He wished there was light. A man shouldn't have to die in the dark.

God obliged, switching on the lightning for a couple of seconds.

Not long, but long enough for Joe to see he was, as so often, both wrong and right. It wasn't a death blow because what in fact he'd been hit by was that bluntest of instruments, a set of actuarial tables.

Beryl was holding it. Fleet of foot as well as mind, she had somehow contrived to thrust it in the path of the flick knife which had driven into it with enough force to knock Joe over while the book remained impaled like a loaf of bread on a toasting fork.

Nor did her talents end there. As Rocca (Joe had given up all hope that it might not be Rocca) redirected his assault, Beryl ducked under his sweeping arms, seized his left ankle, rose to her full height and tossed him lightly backwards. His head hit the door jamb with a crack which in another place at another time Joe might have found sickening. Here and now it sounded almost melodic.

'You all right, Joe?' she said anxiously, kneeling beside him.

It would have been nice to relax and let himself be cradled to that warm and generous bosom, but this was no time for such languorous delights.

'Fine,' he said, pushing himself upright. 'Let's get out of here, fetch help.'

But, reassured he was OK, Beryl now began examining the prostrate Italian. So it was only professional interest after all, thought Joe glumly.

'You go,' she said. 'I'll stay here.'

'With him?' he cried. 'That's Rocca. He's killed four people that we know of.'

'He's harmless now,' she replied. 'Also he may have cracked his skull. He could vomit and choke on it if we leave him. You go, Joe. Get an ambulance. Hurry!'

The weight of her authority sent him staggering out of the lock-up. He stood there a moment taking in deep breaths. The storm seemed to be retreating. He turned towards the mouth of the cul-de-sac and saw his troubles weren't.

Under the solitary lamp stood a gang of youths, examining his car. Individual features were impossible to pick out in the lurid sodium glow, but their shaven heads and Union Jack T-shirts told him who they were. The Hermsprong Brits. And he didn't need a dictionary to tell him why they were here.

They hadn't yet spotted him, but Whitey was in the car and there was no way he could step back from this.

'Hey!' he cried.

Darkness returned, followed almost instantly by another flash.

And now they were all looking his way.

'It's him!' someone yelled. 'Saves us the bother of flushing him out!'

So they'd come specially. He might have guessed that the yobs who'd assaulted him the previous night wouldn't lie down quietly under their humiliation by Blue and Grey.

They were moving towards him, not hurrying, confident that there was nowhere for him to run to.

He went forward to meet them. It wasn't courage, just a hope that he might be able to keep them from spotting Beryl.

Now he could recognize last night's attackers, one of them had his arm in plaster. At their head was Glen Ellis. So much for acting like a man of principle and alibi-ing the young thug from Mr Nayyar's fire. God had funny ways of rewarding virtue.

'What's your problem, boys?' he said.

'Boys? Who are you calling boys? That's what we call you lot, Sambo. Hey, boy! Bring us another beer and make sure you wipe your big lips clean before you kiss my ass!'

This pearl had them all hooting with laughter.

Then one of them said, 'Hold it. Someone's coming!'

For a heart-lifting second Joe thought it might be the US cavalry riding to the rescue. Then he saw that he'd been half right. It was cavalry all right, but home grown and extremely superannuated. Striding round the corner, wearing an ancient riding mac and a battered deerstalker, came the Major. In one hand he carried his shooting stick, in the other a torch whose broad beam he directed over the Brits.

'Right, you chaps, what's going on here?' he said. 'Bit off your patch, aren't you?'

So he knows who they are, thought Joe. That's hopeful.

'What's it to you, dad?' asked one of them.

'A great deal perhaps. It's bad enough to have our own people scrawling on walls and peeing on stairways without having strangers messing up the place.'

'Why don't you piss off, you daft old git, before we stick your stupid hat down your stupid throat!'

The Major looked at the speaker gravely.

'Young man,' he said. 'I observe you are wearing a facsimile of the Union Flag. I have served that flag in many strange places and against many fearful foes, and up till now, whenever I saw it draped round a man's body, it was because the man was dead and had died honourably. I suggest you go away and think about this and find another way of advertising your patriotism.'

'What you on about, you silly old wanker?' demanded the youth.

'I should warn you, I'm not alone,' said the Major.

For a moment Joe's hopes rose again. Then he glanced towards the pool of light around his car. It was true, there were figures there, three of them, but they were hardly the stuff relief columns were made of.

It was the Major's hardcore vigilante patrol—Auntie Mirabelle, brave as a bulldog, but rising seventy and carrying all that weight; Mr Holmes from 718, still using a stick since his hip replacement; and Sally Firbright from 54, in her twenties but so short-sighted she wore spectacles like the bottom of a beer glass.

If only one of them had had the sense to go and call the cops!

The Brit looked at the vigilantes too, summed them up, and laughed.

'What you going to do with a fat old nigger, a cripple and a four-eyed kid, grandad? Why don't you just... aaahhhoww!'

The Major's stick had swung up sharply between the youth's legs, doubling him up in eye-popping agony.

'You need to learn some manners, young man,' said the Major.

And you need to learn some sense, old man, thought Joe desperately. Talking, there'd been just a chance the Major might convince some of this lot they didn't want to commit mayhem in front of witnesses. But now he'd started speaking their language and the Major was no Blue or Grey to frighten them into submission.

'Let's give the old bastard a good kicking,' said Glen Ellis, and matched his words by swinging his left trainer at the Major's chest. The old man staggered back and almost fell.

'Oh *shoot,*' said Joe, despairing, and prepared to hurl himself forward in a useless effort at defence.

Ellis flung another kick at the Major's head, sending his deerstalker flying.

Then there was a sound of running footsteps and a voice screamed, 'Glen! The filth's coming!'

They all looked again towards the vigilantes. A fourth figure had joined them or rather had been forced to join them. It was Suzie Sickert struggling in the powerful embrace of Mirabelle and still screaming, 'Run, Glen, the pigs are coming. Run!'

Her warning was already superfluous. A chorus of sirens was crescendoing down Lykers Lane, and next moment headlight beams turned the shadowy yard into a floodlit arena. The Brits scattered in panic, but there was only one route out and that was rapidly filling with uniformed figures. Glen Ellis sprinted past Joe into the open door of

No. 5 and almost immediately came bouncing back as if he'd hit a brick wall.

Beryl followed him, nursing her fist.

'I think maybe we're both in the wrong business,' said Joe.

She shaded her eyes and looked into the headlight beams.

'I don't see no ambulance,' she said reprovingly.

A group of policemen came running up. One of them was Sergeant Brightman.

'You all right, Joe?' he asked, breathlessly.

'Fine,' said Joe. 'Is the Major OK?'

'Will be when he's finished taking his medicine. Look for yourself.'

Joe looked. The Major, upright and hatted once more had produced an old gun-metal flask which he was apparently trying to swallow whole.

'That's good,' said Joe, relieved. 'Sarge, where's Chivers? There's something he might . . . Oh shoot!'

He reeled back as Auntie Mirabelle folded him into her brawny arms.

'Joseph, why are you always getting into these scrapes? And Beryl. You here too?'

Her eyes moved from one to the other, full of lively speculation.

'We're fine, Auntie,' said Joe, disengaging himself. 'And thanks for ringing the police.'

'I never rang no police,' said Mirabelle as if accused of something shady.

'No? Who then . . . ?'

'Anonymous tip-off,' said Brightman. 'Sounded like a young girl, said there was going to be a ruck in Rasselas and that some nosey black dick was going to get his stupid head kicked in if we didn't get down there quick. End of message. Good job I was around, Joe. The others mightn't have recognized the description.'

'Thanks,' said Joe abstractedly. A young girl's voice . . .

He looked towards the police cars. Suzie Sickert was being manhandled into one of them. Her head turned his way and for a moment their gazes met. He raised a hand in a gesture of acknowledgement. Perhaps God did reward virtue after all. In reply she tore one arm free and flung him a hugely derisive V-sign.

'Friend of yours?' said Beryl Boddington curiously.

'In a manner of speaking,' said Joe Sixsmith.

TWENTY-TWO

THE SUN WAS SHINING, the birds were singing, the sky was blue. The only clouds were metaphorical, but they were somewhat bigger than a man's hand.

The first was Desmond Boddington, strapped into a child seat in the rear of the Morris but already looking as if he was after Houdini's record for rapid escape. Whitey, curled up alongside, eyed him with baleful disbelief. To be relegated to the back seat was always cause for complaint—but to be expected to share it with *this!*

The second cloud, larger still, was Auntie Mirabelle. At least she wasn't in the car, but when Joe arrived to pick up Beryl, there she was standing on the pavement, arms folded under her pendulous bosom, and her face lit with a smile like God's on the seventh day.

'Now isn't this a sight to warm the cockles of my poor dead sister's heart?' she asked various of her cronies who'd gathered like ghouls round a newly dug grave. 'Joe sitting there, fine and dandy, with Beryl by his side and the baby in the back. Don't he just look the real family man!'

Joe gritted his teeth as he unwillingly acknowledged that, as so often, he'd fallen into a trap of his own device.

Inviting Beryl on a day out had seemed the least he could do after the help she'd given him.

'I'm thinking of running up to the National Exhibition Centre in Birmingham on Saturday,' he'd said. 'There's a Security Fair. Lots of hospitality freebies. Idea is to get me so drunk I'll sign anything and everything, and it'd be nice to have you along to stop anyone taking advantage.'

'You really know how to smooth talk a girl, Joe Sixsmith,' she replied.

'No, look, I'm sorry,' he said. 'What I mean is, I'll probably look in for an hour, it can be really interesting, if you're
interested. Then we can go somewhere for lunch, have a
drive around the countryside, run down to Stratford maybe.
Of course, if you're working...'

'No, it happens to be my day off,' she said. 'Only my sis-
ter Lucy and her man, they're going to be away too, so I got
Desmond to think of... Look, let me have a word with
Mirabelle. I'm sure she'd be pleased to help us out...'

Oh yes, thought Joe. More than pleased. Gloatingly delighted! And when he explained this wasn't a big romantic
thing, just a guy paying off a friend's favour, she'd smile
even more complacently...

He said, 'Hey, no need to bother Auntie Mirabelle. Why
don't you bring the boy along too. Lots of flashing lights
and buttons to press, he'd probably love it.'

'You say so? OK. Why not?'

He should have known there was as much hope of keeping a royal scandal from the tabloids as such good news
away from Mirabelle. And so he ended up with the worst of
both possible worlds, with the kid yelling in the back and his
aunt beaming on the pavement.

But for all that, the sun *was* shining and the sky *was* blue,
and Beryl Boddington was strapped in at his side, so he
found himself driving up the M1 in much higher spirits than
that thoroughfare normally engendered.

'Everything sorted now about that Casa Mia business,
Joe?' said Beryl.

'Sure. Willie Woodbine was most complimentary.'

The DCI, rapidly grasping that any attempt to slag Joe off
just left the police looking really dumb, had grappled him
to his bosom and sung his praises loud and long, somehow
contriving the impression that Joe had been working unof-
ficially under the aegis of the CID. Which Joe thought was
a bit cheeky. On the other hand, Chivers hated this, which
was a great big plus.

Rocca was pleading temporary insanity. He'd got to Biggleswade that morning, found the electrical suppliers who were interviewing him were closed all day, realized he'd got his dates mixed, and spent the rest of the morning driving around aimlessly, brooding on the rottenness of his luck, the spleen of his wife, and the meanness of his in-laws. He ate nothing, drank a lot, and got home to find the Tomassettis at their tea. News of his abortive trip had pricked his wife to abuse. He had replied in kind. Old Tomassetti had joined in and then abused in his turn. Gina had attempted to calm things by saying she would brew some more tea, but while she was out in the kitchen things had been said about Rocca's manners, morals and manhood which had made him snap. He claimed to recall nothing of killing the trio in the lounge, nor of running into Gina in the passageway and killing her too, though this made it hard to explain why within a few minutes of driving away, he had stopped at a phone-box and rung the police, saying he was Andover and he'd just killed his family.

'He must be really round the twist to think that would do any good. I mean, hadn't Doberley just seen him go into the house?' said Beryl.

'It was probably meeting Doberley that gave him the idea,' countered Joe. 'Asking questions about Andover's state of mind and reminding Rocca of that crazy dream.'

'You mean in a way it was the dream helped cause the killings rather than the other way round?'

This was too clever for Joe.

'I expect it all just seemed like a good idea at the time,' he said, with the sad sympathy of one whose life seemed packed with such mental deceptions. 'And it seems he hated Andover. Reckoned he'd weaseled his way into the old man's good books and was set to clean up when he died.'

'And he'd been hiding out in the lock-up ever since?'

'More or less. He had to come out to get some grub. I saw him, I think. Only I didn't know who it was, of course, seeing that it was dark and I was being chased by Blue and Grey.'

Beryl laughed at his defensiveness and said gently, 'Joe, you didn't know who it was when he was standing right in front of you! I nearly died when you started calling him Stephen and pulling his moustache!'

It took Joe a moment or two to join in her laughter but when he did it was without resentment.

He said, 'Thanks for keeping quiet about that.'

'My pleasure,' she said. 'And I could see how you got confused the garage being in Andover's name and all.'

'Yeah. What happened was—'

'Rocca saw his business was going under,' she interrupted. 'So he knew that when he went bankrupt, everything he had would be seized and sold off to help pay his creditors. So he rented that lock-up, using his brother-in-law's name, as that was the first thing came into his head, and he started stashing a lot of his stock there out of the auditor's way, to be sold later against a rainy day. Simple when you think about it. Not worth paying anyone for.'

'I wonder if I'd make a good nurse,' said Joe dolefully.

'You should do,' she said to his surprise. 'You're concerned about people. And this thing you got, that seems to steer you right even when you set out wrong, there's a name for it . . .'

'Serendipity, you mean,' said Joe. 'That's what this old lady told me once. I thought she meant I was sick till I looked it up.'

'Whatever you call it, there's better ways to use it than going around pretending to be something out of an old movie.'

'You've been talking to Aunt Mirabelle again,' he said, determined not to get into a quarrel.

'No, she's been talking to me. I think her conscience is bothering her.'

'Her conscience? What conscience?'

'Well, she's a fair woman and wouldn't like to feel responsible for me marrying some feckless no-income PI,' said Beryl.

Joe's foot jabbed spasmodically on the accelerator with the shock, and he nearly ran into the back of a truck. The consequent jerk as he braked brought Desmond, who'd mercifully dozed off after ten minutes or so, back to noisy life.

'I wanna pee-pee,' he boomed.

'Better stop soon as you can, Joe,' said Beryl. 'It's an old tradition in our family. You get fair warning, and after that, anything goes.'

He glanced at her and saw her eyes were bright with mischief.

At least he hoped it was mischief.

Desmond's fair warning hadn't run out when they reached the next service station and he went off happily with his mother.

Leaving Whitey to look after the car, Joe wandered into the shopping area and bought the cat a packet of cheese-and-onion crisps and the boy a bag of boiled sweets, choosing non-chocolates on the grounds of damage-limitation.

Then he spotted a shelf full of toys. There wasn't a great selection but what really caught his eye was a range of soft felt animals, among them a large brown and white bull.

He bought the bull, and a bear which was more grizzly than teddy. When Beryl and Desmond reappeared, he presented the bear to the little boy who was clearly delighted with its ferocious appearance.

'You shouldn't waste your money, Joe,' said Beryl. 'But thanks a lot. He likes something to cuddle up to in bed. That why you're keeping the bull for yourself, Joe?'

These jokes, Joe decided, were good news. Beryl's one brief reference to Desmond's father hadn't suggested she saw matrimony as any laughing matter.

He said, 'That kid, Amal, the one whose toy bull caused all that hassle. Well, it ended up in shreds and I feel I owe him. When I saw this, I recollected his mother saying she worked at the Sheldon Airlodge, and that's only a few minutes along the road from the Exhibition Centre. Mind if we make a short diversion to drop this off?'

'It's your party, Joe,' she said indifferently. But when they got back in the car she reached across and squeezed his hand and said, 'You're a really nice man,' in a tone so free of mockery that Joe felt simultaneously flattered and alarmed.

Serving both the airport and the Exhibition Centre, the Airlodge was very busy and Joe had to park a good way from the entrance.

'Won't be long,' he said.

Swinging the bull debonairly in its plastic bag, he hurried between the rows of cars towards the hotel.

He recalled Mrs Bannerjee saying she was part-time so he guessed he'd be lucky to find her, but his luck was in. There she was, distinctive in her sari, one of four women behind the long and busy reception counter. Joe got in line behind a very large American who seemed to be having problems with the concept of Scotland.

'We're *how* far from Aberdeen? But they told me once I got here, nowhere was further from anywhere else than the Bronx from Brooklyn.'

Finally convinced that he had more than an afternoon stroll ahead of him, the American moved aside, leaving Joe exposed to the full heat of Mrs Bannerjee's welcoming smile.

It froze with recognition.

Why the shoot should she look so worried? wondered Joe.

'Mrs Bannerjee, remember me?' he said unnecessarily.

'Yes. Mr Sixsmith. You were very kind to us. We thank you,' she said recovering.

'I was in the area and I remembered you saying you worked here,' he said in his best PI's never-forget voice. 'I was pleased that everything worked out for your husband. Back at work, is he? Still with Mr Herringshaw?'

'Yes. Please, Mr Sixsmith, what is it you want?'

Whatever it is she thinks I want, she doesn't think she's going to like it, thought Joe. Must be the way I smile.

He said, 'Amal left his bull, remember? And I thought, I bet he misses it. So, being in the area, like I say...'

He lifted the carrier bag up and placed it on the counter.

Her expression softened with gratitude. And relief.

'You have brought back his bull? Oh, he will be so pleased. This is very kind of you, Mr Sixsmith.'

'Well, it's not exactly *his* bull. The one you got in Spain got sort of damaged. In fact it got all cut up, some silly idea they had about there being drugs in it...'

Suddenly the relief and gratitude were gone again.

Now Joe heard a voice in his head. It was his own voice and it was saying, *He chose somewhere nice and busy, lots of people, lots of mail...*

His gaze drifted to a high rack of pigeonholes, lots of them feathered with envelopes, while down below at ground level ran a shelf for broader packets and parcels. It was quite full.

Sixsmith, you've done it again, he thought.

He said, 'He did pack it up and post it here, didn't he? Made up a name. Marked it *To Await Collection*. Only you were going to collect it...'

She said, 'No. Please, believe me, I did not know.'

He studied her face, believed her.

He said, 'But you know now.'

She said, 'Yes. He has told me everything. It was all a stupidity. There was a plan. He was told it was foolproof. He would be given the bottles and in the duty free he would buy two similar bottles so that he had the proper receipts. And these he would leave at Malaga Airport and take the others through the Customs at Luton. Only he was very frightened...'

'Not so frightened he didn't agree to do it in the first place?' said Joe.

'He was even more frightened of Herringshaw.' She hissed the name viciously. Something had happened here.

'Because of his job? Shoot, it's only a job. Things will get better,' said Joe, probing for the truth. 'A job's not worth becoming a criminal over.'

'There is more. His papers, when he came here twelve years ago, there was something not right. Herringshaw has helped, but if he wants, he could still let the authorities know, and Soumitra would have to go back to India. This too I did not know, not till we talk last night.'

No wonder the poor sod got so scared in custody, thought Joe. They were just rattling his bars to get him scared, but he knew there really was an immigration problem.

'So what happened with the drugs?'

'He decided he will not do it. Too much risk. But he must make Herringshaw think he tried, so he invents a story that his baggage was interfered with and this made him so worried he poured the drugs down the toilet at Luton before he went through Customs.'

Joe Sixsmith, you should start backing horses, thought Joe.

'And he rang from Spain anonymously, giving a tip-off against himself so's he'd get picked up and Herringshaw would be convinced,' he said.

Except that it took rather more than that to convince a man like Herringshaw.

'That is right. Then Soumitra—he is not a wicked man, just foolish, always wanting to do things better for his family—he thinks that these drugs are worth so much money, it is foolish to destroy them, why should not he and his family have the profit from them?'

'And he packs them up and simply posts them here. And last night he finally confesses to you. So have they arrived, Mrs Bannerjee? And if not, what are you going to do about it when they do?'

Her eyes flashed angrily.

'You think I too will be greedy for money from drugs? I would rather join all those others I see begging in the street.'

'And your kids, would you see them beg in the street too?' asked Joe mildly.

It wasn't the time or place to be making debating points, except that at this time in this place it was more than a matter of debate. Joe had met neither Herringshaw nor Bannerjee but in that sensitized area of his being that Butcher called blood sympathy he felt he knew them both: Herringshaw, the kind of man who, given power, would eventually abuse it; and Bannerjee, living in perpetual fear and finding so little protection in the law that when finally the time came to act, he would have no qualms about breaking it. Mr Nayyar had been the same in a smaller way. It wasn't just power that corrupted. Daily indignities did too, so that when the big indignity came and the abused decided to fight back, they didn't know any way better than the methods of the abusers.

Maybe I became a PI because the only other way out I could see was to become a crook, thought Joe Sixsmith. And, with that saving grace of self-mockery which had always kept him sane, laughed riotously at the thought of what a lousy crook he'd have been.

But only inside. His expression was serious and sympathetic as he watched Mrs Bannerjee examine his debating point.

He guessed that when her husband had finally come clean last night she had flipped her lid and piled abuse on him from a great height. Poor Bannerjee. He'd probably been hoping for some kind of absolution, or at least of understanding that a father, believing his own destruction would mean the destruction of his entire family, might be justified in taking any action, no matter how extreme, to get off the hook. He guessed that Bannerjee's life had been full of small borderline criminous acts performed as 'favours' for his boss, and that with the distorted logic of the abused, he had decided if mere terror could turn him into a drug smuggler, it must be positively virtuous to do it out of love. What fantasies must have filled his mind; of using the money to escape from Herringshaw's clutches, of setting up his own business, of God knows what. 'A dreamer,' Butcher had called him, a man who saw one last hope of making his dreams come true.

Till his wife had screamed at him that dreams built on drug money were worse than the foulest nightmares.

But now Joe's question, and perhaps her own calmer thoughts since the explosion, were making her see things through her husband's eyes. And perhaps she was finding the distortion not quite so great.

But still great enough.

She swept the plastic carrier off the counter, turned, tipped the bull on to the parcel shelf and in the same movement pulled a neatly wrapped package into the bag.

'Here,' she said. 'This morning it arrives. You take it, Mr Sixsmith. It is yours. Do what you will with it. And thank you for Amal's bull.'

And she turned away from him to greet another inquirer with her wide professional smile.

Oh shoot! thought Joe Sixsmith as he walked towards the exit door. Here am I, strolling along with enough heroin in my possession to get me put away for the next ten years. Or, put it another way, to set me up in comfort for about as long. What the shoot am I going to do with it?

One negative answer came straight away. Not carry it around in a car which also held Beryl Boddington and her kid.

First thing was to be sure he'd got what he thought he'd got. Best place to check that was the Gents, which was also the best place for dumping it if that's what he decided. Luton rats' loss would be Birmingham rats' gain.

He did a swift turn in search of the toilet, and found himself looking straight at Mr Grey.

'I always knew you was bent, Sambo,' said the thug complacently.

He looked to have regained full vulgar health after his bewitched belly-ache, if that's what it had been. If Joe had had the poppet in his hand, he'd have bitten its head off now without hesitation. But in the absence of supernatural aid, he opted for the human touch and kneed Mr Grey very hard in the groin.

Beryl Boddington, impatient at being abandoned for what was becoming an unmannerly length of time, had got out of the car and was strolling through the parking bays with Desmond when she saw Joe come running out of the hotel. Behind him came another man, about twice Joe's size, his face flushed with rage or pain or both, and running with a strange hobbling kind of gait.

'What's he doing now?' Beryl asked her son in exasperation, and the boy indicated by a delighted laugh that whatever it was, it beat being strapped in the back of a car with an unsociable cat.

Joe glanced back, saw to his amazement that Grey was following—he must have a groin of granite!—but estimated that the handicap was enough to give him time to reach the Morris and make his getaway.

Then he looked to the front again and saw Beryl.

'Get in the car!' he yelled breathlessly. 'In the car!'

'What? Why should I wait in the car?' she called back indignantly. 'We're your passengers, not your prisoners.'

With a groan of dismay, Joe changed direction and was immediately knocked down by a vehicle moving slowly along the parking bays. It wasn't a hard blow but enough to make him drop the bag and by the time he had scrambled after it on his knees and picked it up, Grey was almost upon him. He pushed himself to his feet and dodged behind the car which had hit him. Across its dirty white roof, he and Grey confronted each other.

'I'm going to flatten your black skull and use it as a frisbee,' said Mr Grey, extreme emotion mining an unsuspected vein of poetry.

'Help,' said Joe. It came out as a croak, but it wouldn't have made much difference if it had come out as a clarion, for the Great British Public was performing its usual trick in face of disturbance of carrying on as if nothing was happening. This was an admirable quality when the disturbance was the Blitz, or a Tory Election victory, or some great natural disaster, but it could get right up a PI's nose when it was his personal destruction.

Grey lunged forward, his outstretched hands almost catching Joe's head, and the weight of his body making the little white car shake.

Joe shot back. At his waist level the driver's window opened. Perhaps after all help was going to be offered. An Englishman's car was his castle and you attacked that at your peril. Then a hand came out of the window, dipped into the plastic bag, plucked out the package and withdrew it into the car.

'Hold on!' cried Joe, stooping to the window.

''Afternoon, Mr Sixsmith,' said Mr Blue, his smile showing teeth like a portcullis. 'Knew we could rely on you to keep a bargain. That cat of yours all right, is it? *Are you getting in or what?*'

This last, very bad-tempered question was directed at Grey who, with many a longing glance towards Joe, doubled up his bulk and squeezed it into the passenger seat.

'Wait!' yelled Joe, leaning in through the open window and trying to grab at the package.

Blue had set the car rolling slowly forward, so Joe found himself running sideways, half in, half out, with the package just out of his reach. Then Grey's huge hand wrapped itself round his face and he was hurled backwards. He crashed painfully against the bonnet of a black BMW and slid slowly to the ground.

Scooping up Desmond in her arms, Beryl came racing towards him.

But she wasn't first there. A well polished pair of shoes and a nicely creased pair of trousers slid out of the BMW into Joe's view.

'You all right?' asked a faintly familiar voice. And he looked up into the smiling face of Detective-Inspector Yarrop.

'I think my nose is broken,' groaned Joe. 'They're getting away! And they've got the dope!'

'Yes, of course they have,' said Yarrop. 'That's why we let them loose, wasn't it? And soon they'll be handing it over to Mr Charles Herringshaw. And that's the point when we'll scoop up the lot of them.'

As if in illustration, he reached down a hand and pulled Joe to his feet, then stepped back sharply as blood dripped on to his shoes.

'You mean you deliberately let this happen to me?' gasped Joe. 'I could have been killed!'

'Or you could have been picked up carrying two kilos of smuggled heroin,' said Yarrop reasonably. 'Which wouldn't have looked very good.'

'I was going to hand it over to you,' protested Joe feebly.

'That's what they all say,' said Yarrop. 'Naturally I tend to believe you. But I've got a boss who likes a result above all things, so if push came to shove, I might have had to offer him you, and of course the Bannerjees.'

Joe looked for signs that he was joking, but Yarrop only smiled and dusted the bonnet of his BMW. The smile vanished as Beryl arrived, dumped Desmond on the car, and started examining Joe professionally.

'Why do you do these things, Joe?' she demanded as she probed his nose. 'This is a game for young, fit, and very stupid men, and you don't qualify on at least two counts. Does that hurt?'

'Only when I breathe,' said Joe.

'He may not be young, but he takes his punishment well, you must give him that,' said Yarrop, gently prising a windscreen wiper out of Desmond's fingers. 'As for stupid, he got that Eytie killer, didn't he? And he worked all this out for himself. Luckily so did we, else things could have been very different. Always share with the professionals, Joe. Let that be your motto. Always share. Now I've got to be off. I've got an appointment with Mr Herringshaw.'

'I don't think it's broken,' said Beryl, abandoning the nose. 'What we need is some ice.'

'In a minute,' said Joe. 'Mr Yarrop, what will happen to Mr Bannerjee?'

'He'll be all right. He came to us this morning after his wife bawled him out. Told us everything.'

'So that's why you're here,' said Joe. 'You didn't work it out.'

Yarrop smiled.

'Didn't need to. The package got sniffed out at the Post Office. We told 'em to let it through so's we could see what happened. Bannerjee was lucky his wife reacted like she did, otherwise he'd have stayed right in the frame. There's nothing like the love of a good woman, so they say. But sometimes the nagging of an angry one does us more good. You think about that, Mr Sixsmith, if you ever get thoughts of matrimony. This belongs to you I think, madam.'

He deposited Desmond in Beryl's arms, touched his hat and got into the car.

They stood aside and watched him drive away.

'Where's it going to end, Joe?' said Beryl softly.

'I don't know. I hope Bannerjee'll be OK but I'd better let Butcher know so she can watch out for him.'

'Sod Bannerjee. I'm talking about you. Where's it going to end for you? I mean, you can't go on for ever like this. I've only known you a couple of weeks and I've seen you with your face split open, and being attacked by a mad Italian with a knife, and knocked down by a goon in a car, and punched in the face by his partner...'

'It's not always like that,' said Joe. 'Usually it's exciting.'

She looked at him sadly and said, 'You're talking telly-speak again.'

'Am I? Don't know how. I never have time to watch it. Do you reckon they'll let us have some ice here?'

'If you promise to leave quietly without starting any more fights, they'll probably give us a choice of flavours,' said Beryl.

With the bleeding staunched and his nose confirmed as unbroken, they returned to the car. Whitey was sulking at having been left for so long, but in compensation, Desmond had been so impressed by Joe's entertainment potential that he was now putty in his hands.

'Tell you what,' said Joe. 'I think I've had enough of the security business for one day, and dragging you round an exhibition was never a good idea anyway. Let's buy some grub, head down to Woburn or somewhere, look at the animals, have a picnic.'

'That sounds good,' said Beryl.

'Yes yes yes!' shouted Desmond. 'Uncle Joe gonna fall down again?'

'I wouldn't be at all surprised,' said Joe.

They had a great day all things considered. There were times when Joe felt the chaperoning presence of Desmond to be a definite drawback, and times when it was a source of considerable comfort, though whether he was frightened of making a pass at Beryl, or frightened of being rebuffed if he did, Joe wasn't quite sure.

However, if there were options open, it seemed silly not to keep them that way, so when they got back to Rasselas in the early evening, he pulled up round the corner from Beryl's block.

'Don't want Auntie hanging over her balcony,' he explained.

'She's ten storeys up!' objected Beryl.

'You don't imagine she ain't got a telescope, do you?'

Beryl laughed and said, 'Anyway, what's going to happen you don't care for her to see?'

Joe knew a cue when he heard one.

'This,' he said. And leaned over and kissed her.

For a moment it got interesting, then as their mouths manoevred for maximum contact, their noses clashed.

'Oh shoot!' cried Joe, pulling back.

And Desmond clapped his hands with glee at this latest comic turn.

'Let's do it again some time,' said Beryl, unstrapping the boy and getting out of the car.

Uncertain what she was referring to, but certain of his answer, Joe said, 'Yes.'

He didn't drive straight round to his block. Instead, almost as if on automatic pilot, he found himself driving back through town and out past the University till he reached the Stemditch Industrial Estate. Here he brought the Morris to a halt with its front bumper against the rusty security fence surrounding the deserted and desolate buildings of Robco Engineering.

'What the hell are we doing here?' howled Whitey, who had none of Joe's conditioning against swearing.

'She wants to know where it's going to end,' said Joe. 'That's a good question, Whitey. I don't know a good answer though, except, not here. They tried to make it end here, but they didn't, and they won't, that's for sure.'

It wasn't a very articulate expression of the tumult of defiance he felt welling up inside him, but, as with crosswords, he was better at answers than explanations.

Suddenly the door was dragged open and a huge figure blocked out the evening sun. Thoughts of Blue, Grey, even Rocca, escaped from police custody, ricocheted round Joe's mind.

Then Merv Golightly said, 'Joe, my son, if you're here on a stake-out, I reckon you got the wrong address!'

'Merv. What the shoot are you doing here?'

'Just dropped a client close by, thought I'd take a look-see at the old place.'

'Me too,' said Joe.

The two men looked at each other, knew they were lying, knew they both knew, and knew it didn't matter. A shared defeat, whether in war or in work, binds men together but doesn't leave them needing to talk about it. Here where they had spent years feeling themselves useful they had at last been told they were useless.

Where else should they come to express their defiance?

But defiance needs other sustenance than a view of dereliction, else it can simply waste away to yet another defeat.

'Here, Joe,' said Merv with sudden brightness. 'It's Race Nite tonight down at the Glit. Fancy losing your money over a couple of jars?'

Joe looked at Whitey whose eyes grew round at the prospect of bacon fries and ashtrays full of beer.

'Why not?' said Joe Sixsmith.

Fare Play
BARBARA PAUL

First Time in Paperback

A Marian Larch Mystery

HAZARDOUS AT THE TOP

Newly promoted to lieutenant in the NYPD, Marian Larch must take everything that comes with the job: prestige, pay, problems...and diabolical murder.

The first victim is an elderly gentleman shot on a crowded bus, silently and skillfully. But why did no one—including a detective who was tailing him—see anything? The next victim is a young woman on a subway. Same MO—a sneak attack, no chance for the victim. Marian suspects a hired killer is involved.

As she wages private love and war with former FBI hacker Curt Holland and tackles an overzealous fan of her actress friend, Marian uncovers a murder ring that leads her to a killer—and to those willing to pay for his services.

"Zingy from page one to the finish..."—*Publishers Weekly*

Available in August at your favorite retail stores.

WORLDWIDE LIBRARY®

FARE

Take 3 books and a surprise gift FREE

SPECIAL LIMITED-TIME OFFER

Mail to: The Mystery Library™
         3010 Walden Ave.
         P.O. Box 1867
         Buffalo, N.Y. 14240-1867

YES! Please send me 3 free books from the Mystery Library™ and my free surprise gift. Then send me 3 mystery books, first time in paperback, every month. Bill me only $4.19 per book plus 25¢ delivery and applicable sales tax, if any*. There is no minimum number of books I must purchase. I can always return a shipment at your expense and cancel my subscription. Even if I never buy another book from the Mystery Library™, the 3 free books and surprise gift are mine to keep forever.   415 BPY A3US

Name	(PLEASE PRINT)

Address	Apt. No.

City	State	Zip

First Time in Paperback

Jeanne McCafferty

A MacKenzie Griffin Mystery

CLIMBING THE CHARTS IS MURDER...

Murder scenes aren't supposed to look this good. The lighting, the staging, the arrangement of the body, even the clothes are eerie recreations of pop superstar Peter Rossellini's hot music videos. In fact, each victim resembles the sexy singer.

Clearly, the killer is obsessed. But is Peter the next intended victim? Criminologist MacKenzie Griffin fears just that. Mac has no shortage of suspects. And one is setting the stage for a hit that's to die for.

"A highly recommended first novel."

—Susan Rogers Cooper, author of
Dead Moon on the Rise

Available in August at your favorite retail stores.

WORLDWIDE LIBRARY ®

STAR

CRIMINALS ALWAYS HAVE SOMETHING TO HIDE—BUT THE ENJOYMENT YOU'LL GET OUT OF A WORLDWIDE MYSTERY NOVEL IS NO SECRET....

With Worldwide Mystery on the case, we've taken the mystery out of finding something good to read every month.

Worldwide Mystery is guaranteed to have suspense buffs and chill seekers of all persuasions in eager pursuit of each new exciting title!

Worldwide Mystery novels—crimes worth investigating...